A CALL FOR DR. BARTON

A CALL FOR

Dr. Barton

By ELIZABETH SEIFERT

DODD, MEAD & COMPANY

NEW YORK

Library of Congress Catalog Card Number: 56-10919

Printed in the United States of America
by The Cornwall Press, Inc., Cornwall, N. Y.

For
BEVERLY

*The characters, places, incidents and situations
in this book are imaginary and have no relation
to any person, place or actual happening*

A CALL FOR DR. BARTON

CHAPTER *One*

PICTURESQUE, decided Grady. That, exactly, was the word for the town. It was small, and built upon the sides of steep limestone hills; the streets seemed to run straight up and down. Houses, and many of the business buildings, were constructed of cut and fitted limestone blocks which had taken on a fine patina through the years. The place was clean, and, yes, picturesque—what with the blue waters of the lake, the fields and woodlands behind the town, the swept streets and the polished window fronts. The tile-roofed church was of limestone, too, and the parish house next door had blue shutters, with geraniums red in its window boxes.

The filling station was of white stucco, with a blue roof.

"You've a pretty town here," the traveler said to the young man who came out to service his car.

"Yes, sir. Thank you. We like it."

"How big a town is it?"

It was a minute before the attendant answered him, his first attention seeming to be on something going on within the small building. "We're about a thousand," he

1

said then. "In the wintertime." His chamois made swirl-
ing patterns on the windshield, came to a sticker, slowed
and stopped. He stepped to the window and leaned
through it.

"*Are* you a doctor?" he asked intently.

"Yes. Yes, I am. . . ."

"Ah—would you come inside for a minute? Mr. Seddens—" His cap tipped back toward the building. "He's
having a spell in there."

Before the last syllable was spoken, Grady was on his
feet, his hand reaching for the small bag in the back part
of the car. He strode with confidence across the stretch of
concrete, ducked his tall head instinctively for the door
lintel, blinked to adjust his eyes to the dimmer light and
moved forward again.

Seated in a chair was a gray-haired man—gray-bearded,
too, as one does not often see a man bearded these days.
A Vandyke beard, precisely trimmed. More important
now, his face was suffused and his breath came with difficulty. Grady bent over him, his fingers on his pulse.

"He's a doctor . . ." the uniformed man was explaining
to others in the station.

"I'm Dr. Barton," said Grady to the distressed man,
speaking in a firm, clear voice. "Just take it easy, sir."

He turned to open his bag and take a stethoscope from
it.

"He came in here a few minutes ago." An older man
came to the doctor's side. He too was wearing the green
uniform of the gasoline service. "He asked for a glass of

water—I gave it to him, and he sat there in that chair. He seemed so ill—"

Grady's uplifted hand silenced him. The doctor's head bent, he listened, then nodded. Swiftly his fingers loosened the knotted tie, the collar, unbuckled the belt. Mr. Seddens sat, still breathing hard, his eyes on the stranger. Dr. Barton turned again to his medical kit and intently prepared a syringe. With it in his hand, he bent over the patient.

"We'll get that blood pressure down, sir," he said, even as he sent the plunger down. He straightened and stood watching the distinguished-looking man. Neat gray suit, black knit tie—and that pointed beard.

The doctor glanced up at the others in the small room. "I think," he said, pleasantly firm, "if he could have a little air—and quiet. . . ."

The men filed out, their heads together, their eyes turning backward from the door.

Within ten minutes Mr. Seddens had received so much relief that he was adjusting his own tie. "You're a fine doctor!" he blurted to the big man who had seated himself on a bench under the small-paned window.

The broad shoulders lifted in a shrug and the smile was deprecatory. "Any doctor would have helped you, sir."

"Hmmmn," said Mr. Seddens.

Grady stood up. "Better take it easy for a day or so, sir," he advised. "Cut down on salt—and keep in touch with your physician."

Mr. Seddens looked up at him. "My physician lives fifty miles away," he said flatly. "That's too far, isn't it?"

"It was a good idea this morning," said Grady, "to have a doctor closer than that."

"Yes!" The bearded man had taken out a billfold, and now he sat regarding the bill edges to be seen within it.

"There's no charge, sir," Dr. Barton told him.

"Of course there's a charge. I was just wishing I knew how much it would take to keep you here in our town." He turned keen blue eyes upon the young doctor. They asked a question.

Grady Barton was a big man—something over six feet—with wide shoulders, a thick neck and straight, strong limbs. His hair was a dark, rich auburn, growing to a peak upon his forehead. His features were regular and strong rather than handsome. A slight cleft marked his chin, a deep line was graven between his nose and upper lip. His mouth was especially firm, with lines of restraint etched around it.

"You wouldn't be interested, would you," Mr. Seddens voiced his question, "in coming here to live?"

"It's beautiful country and your town is most attractive. Living here sounds like a pleasant suggestion."

"I'd make it more than a suggestion—if you'd give me the chance," said his patient, standing up.

Grady went to his side. "I'd like to take you to your home, sir," he said courteously. "You're nicely over that slight edematous attack, but, as I said, caution would be a good thing for a day or two."

It appeared that Mr. Seddens had walked to town—as, he said, he did most days—for his mail. Grady offered to drive him to his home, which proved to be an attractive,

veranda-girdled house built just above the beach of the
pretty lake. Miss Nellie, his sister, invited the young doctor to stay for lunch; Grady accepted with pleasure.

The two men established themselves comfortably upon
the screened porch, and Mr. Seddens gave Miss Nellie a
glowing report of the way Dr. Barton had "saved my life,
my dear."

Smiling, Grady repeated his claim that any other doctor . . .

"But we don't have any other doctor!" said little Miss
Nellie, solemnly, her cheeks trembling. "Green Holly
doesn't have a doctor at all!"

A lot of small towns didn't, Grady knew. "Then, sir,"
he said to his host, "you should be especially careful of
your blood pressure." He delivered what he called a five-
dollar lecture on edema: then he took a prescription pad
from his breast pocket and wrote upon it.

"Check this with your physician, sir," he said, giving the
sheet to Mr. Seddens.

Frank Seddens studied the heading on the piece of
paper. "You're on the staff of this hospital?" he asked,
looking up.

"I'm admissions physician there," said Grady. "It's a
big general hospital. Twelve hundred beds."

"Sounds like an important job."

"Well, important in that such a hospital has to have an
admissions physician, sir." Grady's eyes smiled out at the
lake.

"You're up here on vacation?"

"Yes. I've been driving through Wisconsin, stopping off

to fish wherever the notion struck me. I wanted—I *needed*
—to get away by myself for a time." His hand tightened
upon the chair arm and his jaw showed a ridge of white.
"The main idea," his voice resumed its friendly, pleasant
tone, "was to relax."

"I thought that was advice which you doctors gave only
to other people."

Grady's fine eyes smiled. A dignified manservant
brought out a tray of fruit juices and canapés. Miss Nellie
rejoined them, and Grady was nicely responsive to her
fluttering attentions.

"Did Brother persuade you to come here and practice?"
she asked, with the innocent forthrightness of a child.

"He's getting around to it," Grady told her.

"Not with much hope for success," said Mr. Seddens.
"He has a big job in Chicago."

Grady qualified this, but admitted that he did have a
good job—and with good pay. But then he went on to
say that it was not exactly the sort of work he wanted to
do.

The Seddenses exchanged hopeful glances. Grady noticed that they did, and he laughed. "What I want,"
he said, "is to practice in my own office, with a chance to
do some surgery. I did my residencies in surgical service
but—well—we had a war, you know. And when I came
home I somehow got behind the desk I now occupy and
I can't seem to break loose."

"Don't you do any doctoring?"

"Oh, yes. I used the desk-sitting figuratively. My service sorts out the patients who come to us; a large percent-

age are emergencies. And we do that sorting by examination and some treatment, which I supervise or do myself. But we always assign those patients to other services for continued treatment and care. Except that we try not to make mistakes in beginning their course of treatment, we don't get as much satisfaction out of our work as do doctors in other positions. Besides, we're busier than I like.

"You see, our hospital gets a new patient about every twelve minutes, day round, year round—and we get all kinds of patients. A splinter in a little girl's hand, an old man hit on the street by a reckless driver. They come to us by police car, by taxi, in private cars. Some even come in on foot. Now, don't get the idea that I attend to all these cases. Maybe I'd be happier if I did. My job is somewhat administrative, and that is the part I don't like. I would prefer closer contact with the patients. . . ."

By the time they went in to lunch, Frank Seddens was looking more hopeful. And after the nap which Dr. Barton enjoined, he telephoned to a couple of his friends. "Come over and meet a young man who is visiting me," Grady heard him say.

Grady too had napped, stretched out on the cushions of the porch glider, and only vaguely thinking that he should be on his way. He would, he thought drowsily, ask his host about fish in their lake. . . .

There were fish, said Seddens. "Why don't you stay with us tonight and try your luck? I'll see that you get a boat to use—you could have a go at it this evening, or early in the morning—"

"Or both," laughed Grady.

"You'd do it?"

"Oh, yes. Sure. Even without fish, I'm all for the project."

The invited men arrived and, over mild highballs, visited for an hour with Frank Seddens and young Dr. Barton. They were pleasant chaps, one, George Goddard who owned an auto accessory business, the other, Norvell Lee—self-styled as a displaced Texan—who did rock quarrying and crushing. They were cordial to Dr. Barton and under the guise of humor demanded to know why he—or anyone—would want to go back to Chicago when he could stay in Green Holly?

And Grady laughingly said he could not think of a valid reason, offhand. Mention was made again of the fact that Green Holly, and adjoining Holly Neighbors, had no doctor. Together the towns were spoken of as "The Hollies."

Grady talked of the various ways in which medical schools and medical associations were trying to solve the problem which was not theirs alone.

"The big trouble," he explained, "is that young doctors, who might be interested in such a location, have had an expensive education; many of them are in debt for it and cannot face the risk of a practice which might not give them a living or pay for the equipment they'd need to set up in business."

The three men nodded—that would be a problem. They then talked about their town, how it was founded because of the limestone to be quarried and sold. There was good dairyland close by. The lake and the scenery brought in summer visitors, and some of them stayed on. Holly Neighbors had a few industries. Together the towns ran to about 3,000 people, with another 500 or so coming in every summer to live in cottages along the lake.

A wave of the hand indicated some of these cottages. Mr. Seddens' home had once been just that. But insulation, storm windows and a new furnace had converted it to full-time living when he'd retired from his work as sales manager for a dairy supply company. There were mild jokes about how little he knew of cows. "I didn't need to know cows!" he defended himself. "I knew all about the machines that got their milk and handled it."

It was a very pleasant hour; at the end of it, Mr. Lee agreed to fix Grady up with a boat—he had a fairly reliable outboard—and he showed Grady where to pick it up.

So, with the sun still an hour from setting, Grady found himself dressed in dungarees, guiding the small boat out upon the sparkling water of the lake; soon a fishpole was in his hands, a pipe in his mouth and the view of the two Hollies lay spread out before his contented eyes, Green Holly particularly, Holly Neighbors being little more than a blur and a smudge on the far tip of the shore's crescent. He'd judge the towns were six or seven miles apart—with beach homes dotted between them, sand dunes, even a dance hall and pier of not much magnitude nor magnificence.

He had a bite and lost the fish—cast again and smoked. Green Holly lay like a toy village in the level rays of the sun. The western faces of its buildings were pink tinged, the eastern ones empurpled with shadow. Behind the town, hills rose in a gentle swell—fields and woodland, a red barn, roads and the shine of a smaller lake and a twisting river.

With the setting sun, the air grew chill and Grady reached for his jacket. There were a few other boats dotted upon the quiet surface of the lake; he could see people moving about on the beach and in the town, but no one seemed to hurry, or—well . . .

At dark he went home and smiled at the word he used for his destination. He watched television with his host and hostess and was in bed by ten, with an owl hooting somewhere in the distance and the smell of the close-by water clean in the air which stirred the curtains at his window.

He slept like one dead—deeply, dreamlessly—but was up again at daybreak, tiptoeing through the house, going down to the lake for another three hours of fair luck and abundant rest and refreshment.

Beaching the boat, he cleaned his string of three fish, took them up to the house and gave them to John; then he bathed, shaved, dressed and packed his bag. He joined Mr. Seddens and Miss Nellie for breakfast on the porch, with sunlight twinkling on the coffee urn and the folded newspaper ready at his left hand.

"You're too good to me," he assured the kind couple. "I find myself wishing that I'd spent my entire vacation here and definitely dreading my return to the city. The skyline of Chicago is not going to look very good after this—" His hand swept outward to include the azure sky, the golden beach and the diamond-dusted lake.

"You know you could stay here," said Miss Nellie in her soft, breathy voice.

Grady smiled at her. "Except that I'm expected on duty tomorrow morning at eight."

"On Sunday?"

"People get sick or hurt on Sunday too."

"I wish I could see you in your white clothes, in that big hospital," mused the little old lady. "I'll bet everyone likes you."

Grady laughed. "Oh, I'm afraid not. In a hospital of that size your chiefs work so hard and so fast that all anyone can accomplish is something approaching efficiency. No, Miss Nellie, I have to get on the backs of my interns too often, I have to jack up the ambulance men and dress down the orderlies and the nurses. Because, you see, we all have to keep on our toes. Me too. And if you've ever tried walking on your tiptoes for eight or twelve hours a day. . . ."

"Oh, I couldn't do that," she said, quickly. "I have bunions."

Her brother and Grady laughed. But Grady's face had tightened just to think about, and talk about, his job in the big hospital, a place where emergency was the rule rather than the exception, where urgency and desperate need set the pace of his days.

Without a note of whining discontent, he quietly explained that the strain of big-city-hospital medical service after his sort of war duty had been rather hard on him. *Rough* was the word he used.

"What was that war duty?" asked Mr. Seddens. "In Korea?"

"No, sir. I'm older than that. I did my intern service in the forties, with the airborne troops. In Italy and then in Holland and Belgium."

Mr. Seddens leaned forward. "But that sounds as if . . ."

Grady nodded. "Yes, sir. I did jump—even managed to break a leg in a bad jump. That service taught me a lot, sir, but I paid for the schooling. You see, that one bad jump got me behind enemy lines—and I—well, let's say I suffered from the experience." He smiled, but again there was that tautness of hand and face. His hosts saw it. Grady felt it.

Against his will, despair crowded his mind and clogged the vessels of his heart. Gisela was in Reno, Grady was here in Wisconsin on vacation. These two weeks, ending tonight, had been dedicated to the purpose of forgetting what was past, to shake off regret and hurt—and shame. To "get over" things. But he'd discovered that two weeks were scarcely time enough to let a man become accustomed to failure, to put his feet firmly on the ground, straighten his shoulders, look about him and get set to start anew.

Grady had hoped to accomplish that much, but . . .

Kind Miss Nellie was hoping to relieve the tension. "No wonder," she said, her eyes twinkling, "that it's hard for you to walk on tiptoe—with a broken leg, I mean."

"Yes," agreed Grady, after they had laughed at her joke. "Their doctors. . . ." *And their nurses!* "Well, anyway, I might have learned as much if I'd been assigned to duty with independent families at some base hospital. But I just didn't happen to be. They trained me for emergency medicine and surgery—and that's what I did. When I got home, that was still what I'd been trained to do and it's what I am still doing."

"And you say it is hard on you?"

"On my nerves, yes. A stretched rubber band wears thin."

"I hope your fishing vacation has helped you," said Miss Nellie politely.

Grady answered her in kind. "It has," he said warmly, "thanks to you."

For a moment it seemed that the little old lady might kiss him. "I wish you could stay longer," she said tremulously.

Grady turned his chair a little away from the table, and his gaze went out to the lake, to the sunny stretch of beach. Down on the sand children were going busily about their affairs with rocks and buckets and shovels and castles. Young people ran and played—or sunbathed— with earnest grace. There were some swimmers. A breeze frilled the blue waters with narrow lace and brought a decorative cloud or two into the blue sky. Grady sighed. "I wish I could stay," he agreed.

"Doctor," said his host, "have you ever really considered rural practice?"

Grady accepted a cigarette from the case being offered him, and took out his lighter. "A man," he said gravely, "without resources other than the work of his hands often cannot afford to 'consider' too much of anything. I mean,

such a man takes the best job offered to him and he stays
with it—lest he have no job at all. My life's main dream,
my ambition, and my fight, was aimed at getting an M.D.
I did get it, and I'm doing fairly well. But, as I said, I
haven't been able to afford consideration of what I would
like to do, at the risk of losing what I already am doing."

"Well, then, let's put it this way: If there were some
security afforded, would you consider such practice?"

Miss Nellie gave a little bounce of excitement and her
brother shook his beard at her. So she put her ringed old
hand over her mouth.

Grady was again looking at the beach. "Just what do
you have in mind?" he asked, putting his cigarette again
between his lips.

A cloud-shadow passed over the scene before him. It
made the regained sunlight seem all the brighter. He
smiled at the brightness, smiled at the boy-haired young
girls who ran along the sand, smiled at three crop-haired
boys who played leapfrog in the hope of attracting the
attention of those girls, then he moved his gaze to what
could be seen behind him of the hills and the dark green
woods.

Frank Seddens watched him and saw the peace which
came to the younger man's face and into his eyes. Seddens had been a master salesman; he knew how to present his product or his proposition and then wait for the
proper time of reaction in his customer . . .

Now, when that minute seemed to have come, he said,
quietly, "The Hollies need a doctor, Grady. Our little
town here—Green Holly—has none, which is perhaps to

be expected. We're too small to support a doctor. We're only a thousand souls, with some claim to the 500 folk who come in for the summer season. That runs to ten weeks, about.

"But Holly Neighbors has no doctor either—and it's bigger. There are at least 2500 people there. Which, if you're good at arithmetic—as I am—means there are 3500 people here the year round. And that's quite a lot of people, old and young and in between, to try to get along without direct medical help."

"You forget Dr. Stone," murmured Miss Nellie.

The jutting gray beard seemed to bristle. "Stone!" barked Frank Seddens. "He isn't as much help as a good veterinary would be!"

Grady leaned forward in his chair.

"He *says* he is an osteopath," cried Frank Seddens. "I *know* he is a charlatan!"

"*Brother!*" protested Miss Nellie.

"Well, he's no doctor!"

"Oh, no! No, he isn't, dear."

"Well, then!" Her brother straightened the set of his coat lapels. "Where was I? And don't interrupt, Nellie!"

"You were saying a lot of people had to get along without . . ."

"Yes!" He turned again to Grady, who was smiling only faintly. "Now, Doctor, if it would be possible for you to imagine such a condition, try to picture those 3500 I mentioned as individuals, some of them needing medical attention constantly, all of them needing it occasionally. Then bring your consideration down to me and my high blood pressure, or hypertension—whatever you'd call it. It still amounts to a chronic condition which needs medical guidance and care.

"Two years ago I retired and decided to live here the year round in the summer home which my wife and I had loved so dearly—where we'd had so many happy times." He paused for a moment of regretful memory, then lifted his head and continued briskly, "I didn't give the matter of medical service much thought. But now—Nellie and I aren't getting any younger, and maybe—" He sighed and shook his head. He was a handsome old gentleman.

"But what do people do?" asked Grady. "How *do* they manage?"

"When they are ill?"

"Yes, or hurt."

Mr. Seddens nodded. "Well," he said thoughtfully, "an emergency goes by ambulance to the nearest doctor or hospital. That's thirty-five or fifty miles. Here in town we have an undertaker with an ambulance—"

"Without a medical attendant?"

"That's right."

Grady's tongue circled his cheek.

Mr. Seddens nodded. "For general medical care and advice, our people go to Mayo's, to Madison or Milwaukee —or even to Chicago. Mild cases—colds and headaches and minor accidents—appeal to the druggist."

"Hmmmn," said Grady. "I'd think you'd need a bit more than that."

"We do. We're a normal cross section of people. We have babies . . ."

"Brother!" said Miss Nellie, and the two men looked at her blankly, then laughed.

"Not me, personally, of course," conceded Mr. Seddens. "But once born, these babies get the croup and the measles—so, yes, we need more medical care than we have close at hand. I do, I'm sure. To get it—while I don't want to move, I may have to move. Miss Nellie, too, for a man likes to feel he has some protection for his family and for himself. For instance, I want to feel that such protection and care would be quickly available when I have my stroke. . . ."

Grady's head snapped up, his eyes keenly studied his host's face. "A man with your essential hypertension," he said quietly, "does need constant medical supervision. That's true enough."

"If he just wouldn't worry about so many things," suggested Frank Seddens' sister. "He frets too much, makes too many things his concern."

"I'm sure you're right," said the doctor. "Still, Mr. Seddens is the kind of man he is. Good, intense, with a feeling of moral responsibility. I mean, certain types have certain diseases. That's been definitely established."

"*You* don't look like the nervous sort," said Miss Nellie shrewdly.

The big young man nodded. "I shouldn't be," he agreed.

His mind darted, lightning swift. Self-disgust was what he had to cope with, and anger at the mess a young man could make of his life, a mess which he must carry with him and learn to handle—or try to forget. His big shoulders lifted.

"I *shouldn't* be nervous," he repeated, "Or even tense. That's why I think I should, perhaps, make a change in the life I live and the work I do. It's why I'm interested to know if your brother is suggesting an offer of some kind to me."

Mr. Seddens nodded. His initial judgment of this quiet, self-contained man was proving to be sound. "I'm afraid I'm not ready to offer much," he confessed. "As things stand now, if you'd come here and set up practice, I could promise you one case of high blood pressure. Beyond that, just at the minute, there's the countryside, the lake. Quiet. Friendly people . . ."

"That's a lot," said Grady.

"Yes, it is." Mr. Seddens watched the younger man's face. Grady's eyes were lowered; he was watching his fingertips rub the edge of the newspaper page.

After a minute of this, he glanced up. "I'm not much of a gambler, sir," he said regretfully. "I own some instruments; I have a few dollars saved, but I think at my age, I'd need to be sure of a living to do good work. I'm a conscientious guy, and bills bother me, things like that."

"They should!" agreed Mr. Seddens. "And—well—of course I'm giving a good bit of thought to being able, in the future, to make a more attractive suggestion to you than I could right now. I'll have to do some work on it. For instance, we'd have to work out some sort of guarantee to give you, at least for your first months here. After you were here—if you came—I'm sure things would work out for you. A practice would build up. The factory at Holly Neighbors would probably use you as their physi-

cian. I don't even know if they'd pay a flat fee, or by
case . . ."

Dr. Barton laughed. "I think there are various systems.
A flat fee perhaps for fixed services—oh, you know, insurance examinations and that sort of thing, with additional pay for additional work, though the workers would
probably pay their own bills from health insurance and
sick benefits. Anyway, it would be a known source of income."

"Yes! And the rest of it—well, look. You leave me your
address. And I think you may be hearing from us."

Grady stood up. "I hope I do, sir! In the meantime, I
must be moving on now toward the job I do have. You've
all been most kind to me. I hate to leave—I hope I may
come back."

It took a bit more in the way of farewells. But within
another hour, he was driving out of the Seddens' place,
turning his car toward the town which he had seen for
the first time less than twenty-four hours ago, and which
he now looked at as consideringly as if it were his home,
and would be.

Beyond the cluster of business houses and homes which
marked the center of the town, when he was about to turn
into the main highway, he slowed his car and stopped it
for a long backward look at the steep streets and the limestone houses. Somehow the place reminded him of Switzerland. Without the Alps, of course, but there was that
same quaint air of cleanliness and outdoor living, of good
cooking and, too, there was the turquoise lake. The quiet

of the wooded hills, the murmur of the forest trees—cows stood about in green fields, there were red barns and farmhouses, with flowers blooming in every dooryard—friendly people. . . .

A man living in this town and working here could put down roots. He could have one of those limestone houses, with geraniums in his window boxes; he could have his own boat down at the lake—a little boat, like the one that girl was pulling up on the sand. . . .

Grady leaned forward across the wheel. But what a *pretty* girl she was! Slender—with short, curly brown hair —she was graceful—she wore a red and white striped shirt with faded blue pedal pushers. Her brown hands were strongly sure with the beaching of her boat and the line with which she tied it up. She shipped the oars neatly, snapped a padlock, then picked up a sweater and walked swiftly, gracefully up the beach. A pretty girl, pink cheeked, smiling, capable—a girl such as Grady Barton would like to know.

With a sigh, he reluctantly started the motor, turned the car wheels into the far lane of the highway and drove past the sign which told him how many miles he must drive to reach Chicago.

CHAPTER *two*

It was raining. The people who came
into receiving were damp and draggled. Slickers rustled
and dripped, the ambulance orderlies' ducks were mud
spattered and there was the smell of wet wool throughout
the tiled corridors and rooms of the receiving ward.

Dr. Barton was busy—and the medical director had just
made him busier by choosing to come down for a routine
"walk" through his department. This occasion was always
as ceremonial as a parade, the director in his dark suit,
the white-clad intern, Dr. Barton in his crisp white jacket,
trousers and shoes—and a nurse. Not the supervisor this
morning. Admissions were coming in at a fast clip and
both she and Dr. Barton could not easily be spared for
the walk.

In his own good time, the director went off satisfied—
Grady thought. He mentioned a missing light bulb and
asked the chief how Dr. Lattimore was shaping up.

Dr. Barton was happy to say that she was doing fine.
While on medical service, Annie had had a little run-in
with an attending. But, except for getting a little tired
toward shift-end, the girl was doing all right in receiving.

21

Of course, in receiving the resident was Dr. Barton, and down here one didn't have much trouble with staffs and attendings.

So now Dr. Barton could give a good report on Dr. Lattimore, and the director was relieved to get it. He went off on that pleasant note.

Which let Grady sit down at his desk for a minute and make a wry face at the police mama-sheets which had accumulated in his brief absence. His desk was strategically placed. From it he could see his whole department, and be seen by his co-workers; by the entering patients, too—and by their families who sat anxiously upon the hard benches in the waiting room. This morning someone in there was praying out loud—they often did that, the sound mingling with the occasional weeping, the half-hysterical talk. Anxiety and fear had a sound as well as a smell. And of course it had a typical appearance. A doctor in Grady's position didn't let those things get to him. Couldn't. His concern and interest must be kept for the patients, for the injured and the sick, upon whom these other people waited.

In the watery gray light of this rainy morning, the smells and sights and sounds were all particularly intensified. There were times like that; there had been such times for Grady during the war. Times when the grass and the trees were greener than usual, and the voices of the soldiers were louder, more clear. . . .

"Six—O.K.!

"Five—O.K.!"

❋ ❋ ❋ ❋ ❋ ❋

"Is *ev*-er-y-bo-dy O.K.?"

"*O.K.!*"

Today, half below ground, and in Chicago, Grady filled in the proper blanks on a police record sheet and was keenly conscious of the wide-armed gesture which the "supe" made as she directed a worried young mother who carried a blanketed baby. A sick baby, Grady supposed. At the door, beyond this group, stood an orderly awaiting the next ambulance. And today Grady was sharply aware of the way this man stood, alertly interested and ready. It was perhaps the thousandth ambulance he had so awaited; Schulte was in his fifties and an old hand at City General. The ambulance arrived with a wet smacking of tires upon concrete, and the case came out.

Dr. Barton stood up; the sounds from the stretcher indicated a psycho, and Lattimore was up next to receive it. Broad shouldered, quiet, Grady stepped to the young woman-doctor's side.

"Ever present aid in time of trouble," said Annie, under her breath.

The case was a woman; her body was bound with restraining straps, she was escorted by three uniformed policemen. She chattered and screamed on a high, piercing note and endeavored to claw her hands. Grady took one of these and fastened a strap to its wrist, then fastened that strap to the cart frame. He gestured to Schulte, glanced at one of the policemen and went back to his desk. Annie took the phone and called psychopathic. Grady pulled a form from the proper desk drawer and tipped his pen toward the chair where the officer was to sit.

All without one word being spoken, he realized, with a grim smile. Tragedy of the first order had been so customarily handled that— *Oh, dear!*

His hand rubbed up over his face and smoothed his thick hair.

Schulte came downstairs again and wheeled a cart from a treatment room along the shining corridor toward the elevator; her pain mercifully dulled and her cuts sewed, that woman was being taken to a ward for rest and later treatment. Somewhere in the pile under Dr. Barton's hand was a report on the auto wreck. "Her auto wreck," they called it in receiving.

The morning wore on. Dr. Penn and Dr. Lattimore, the interns, worked under Dr. Barton's supervision; they did what he told them to do or what their instincts and training told them, should he be busy, as he often was.

Nights were sometimes worse in receiving, but the day-duty staff kept out of mischief. Humor sometimes relieved the tragedy of their work, absurdity brightened the monotony of cuts and abrasions, drunks that fell down and babies that did the same. In any circumstance, the emergency rooms kept full, and sometimes injuries must be dressed in the examination rooms.

Tragedy or humor, dull misery or violence, always papers and reports must be filled in, with the duplicates properly distributed. Morgue tags must occasionally be made out.

A lost child was brought in. A little boy with staring,

hungry eyes and a too-grim mouth for three. That early morning he'd been found wandering along a dark street; the patrolman had canvassed the neighborhood without discovering his home; he was taken to the precinct station and now had been brought to City General. Grady examined the mite and asked for a photographer to take his picture. Published in the newspaper, it might locate his family—if they wanted to be located.

Poor baby. He tore at a man's heart. He was not attractive, but with love and care he could have been. All three-year-olds should be attractive. Appealing.

"I'd like to take him home and cuddle him awhile!" cried Annie Lattimore. She was a nice person, was Annie. A little brisk and self-assured—as women-interns had better be!—but a nice girl withal. She'd make some lucky man a good wife. Grady had thought quite a bit about that lately. An American girl, like Annie, would very likely be the proper antidote for Gisela.

The child didn't cry; he didn't smile either. He just sat cross-legged on the table and gazed unblinkingly at the photographer. He refused all offers of toys or food.

His striped T-shirt and red boxer shorts were exchanged for a hospital pajama suit, and he went off to the children's detention ward, leaving the doctors and nurses and clerks on receiving with a hollow feeling of guilt that a baby could already know so much of tragedy.

By lunchtime Grady's head was beginning to ache. Only it wasn't lunchtime in any normal sense of the word. Personnel on receiving ate when they could go no longer without a break or when, miraculously, a break came.

That day, one did come near enough to one o'clock to be called lunchtime, and Grady took advantage of it. "Better come along," he said to Annie as he passed her.

She swung into step, a tall girl with short-cropped hair. She was ten years younger than Grady. They knew that the whole staff was watching them with what they considered a knowledge of something "cooking" between those two. It might be, too. Grady had often thought about marrying Annie. And of course hadn't, couldn't. Yet.

Lunch was good—he guessed. It was pot roast, with dumplings and what Annie called boiled cucumbers.

"Squash," said Grady with an obliging smile.

"Tired?"

"Aren't you?"

They talked about cases and about Dr. Penn's good looks—and the chances that their part of the hospital would be air-conditioned during the winter.

And the bitch box began to drone. "Call for Dr. Barton. Call for Dr. Grady Barton. Call for . . ."

"Oh, shut up, will you?" growled Grady, as he strode across the dining room toward a house phone which hung upon the tiled wall.

He turned back toward Annie and made gestures to her to indicate that he had a gun-shot case—forefinger to temple and crooked thumb—and went out. She ate his piece of pie as well as her own and leaned back for a cigarette, not even curious as to who had shot whom or why. . . .

"This is certainly a dizzy place," she thought. The din-

ing room was half-filled with white-coated, white-uni-
formed people—or those wearing the green of surgery.
Ten years before, such companions would have struck a
thrill into her breast. Now she didn't see them. Not as
white coated. Just as she didn't "see" the test pan which
the lab worker had brought with her to table or "hear"
the talk at a table of med students behind her.

Instead she thought about Grady Barton—the big, red-
headed guy!—and wished she knew a way to get through
to him how swell he was. How much everyone liked him,
especially Ann Lattimore.

It was, she supposed, the way of a decent man to be
tight-lipped about all he had gone through—during the
war, and since—but surely it would help Grady to know
that his friends were behind him and ready to give him
a hand up and out of his personal hole!

If that tall blonde wife of his didn't appreciate Grady
Barton, there were women who did. Especially Ann Lattimore.

More concerned at having his lunch interrupted than by
the fact of someone's having been shot by someone else,
Grady traversed the huge building, hoping as he drew
near receiving that it was not a child. . . .

But it was not.

In fact, the patient was a woman, large and about
seventy—and, in her excitement, unable to talk English.
She had a small puncture wound over the right eye. Dr.
Penn had applied a dressing and he told Grady that there
had been excessive bleeding.

"How'd it happen?"

"It's anybody's guess. She can't make anyone understand her, and the padre out there is no better."

Grady went out of the examining room to talk to the policeman. He'd been called, this man said—the woman had run screaming down from her second floor apartment, blood trickling between her fingers, and had lit into the priest in the schoolyard next door. Seemed he'd taken this gun here from a pupil, and it had gone off—he was sure he hadn't shot anyone. . . .

"Ricochet?" suggested Grady.

"Could be. Off the building wall, huh?"

"If she was near a window. . . ."

The man shrugged. "Who knows? He talks a little English. How you going to make a report, Doc?"

Grady smiled. "I have to make one."

"Yeah. So do I. So—what nationality is it?"

"Polish, I think. Though of course I'm not sure."

Grady went next to talk to the priest who was, in his own way, as hysterical as the wounded woman, but by dint of extreme patience and some sternness the doctor got the priest to speak some English and admit he was Polish.

Frown lines deep between his eyes, Grady went back to his desk and took up the house phone. They had a patient up on men's surgical—ambulatory—who might help. Grady had been interested in the man.

"Yes," said the nurse at the desk in that distant ward, "Dr. Tomyanovic *is* ambulatory. But I'd need permission to let him— All right, Doctor. I'll be glad to help."

Tightly cursing the red tape necessary to a large hospital, and certainly to a municipal institution, Grady did the things required to get this patient down to receiving. It took time, during which period Grady listened with half an ear to the frightened sobs of a child being taken into the emergency room and thought about the plight of a displaced person who also was a trained and capable doctor, not allowed to work.

Particularly he thought about Stanley Tomyanovic, Polish, a veteran of Nazi labor camps, two years in America as a displaced person and not yet able to establish himself here as a practicing physician.

Ten days before, this man had walked into receiving, already an advanced case of peritonitis; he'd diagnosed his own condition and that of his pocketbook and then had come into City General where he was immediately sent up to surgery.

He was a pleasant little cuss—and in a bad spot. He should be allowed to do the work he was trained to do, but even preliminary inquiry on Grady's part showed that there were tremendous barriers to that happy solution.

"Tommy," as the hospital called him, had been working in a shipping room to feed himself, trying, and hoping of course, to use his education and his ability. Grady had determined to help him, once the man was over his critical illness.

After an anxious week, he now was doing fine and the hospital personnel all liked him. Surely there could be made a place in this big hospital for Tommy!

Right now he was on his way down to receiving as an interpreter. And doing a bang-up job the minute he got within range; stocky, broad-shouldered, bullet-headed, swathed in a terry cloth robe, he was immediately *en rapport* with the excited priest.

"Never smelled so much stuffed cabbage down here before!" laughed Dr. Penn to Grady.

"From where I sit," Grady assured him, "stuffed cabbage sounds fine!"

The policeman nodded. "It's hell to fill out reports on these Bohunks," he told the handsome intern.

The priest's story was taken down, and they moved Tommy in to their patient.

There the tempo quickened and the noise lifted an octave.

It seemed the woman had been sitting at her window reading the newspaper—as, she claimed, she thought she had every right to do!—when all of a sudden-like, she felt a sting on her forehead, and blood began to run down her face and nose. . . .

The facts established, the reports made out, Grady sent the woman, a Mrs. Janski, to a ward bed for a twenty-four-hour rest from shock. The priest got into the patrol car and went back to his school.

And Dr. Barton leaned back in his desk chair to grin at Dr. Tomyanovic.

"I could do more for that woman than interpret her Polish," said Tommy.

"Of course you could," Grady agreed. "I've been looking into your case. It seems there are examinations . . ."

"I have taken their examinations," said Tommy spunkily, "and passed them, too! A lot of D.P. doctors don't."

He spoke English freely and easily, but with an accent as thick as cheese.

"Yes, I found that out, too. Then, in some states, there are citizenship requirements."

"I have my first papers. It takes five years. So I pack boxes until."

"There should be work in this hospital for a man like you."

"If I don't serve as a doctor. But, here, Dr. Barton . . ."

"I know," agreed Grady. "You'd be tempted."

"I'd be—" Tommy hunted for the word. "I'd be *driven!*" he cried. "Oh, Doctor, I am so *hungry* to do medicine!"

"I know," Grady consoled him. "I understand."

"But you do not! You cannot. Unless you too some time have had your hands tied as mine are tied." Wrists close together he lifted his hands as if they were bound in shackles. "One reads of shortages—in doctors, you know? And yet—" He shrugged. "I have tried so hard, Dr. Barton. I have taken their examinations. I have applied for citizenship. I have put my name down for an internship, such as is required in Michigan, and I have asked, even, to do the last year of medical school over again. *That* is required in some places. But the schools are all full, the internship is never available.

"I go to the offices of your big central medical society—"

"So did I," Grady confirmed. "The A.M.A. is on record as wanting to help you chaps. But the matter lies with the state societies, and there you have trouble."

"But they *need* doctors! They say they do."

"Yes. Just as they need teachers. Yet I heard, the other day, of a town in Missouri which had refused contracts to ten good Negro teachers when they integrated their schools, although they had vacancies in their list of white teachers. It doesn't make sense, Tommy. This country . . ."

"It is a very fine country," said Tommy stanchly. "Just, when a thing is so big, it isn't—" Again he hunted for a word.

"Co-ordinated?" suggested Grady, thanking the runner who brought in the mail. He drew his stack of reports closer. "Thanks for helping us on this one." His pen tapped the form on top. "Police cases have to be done rather carefully."

"What will be done about that?" asked Tommy eagerly. "Will it become a police case?"

"All gun-shot wounds become police cases, of a sort."

"Yes, but what sort? Can it be called criminal?"

Grady smiled, his first attention upon an envelope which he had found among the mail. "I could call in the duty doctor to tell us," he said idly.

Tommy leaned forward. "Beg pardon?" he asked eagerly.

Grady stood up; Penn wanted him in emergency. "In a city hospital," he explained courteously to this eager man, "or, I suppose, in any large hospital, there are certain staff doctors who are on call during a fixed period, usually for a month at a time. They are called 'duty doctors,' and the residents can call on them if an emergency seems to require it, for diagnosis and advice. In the matter of classifying this gun-shot case, I was attempting a small joke."

Tommy smiled obligingly and watched the big doctor go into the emergency room. There Penn had a baby with a split lip—the child had been injured in a fall. Quick first aid would reduce the possibility of a permanent and disfiguring scar. Grady supervised Penn in giving this aid, looked in on Annie who cheerfully said she had a school-yard injury. "Three fractured fingers," she announced blithely.

And then the doctor went back to his desk. Tommy had returned to his ward bed. Grady would look in on him before going home that evening, and if he had a chance—when he had a chance—he was going to speak to the director about the guy. There surely was a place here for him!

He reached his hand again for the letter he so wanted to read. It was personal, but—swiftly, he slit the long envelope, swiftly drew out the single, folded sheet of paper, swiftly let his eye run down the page. He bit at his upper lip to control his rising excitement. He folded the letter again, put it into its envelope and the envelope into his coat pocket. He had read enough.

Frank Seddens had not forgotten him! Silly of Grady to think he had. Or would. These things took time! A month was not long. And now—*now*—Mr. Seddens had written to Dr. Barton. Would he please come to see them? Miss Nellie hoped that Dr. Barton would stay with them as

their guest, and Frank himself had a business proposition
to discuss. . . .

"Feel like I did on my first date," growled Grady to his
quickening pulse, his sense of exhilaration.

The rest of the afternoon was got through with the
crackle of that fine bond paper in his pocket.

"Nothing may come of it!" he admonished himself.
"And you mustn't risk too much! You've got a good job
here. Don't dive into strange waters."

But the letter was enough to allow him to approach the
director with more confidence than he might have done.
He stated Tommy's case firmly and with avowed purpose.
"I know you can't assign him to medical duty, sir, but
surely there are clerkships, administrative jobs. . . ."

"He wants to practice, doesn't he?"

"Yes, sir, he does. But—he'd work as an orderly, just
to stay within reach of his profession."

"Has he gone to the medical societies?"

"All of them. Their systems are as screwy as could be
devised. Here's a capable doctor, anxious to work and no
work permitted him. Why, sir, I know of communities
where there is no medical service closer than thirty-five
miles for 4,000 people!"

"Oh, yes, Barton, that's true. And many times over.
But—" The director shrugged. "I have my own problems
to solve."

"Yes, sir."

"I don't mean to brush you off, Barton. I know you are
earnest in presenting this young man's cause—"

"It could be my cause, sir, if conditions were reversed. I mean, sometimes a doctor's license is suspended or re-voked—for various reasons—and a doctor doesn't know other trades. I wouldn't. Tommy has been put on the shelf unjustly—I mean, through no fault of his. Why should a few narrow-minded policy-makers condemn some community to live without medical service when a doctor like him would be available?"

"Would he go into rural medicine?"

"He'd do anything! I'm sure he would!"

The director made a note on his pad. "I'll see about putting him to work," he agreed. "And you and I to-gether will see what we can fix up about a license for him."

"Thank you, sir; you've been very kind to give me so much time."

"I have my own purposes. I want you to think about a position of your own in this office."

Grady sat thoughtful. "It would mean administrative medicine," he mused.

"Yes, and I've been told that you are too good a surgeon even to keep down on receiving."

That was honest of him.

Grady stood up. "I'll think about it, sir. As for re-ceiving, it's been a wonderful experience." He meant that; it would stand a man in good stead if he should take up general practice.

Promising again to consider the director's offer, he walked out of the office, now free to read and think about

his letter, to make a decision to go to the Hollies and
see, at least, what they had to offer.

In their hospital, days on duty were so scheduled that
about once every two months, Grady had three consecu-
tive days off. Such a period was due him in mid-October,
and he sent word to Frank Seddens that he would come
to Green Holly on a Wednesday morning. Mr. Seddens
said to come directly to his home where there would be
a luncheon meeting of the "committee."

The weather was perfect, with frosty nights, clear skies
and a warmly golden sun by day. Grady drove north
with a sense of rising excitement. "I'll not be very sensible," he admitted to himself. "I want to do this too
much."

The minute he saw the sparkling waters of Green Lake
he began to think of the pretty girl he had seen beaching
her boat as he had left the town in September. *Began* to
think? He'd never stopped. Her pretty face, her sparkling smile had, for six weeks, floated in his thoughts.

He cherished his memory of that girl much as a very
young boy thinks about the girl or woman he first recog-
nizes as being wonderfully beautiful and desirable. Appearing to Grady on that particular day, the girl on the
beach had filled a place rendered scarred and barren by
Gisela.

Gisela.

Deliberately now, as if he tested himself, Grady turned
his thoughts to the tall, blonde woman, the nurse of the
husky voice and caressing eyes, whom he'd first known as

an injured prisoner in a German hospital and later had married and brought to America.

Had he ever loved Gisela? He couldn't really remember. Any early emotional appeal and response had long ago become blurred and then lost in the quarrels, the demands, the recriminations.

"I thought it would be different," was the song he remembered of his marriage to Gisela. She'd thought everything would be different in America; she'd thought even a young doctor's wife would have constant fun, excitement and glamour. She'd thought she would have both freedom and privilege. She'd thought she would have everything—which she did not have. And when she did not have those things, she quarreled with Grady.

Well, Gisela was the past—along with the war, its glory and its hurt.

But the present was still his, and the future. A future which might hold a pretty American girl who would smile at a man as she tied up her boat, and whose eyes would be clear and honest as she walked with him along the sandy beach. . . .

Of course that girl would not be on the beach today— and she was not—but unless she was a summer resident, she'd be in town, and if Grady came here to practice. . . .

He clutched his soaring imagination, and deliberately considered the changes which a month and a half could make in the colors of the countryside. The pine forests looked more green, the trees stood dark and rich against the golds and reds and tawny browns of the other trees and brush. There was a golden haze upon the pastures, the lake water had taken on a pewter hue instead of the crushed foil sparkle of summer. Growth had departed from the land, and now was come the time for harvest and rest.

When he reached the town, he found that the window boxes were empty or that little evergreen plants had replaced the gayer petunias and geraniums. Sweaters and jeans covered the bare brown limbs of youth; the women wore stockings now, and a few men wore hats.

At the Seddens' home, the rugs had been rolled up from the screened porch and most of the furniture had been put into protective storage. Miss Nellie came to greet Grady with a lavender wool shrug about her shoulders.

"It isn't really *cold!*" she assured him. "I just get a bit shivery when I sit down."

She was glad to see Grady, and so was her brother. There was a fine smell of roasting fowl throughout the house, and Mr. Seddens told him that the committee would be there at twelve-thirty.

This gave Grady an hour to get settled, to inquire particularly about his host's health, and that of his hostess.

In her turn Miss Nellie asked him what church he belonged to, and did he have a voice? Everyone hoped he did, she said. Most choirs needed male voices.

Mr. Seddens said mildly that she was getting considerably ahead of things, and she agreed, laughing at herself.

Grady's experience with the airborne troops had served to intensify in him a natural inclination to stand back and survey a situation before becoming a part of it. That day, as the committee began to arrive for the luncheon meeting, he stood beside Mr. Seddens, acknowledged the introductions, was himself pleasant but not very talkative. During the meal he continued to study the ten men, to listen to them and, of course, he talked some himself while the men listened to him and studied him. He realized that they were doing that, and tried to consider himself as he must appear to the committee.

He was a doctor who had a job but was open to the suggestion of a change in jobs. A change which this committee hoped he would make, and which Grady wanted to make. For various reasons.

Some of which he hoped to conceal.

Especially he would like to hide the sense of humiliating defeat and failure which he'd not been able to shake off since that day, two months ago, when Gisela had demanded a divorce.

She was tired, she had said, of being poor. She was tired of her need to take second place to Grady's work. She was young, she had said—and she was! Thirty-six. She was beautiful—and she was! And—there was another man. A richer man, a much richer man.

So, she wanted a chance to marry this man. She was offering Grady the opportunity to give her this chance, quietly, unsensationally. If he would not comply—she had shrugged, looking very foreign.

He didn't really care. It had been years since he'd been vulnerable to that kind of hurt. So, without further discussion, he'd drawn a thousand dollars from the bank, and Gisela had departed for Reno.

His pride had been bruised; he was a man to hate failure

in any degree. But he no longer cared—really; his only
concern now was a hope that he need not bring any
shred of that past failure with him into this new life.
Should the committee be ready to let him start anew. . . .

He took a deep breath and studied the committee.

John, the houseman, and a maid served them baked
chicken and potatoes, peas and salad, coffee and butter-
scotch pie, and then cleared the table, having passed
cigars and cigarettes. A fine blue haze soon filled the
dining room. Miss Nellie had departed for a "little nap,"
and the chairs were resumed but not again brought
squarely up to the oval table.

There were ten men on the committee; Frank Seddens
acted as chairman, but perhaps not in any official capac-
ity. Evidently there had been several previous meetings
of this group; references were made to things said before
and decided before.

The membership seemed about evenly divided between
residents of Green Holly and Holly Neighbors. A couple
of the men lived in rural areas adjacent to the incorporated
towns.

Grady checked on his memory for names and occu-
pations. Mr. Seddens had been particular to designate
each man as he was presented. That bulky, dark one,
Kopp, was a farmer. The aggressively handsome blond
guy next to him was named Chronister, and called Mo. He
was a lawyer, as was Mr. Cowan who was called Judge,
and probably had been one. It might be that he still was
on the bench.

There was a Mr. Perry who owned, or managed, the

factory at Neighbors. Present were the two men whom
Grady had met on his previous visit to the Seddens' home,
Norvell Lee and George Goddard. There was a banker
named Rapp and an insurance man named Waller. And,
next to Grady in the circle, a clergyman named Cook,
almost always addressed as "Reverend."

Except for Mr. Seddens, who was the oldest, and Mo
Chronister, who looked to be in his early thirties, the men
were middle-aged and probably well established in their
fields. Mr. Cowan would perhaps be as much as sixty.

Grady looked at these men as he would have considered
a room full of patients, making a few preliminary decisions concerning them, but also exerting a genuine effort
not to prejudge by appearances or mannerisms. Still, as
with patients, appearances were informative. Types indicated certain things.

Judge Cowan, for instance, was a gentleman in every
sense of the word. Just as surely, Mo Chronister was an
extrovert of the first water. Like all medical students and
some interns who talked exclusively of disease and anat-
omy, this young lawyer talked a jargon of criminal terms
and police court slang which was intelligible enough to
Grady in the work he was doing, but he couldn't help but
consider it rather out of place here in the sedate dining
room of Frank Seddens' gracious home.

Kopp, the farmer, was a burly man who spoke ungram-
matically and had small social grace. He was the sort to
be aggressively sure that he was as "good as anybody,"
without any effort made to *be* as good. Grady knew him
as a type.

But, still, he would not prejudge.

And anyway, before he could, Frank Seddens undertook to call the meeting to order and to present the matter in hand.

"I've no big surprise to spring on you, Grady," he said in a fatherly tone. "On your last visit to us when, by happy accident, you turned up at a time when I badly needed medical care, we discussed the fact that the Hollies have no doctor. You agreed with me that 4,000 people should have the attention and care of a physician, and our discussion gave me enough encouragement that I have spent a month in talking to all who would listen to me—and a few who wouldn't. But I talked to 'em anyway."

A rumble of laughter rolled around the table.

Grady smiled and lifted his cigarette to his lips, puffed smoke calmly in a steady pencil of white above his head.

"I don't know if we can be called the town fathers or not," Frank Seddens continued. "But in any case, this group is a fair representation of all the people I have talked to, and of those who came together a month ago to consider the situation of our corporate health. It was that meeting which named this committee of ten to serve as a board. The whole group put its mind and its head to the problem, Dr. Barton, and then it put its dollars. A corporation was formed which sold shares at $25 each, until $9,000 was raised. With that money, we have bought a house and an adjoining building which is now in the process of being remodeled into an office or a clinic.

"It is not an elaborate setup, but it promises to be much better from our point of view than these two towns have had at any time previously. Since there is no other medical service here, we think patients can be assured you. The factory has promised to enter into a contract with you, or any doctor who meets our approval and who agrees to come. Our initial contract with you would run for a year, during which time you would have your home rent free. At the end of that year, you would be privileged to buy the house from the corporation; the clinic building would remain ours.

"The house, as it stands, is somewhat furnished, but you would be free to replace those furnishings with your own things if you chose. The clinic equipment awaits your advice to us and will be purchased as need arises and as funds become available. Various items, we hope, will become projects for our civic-minded citizens and organizations. Some of these things have already been underwritten. An examination table. A sterilizer—I think the term is *autoclave*."

Grady sat like a man of stone and appeared to listen impassively. Really, he found that he must exert genuine effort to control the eagerness which pushed against his ribs and trembled in his veins.

"He's a cold one, isn't he?" said Mr. Waller to the Reverend Mr. Cook.

Grady heard him. But he wasn't cold. Not really.

Having stated the basic proposition, Mr. Seddens sat down. There were further elaborations, comments, interruptions and questions. Grady himself asked some questions.

"What about the women of the town? How do they feel?"

"Our wives are behind us," said Mr. Rapp. "Some of them pushing hard."

"My daughter is *shoving!*" said Judge Cowan with a smile.

Grady bit down a silly impulse to ask if the curly-haired girl would be available. . . .

Instead he suggested that the committee would surely want to know something about him—then he volunteered information about his training and experience.

Various ones asked him other questions. Was he, asked Norvell Lee, an all-purpose doctor?

Grady laughed at the term, and told what he was doing in Chicago.

"I know you chaps don't like to be called general practitioners."

"Only because we don't deserve to be. However, my experience has been quite general, both in medicine and surgery."

"You're not a foreigner, are you?" It was the bearlike Mr. Kopp. The question jarred Grady—especially coming from that particular man.

"No," he said quietly. "At least no more than everyone else in this country. My family has lived in upper New York State for two generations. One of my grandmothers was Irish born. I get my red hair from her."

His manner made one or two of the men cast reproving glances at Kopp who, Grady decided, was impervious to glances of any sort.

The Reverend Cook asked about Grady's church affili-
ations; someone mentioned his politics—laughing. Grady
answered both queries courteously. Seriously.

"If you came here," asked Norvell Lee, "would you plan
to stay?"

"If I gave up the good job I now hold to come here, I'd
hope to stay."

"What Lee means," said Mr. Rapp, "is that most of us
feel we want a settled man."

"Do you mean older?" asked Grady.

"Well—"

"I'm thirty-five," Grady told them. "And a doctor much
older than that would *be* settled—somewhere—if he was
any good. As a doctor, I mean."

"Why do *you* want to come to a place like this? You
say you have a good job."

The question was a fair one, and Grady put some
thought into his answer.

He described the work he was now doing, the position
he held. He briefly dwelt upon the status of a hospital
resident. He told about the work which he'd done with
the airborne. "Both jobs have been fine places in which to
acquire experience. A lot of experience and of all kinds.
I've spent a dozen years acquiring that training. Now I
could move up from the job I hold as admissions physician
to one in the medical director's office, serving as his assistant.

"It would mean executive work rather than active
medical or surgical service. I'm not sure I want that. I
could of course continue for a time right where I am.

It is a good job and it pays pretty well—but it is a job of tensions, of constant emergencies, of accidents and trage- dies and heartbreak. All things which a doctor must learn to face and handle, but which should not be taken in concentrated dosage for a too long period. I feel that I have come to a place where I want—where I should— get away from that continued nervous strain."

Kopp's dark face thrust itself toward Grady. "Have you ever been a mental case, Doc?"

Grady's upper lip tightened and turned white. His hand clenched upon the table edge. He was very angry at the tone, at the implication.

But he spoke quietly. "No," he said gravely, "I haven't been. My record—from the time I entered medical school —is easily available to this committee. I have no police record and no medical record of a neuropsychiatric nature. I broke my leg while in service . . ."

"In a parachute jump," Frank Seddens said in a loud voice. "Behind enemy lines."

Kopp leaned back in his chair. "I think we got a right to ask questions; we got our money invested, and our lives —our family's lives—will be risked, too, if we take on a doctor. I think we oughta be damn careful who we get in here. And I still think he should be a settled man! Yes, and a married man, one with a family who'll feel he has to stay put, somebody we can count on!"

Grady looked at the man—ignorant, prejudiced—and he knew that here was a man whom he wanted to fight! To show . . .

He took a deep breath. "You'll have no disagreement

on that score, Mr. Kopp," he said quietly. And then he heard himself say, "I am married. I have been—for ten years."

And this week, his marriage was to be dissolved. Because Grady had failed as a husband? Or Gisela as a wife? Or because the marriage had been wrong from the first? That last, Grady truly believed. But he said nothing of the divorce. He did not say, "I have been married, but my wife was not happy and divorced me."

Kopp's manner had jarred him—into a defense of his personal privacy? He had a right to defend it, but these men also had a right to know the whole truth about their new doctor.

And Grady had not told the whole truth. Was he crazy? He heard his own voice jangling in his ears. He believed it was the first time he had so compromised with the truth. And the deed now done left a hollow spot in his consciousness, a hole which already burned and ached.

He sat back in his chair, overwhelmed at his reckless folly, and now the hand which held a cigarette, which struck a match, trembled visibly.

He was still numb with the shock of his experience when the contract was brought out for his consideration and his "John Henry," as Mo Chronister called his signature.

"Are you attorney for the committee?" Grady asked him, looking up from the paper.

"I'm attorney for anyone who will hire me," said Mo, laughing. "Judge Cowan there can sit back and choose his clients, but . . ."

Grady glanced across at the distinguished looking jurist.

"Would you care to take me on?" he asked. "It won't pay much. . . ."

"That's the kind he can afford," said Mo, laughing loudly.

Judge Cowan reached for the contract and read it aloud to Grady. "If you want to come here to practice," he said in a kindly fashion, "I think it is safe to sign this."

There was in the contract no mention of a wife.

And the contract was put into Judge Cowan's pocket after he had suggested that Grady might wait to sign it until he had looked at his house and his clinic—an advisable procedure.

Grady thanked him. "I chose my adviser wisely," he declared.

Then the meeting broke up in a flurry of mutual congratulations and good will. Judge Cowan had offered to take Grady for a look at the town.

"Towns," someone amended, with laughter.

Something like a tour was quickly arranged; Grady got into the judge's sedate sedan, with Frank Seddens and the Reverend Mr. Cook in the back seat, and they started out. He was shown the whole setup. Holly Neighbors first—its factory built of stone, its homes and its stores, its churches, the dance hall and pier, closed now for the winter as were many of the beach cottages they passed.

He was shown the dark red barns and the silo of the Kopp farm, and taken around the edge of Green Holly to see the showplace which belonged to Mo Chronister's parents. This farm was a model one, with huge barns, white fences and a handsome house of field stone and wide expanses of thermal glass. The elder Chronisters, he was told, spent their winters in Arizona.

Mo, he learned, too, was county prosecuting attorney. Judge Cowan explained that such offices were given to young lawyers. "Like your own service in a big city hospital, it will give him the necessary variety of experience."

"He seems a likable chap," murmured Grady, though he was not so sure that he had entirely liked Mo. Now he guessed that his parents' wealth had endowed the young man with his brash, assertive manner.

They were coming back to Green Holly, planning to go to the doctor's house and the clinic building. These were shown to Grady with a running comment from his three companions; the net result was a general impression that his future home was one of the older limestone houses; it had six rooms and a bath; it was somewhat old-fashioned, but comfortable and adequate. The clinic building had originally been built in the house's back yard to serve as a cottage grocery store. It was of frame faced with asphalt shingles and would do fine as an office and treatment room. The front display windows could be curtained— Grady wondered about finding a nurse or some sort of office help.

"Would you gentlemen," he asked on impulse, "misunderstand me if I asked to be allowed to look around now on my own?"

They did not misunderstand, and Grady watched the Buick drive away with his kind new friends. He turned back and went into the clinic where two carpenters sawed and pounded. Mentally, he set his desk into place—chairs

—and the promised examination table. In time they might equip a small lab; he'd have to do some work of that sort from the first. And do it himself, probably.

He crossed the yard to the house; keys had been given him. He stood and looked up at the place. It was an old house, built in the time of mansard roofs. The limestone walls were silvery, the slate roof had taken on a bluish tone. The frames of the tall windows were painted a dark blue. There was a small, screened porch at the kitchen door, a larger open porch at the front.

Inside, the rooms were large and high-ceilinged. The floors were of wide-planked maple, the wide window sills and doors were of walnut. In its day, this had been a very fine home.

In it now, there was, as the committee had promised, some furniture. Assorted. A stove and a refrigerator, table and chairs and dishes were in the kitchen. The dining room was empty except for a rug and a huge fern on a pedestal set into the bay window. The wide central hall contained a tufted black leather couch which, Grady acknowledged with a smile, possessed a truly professional look. In the living room, again with a bay window and lace curtains, there was a suite—a couch and matching arm chair in dark red cut velour. There was a gas grate, a radio—and a marble topped table. Lamps.

Upstairs were three bedrooms and the bath. One bedroom was completely furnished with a double bed, a dresser, chest and chairs and rug. The windows up there were of the casement type, the ceiling sloping toward the walls. "Got to watch it," Grady told himself. He could stand erect if he stayed near enough an inside wall. The smaller bedroom was empty, and papered in pink. The other large one contained bunk beds, and two chests of drawers.

In his Chicago apartment, Grady had some things which he'd bring here. A TV set, a desk, a leather arm chair. He owned some instruments, too.

"Looks like I'm in business," he said, aloud again. "If it weren't for that family thing, I'd be downright happy." He kicked his shoe at the ball-foot bathtub. What *ever* had made him give the wrong idea about his marriage! He'd talk to Seddens at dinner tonight, or to Judge Cowan when he signed the contract. Maybe they'd understand how Kopp got under a man's fingernails.

Maybe not, though. The man was on their committee; presumably Kopp was a respected citizen here in the Hollies.

Well, Grady would find, and take advantage of, a way to get things straightened out. . . .

He took out a small notebook and began to make a list of the things he must do and get and bring and buy. . . .

Laughing at the futility of doing that now, he put the book away and decided to walk about town.

He went out of the house, checked on the frame garage at the side of it, then walked on down the street, keenly noticing every detail. The houses, their lawns—the people he passed. The beach and the lake. All of these parallel streets ended at the lake. The water had lost the diamond

sparkle of midsummer, and the breeze was now a wind,
chill against his face. He should have worn his topcoat.
He walked briskly to the next street, and up along it to
the main part of town, a matter of three blocks, his eyes
and mind busy. People he passed identified him as the
new doctor, a few spoke to him as such.

He went west again along a narrow, tree-shaded side
street, the sidewalk of herringbone-set bricks, mossy
underfoot, and turned once more down toward the lake.
On this street were large homes, wide lawns, tall trees;
there was a general sense of ease and gracious living.
Here would be the "better part" of town. Even cities like
Chicago had recognizable levels of wealth and social dis-
tinction. All small towns of Grady's experience definitely
had them.

The street here was wider, the elm trees arched heaven-
ward with their branches interlocking midstreet. There
was a large home of buff brick—a charming, low one of
limestone—and . . .

Grady's brisk step slowed, faltered; then he continued
at snail's pace. The house he saw was big, square—white-
painted frame—green shutters—a delicately columned
porch entirely around it—a white picket fence enclosed
a wide smooth lawn, dotted with tall trees and shrubbery.
On the lawn there was a dog—and a girl.

A somewhat-Airedale dog, and the girl. . . . So familiar
had she become to him in the past six weeks of thinking
about her that Grady hardly restrained an impulse to call
out to her. He did watch her, for as long as decency would

let him dawdle, for as many backward glances as pro-
priety would permit him, and a few after that.

Having reached the end of the street, he considered
walking back along the other side. She probably wouldn't
notice. She hadn't noticed him before.

He went clear to the lake's edge, propped a foot upon
an upturned boat and thought about that pretty girl. Today she was wearing a red sweater and a dark blue skirt,
with sturdy moccasin shoes. Her short hair was a brown
curly mop, and her eyes were as blue as the autumn sky.
Exactly that blue. With just a softening tint of gray.

As she had talked to the dog and protested with him
for racing through her heaped leaves, she had smiled, her
teeth sparkling, her curved lips red. Her voice was clear
and musical.

"Candy, you rat!"

He examined that single speech; he considered the
enunciation of those three words, the inflection, the tone
of voice. . . .

One thing was assured! She lived here. *She lived in this
town!* In that fine home—not so much a rich-man's home
as one that bespoke background and taste and respectability. The Seddenses would know the people in that
house, and so Grady could hope to meet them, and—
and . . .

His eyes narrowed, and focused upon the water, upon
a bubble-edged chunk of wood, black and shining as, with
each wave, it lifted and dipped and came closer into
shore.

And *nothing!*

Grady's teeth ground together. What difference could any girl—what difference could that girl particularly— make to him? *He* was a married man!

And the most consummate of all fools! He certainly was *that!*

CHAPTER *three*

ON THE FIRST day of November, Dr. Grady Barton came to Green Holly to live and to work.

His hopes were high; he faced the future with confident anticipation. There would be work here for him to do, people to know, a place in the community to shape for himself. He drove his car into the garage beside the limestone house as a man puts his car away when coming home. He took out his keys and went in through the wide door; the house was warm; the stoker purred a welcome. He brought in his bags and the things which he had brought with him in the car, some instruments to take over to the clinic, some food for the kitchen. But there he found that staples were already lined upon his cupboard shelves, meat and butter and eggs and milk in his refrigerator.

These people were kind. He must not fail them.

Carrying his clothes upstairs, he stowed things away, being a tidy man by nature—and, he acknowledged with a smile, because of his mother's persistent training.

A telephone had been installed, with an extension at his bedside.

He walked about his home, liking it. He decided where to place his own things when they would arrive by truck. He'd have to rig some bookshelves—there were none in the house, and the truck would bring boxes of books.

He went over to the clinic and found it not yet quite finished. Muslin curtains had been hung at the front window, and some furniture had been set into place, but the paint was still wet and an overalled workman was busy with cabinets. Still, Grady could immediately begin to see patients here, and to work. Again he considered the possibility of a lab. He could start with the sink and the autoclave; there was a gas connection.

"Is the phone alive?" he asked the workman.

"Oh, yes, sir. You're the new Doc?"

"I most certainly am. Name's Barton. I thought I'd let someone know I had arrived."

"Won't be no need. Most'll know by now. They been watching for you."

"Good!"

It was good. Everything was going to be good here. He sat down and telephoned to Frank Seddens who said he'd be down to see Grady that afternoon. Was everything in order?

"Couldn't be better," said Grady enthusiastically.

"I'll put a little news item in the paper," Mr. Seddens offered. "Just to let folks know they can pester a doctor now."

Grady laughed and hung up. He sat on at the desk and

began to make one of the lists which were the framework
of his life. He'd need stationery, prescription blanks; he
must check on what medical equipment the committee
meant to provide for him.

The phone rang; it was the editor of the daily newspaper at Holly Neighbors. He welcomed the new doctor
and asked how soon he would be ready for business.

"I can see you at any time," drawled the "new doctor,"
and the editor chuckled.

"We have here an order for prescription blanks," he
went on. "One of the drugstores commissioned the job.
I want to check on how you want your name, and all."

"Maybe I should check first on that drugstore," suggested Grady.

"Now, look, Doc, you're not going to start out by taking
an order away from me, are you?"

"No, I guess not," laughed Grady.

The drugstore was sticking its own neck out to the extent of the bill for that order. If the connection proved
unsatisfactory, or an embarrassment, Grady could stop
using the blanks and order his own.

"Just put it, 'Grady Barton, M.D. Physician and Surgeon.'"

"O.K., Doc. O.K. Good luck to you!"

"Thank you very much." Grady sat back, smiling at
the telephone.

He thought he could see that wished-for luck already
upon the horizon. A good life was opening for him in
this place; he helping the towns, the towns helping him.

Mr. Seddens had said something about three o'clock.

Grady would eat some lunch, get his personal effects completely put away. . . .

At two, the handbell on the carved front door rang loudly. Grady slipped into the jacket of his brown suit and went downstairs. Judge Cowan stood upon his front porch, his dark green felt hat tilted back, a cordial smile upon his chiseled lips.

"Come in, come in!" cried Grady. "You're my first caller, and I hope it's nothing professional."

"You won't make a dime that way," the judge admonished him. He went into the living room and looked around. "See you got the Waller suite," he said dryly, his cane tapping the red plush chair. "Hope they had the spring fixed."

"I don't know," Grady confessed. "I haven't got around to sitting in here."

"Be like living in a Methodist parsonage, I'm afraid," said the attorney. "Or do you have your own furniture?"

"A few pieces—they're coming by truck."

"Your wife with you?"

"No," said Grady. "I'll be on my own for a time."

He had his comments—and his answers—all ready. He had decided that confession to a lie was not a good way to start practice in the Hollies. Too many people had heard him deliberately say that he was married. So—he would clear himself, but by a more indirect route. He'd be careful, but some discussion was inevitable. These people, he had known, would expect his wife to come with him. . . .

So—hating himself for each half-truth—"Gisela" he said

quietly, "has been out West on a family matter. It seems better for her to stay for a time. I've assured her that I'll do fine on my own, and I hope I can make good on that promise."

Judge Cowan said the properly sympathetic things about the undefined "family matter," and reassuring ones about the doctor's ability to keep house alone.

"You'll be lonely of course."

"Not if I'm as busy as I hope to be."

"I thought you came here not to be so busy."

The two men had seated themselves on the chair and couch of the Waller suite and were smoking. The spring had been repaired.

"Oh," said Grady now, "I'm ready to believe that I can be busy here, perhaps even have more actual work to do here than I did in Chicago, and yet not have to meet—and feel—the pressure of big-hospital medicine. That's a rat race, sir. Not only the cases, but the politics that goes on, the wire-pulling, the apple-polishing which is done and comes to be expected, the petty jealousies, the tale bearing, the grievances—real and fancied. The swarms of anonymous people." Grady sat thinking about those swarms of patients, policemen, orderlies, nurses, doctors, families, reporters—all ready to talk to the DOCTOR, and expecting the DOCTOR to talk to them.

"How do you get along with people, Grady?" asked the judge keenly. "I'm sure your friends here won't call you 'Doctor.'"

"I hope not. Well, sir, I get along with people quite well, I think."

"You seem fairly reserved for a young man."

"I know. I am reserved—I don't like to undress in public—literally and figuratively. But that doesn't mean I'm concealing things." Red flared into his cheeks. *"You're a liar,"* his conscience cried. He took a steadying breath. "It's more—well—waiting to express myself until I *know* what I think, and feel."

"A good trait," agreed the judge.

"I try to get along with people," said Grady earnestly. "I like them, generally. It's just that—well—Saturday night on the receiving ward of a general hospital—a big one—can put that liking of people to a test. The drunk, the hurt, the quarrelsome ones and the beaten ones— children and women, men in the gutter—I didn't so much hate the patients. Oh, I didn't hate *them* at all! But you found yourself in a constant foment at the people who were behind their being drunk and hurt and sick."

"I can understand how you would—if you were a man who would bother about the background situation."

"I seem to be that kind of man," Grady confessed.

"You may run into a little background material here, you know."

"Of course I know. But it's apt to be spread out a little thinner, isn't it?"

"I hope," said the judge, rising to leave. "I hope."

Grady arrived in Green Holly on Wednesday. On Thursday he was called twice by telephone, and three people came to his "office" for consultation. On Friday, he was a little busier, and attended a buffet supper at the

Reverend Cook's with a committee of the board, at which time the matter of clinic equipment was ironed out and his small laboratory promised him. Over the salad and sliced meat, the oyster scallop and good coffee, he became really acquainted with Norvell Lee and Joe Perry, and they with the pipe-smoking, red-haired doctor who had a store of interesting tales and a smiling, receptive air for the tales of other men. Judge Cowan was also on this committee and he seemed pleased at the way Grady fitted in.

"He tells us what he wants and gets it—and we think it was all our idea," he analyzed the young doctor's method to his daughter, when he returned home.

"Is he good looking?"

The judge thought about that. Then he nodded. "Yes, I think you'd say so. He's not a pretty man. He's too big and rugged. He has red hair—the dark kind, which he combs neatly. His complexion is the ruddy sort which goes with that hair, and his eyes are brown. There is a deep crease in his right cheek when he smiles."

"Does he dress well?" asked June.

"He's neat. He looks well in his clothes, but any man can achieve that in a well-pressed suit if he has a straight spine and broad shoulders, slim hips."

"The doctor does have those things, I take it."

"He's a fine chap, June."

"I wonder what his wife is like?"

For a long minute the judge was silent, and June looked up from her sewing.

"I was thinking," said her father, "that if I didn't know different, I'd decide that Barton was not married."

"Why?"

"It's not a reasoning judgment. You know, I fancy that I'm able to look at photographs of men in the newspaper and pick out the ones who I'm going to read are dead. I hit it quite often, too. This is the same sort of thing. Marriage seems to give an undefinable air to a man. Barton doesn't have it."

June laughed. "Well, anyway, I do think you like him, and I hope he works up a good practice."

"The indications are that he will."

On Saturday morning, Grady watched a sign painter neatly print his name in gold leaf upon the glass of the clinic window, and below it the hours when he might be found in the office. Mornings, ten to twelve, afternoons, three to five. No office hours on Thursday afternoons and on Sunday.

"Can't we come see you after work?" asked one onlooker.

"At night, you mean?" said Grady.

"Yeah. It's hard on a working man to have to lay off."

Grady smiled. "How long a day do you put in?" he asked the man.

"Eight hours. Five days a week."

"Come in on Saturday."

"I go fishin' on Saturday."

"I see. I do mine in the evenings."

Grady went into the clinic and the workman scratched his head. "He's a cool one, ain't he?"

"He knows what he wants," said the painter.

On that Saturday, Grady had a half-dozen office visitors, and went out on two house calls. He set up a bookkeeping system and began a case file. He took stock of his supplies, and wrote an order to a supply house.

That evening he ate dinner at the hotel in Neighbors, being over there on a call, and drove home in a drizzly rain that promised to become sleet. The house was warm and pleasant when he went into it. He changed into some slacks and a pull-on sweater and piled some reading beside his leather armchair. He had, that day, received his license to practice as a resident of Wisconsin and a bulletin from the state society.

He filled his pipe and stretched out, thinking about the week just passed, the work accomplished, the work still to do, and about the people he had met, those he had come to know better. The town . . .

At ten he began to think about a can of beer and a sandwich. He was still reading at ten-thirty when his door bell jangled.

"Got to put in an electric one," he muttered as he heaved out of his chair to answer the noise.

He snapped on the porch light and opened the door. His caller was a uniformed policeman, and the patrol car stood at the curb.

"Got a drunk and disorderly, Doc," said the policeman. His name was Stone—Obie—Grady had already met him. Green Holly had three men on its police force and worked in co-operation with the larger force at Neighbors, when the occasion demanded that.

"Is your man hurt?"

The slender officer nodded and shrugged, his face and eyes knowing.

Grady felt for his keys, then pulled his front door closed behind him. "Bring him over to the office," he said, going down the steps. "Will you need any help?"

"I expect," said Stone.

So Grady unlocked the office door, turned on the lights and crossed the pavement to assist the single policeman with his "D. and D."

"Just like home," he thought. But, of course, Saturday night, anywhere, was Saturday night.

Like a sack of old clothes, they dragged the rumpled, incoherent man out of the back seat of the patrol car, supported him across the walk to the clinic door and through it.

"Fix him up—good as you can, Doc—" panted Obie Stone when they had heaved the big man up on the table. "It's the prosecuting attorney—he gets a bit warlike when he drinks. Tonight he got himself socked in the eye."

"And how!" said Grady, busy with the man's cut and swollen cheek. Somebody had really hung one on Mo Chronister.

"He'll have to think up a good alibi for this mouse," he told the policeman.

"Won't have to bother. Folks know him."

Grady knew him, too, slightly. He had met the P.A. at the luncheon when he was asked to come to the Hollies—

a handsome, brash young man. He'd seen him since behind the wheel of a sporty car.

After an hour, young Chronister was on his feet, somewhat uncertainly, and ready to be taken home. He gin-
gerly fingered his cheek. "Thanks a lot, Doc," he said.
"I'll do as much for you if you're ever out on the town."

Grady laughed, said good night and turned back to
set things straight in the treatment room. Why, he asked,
should a man like Chronister think it a part of pleasure
and recreation to get into a fight with a truck driver at a
roadside restaurant? One's tastes in "fun," he supposed,
differed as widely as did the individual's tastes in reading, TV programs, women, sports.

Yawning, Grady went across to the house and up to
bed. Between the sheets he remembered that he'd never
got around to that beer. Well, he hadn't really needed it.

The next week was busier and better than the first one.
Grady's office hours were fully occupied, he had established something of a routine of house calls. He frequently
was called out of the office for sudden illnesses and small
emergencies. That week he eased one old person's dying
and brought a baby into the world, noting with satisfaction these mark-stones in the establishment of Grady
Barton as a family doctor.

He did a series of physical examinations for the factory
over at Neighbors and was invited to dinner at the manager's home. Joe Perry was not a native of the Hollies,
and both he and his home were what some Hollies folk
called "citified." Which meant only a fine gloss of sophis-

tication and no snobbishness. Mrs. Perry bought her
clothes in Chicago and employed a full-time maid. Joe's
silver-dusted hair was crew cut and he dressed with
meticulous attention to detail. Their two teen-age daugh-
ters were away at school.

Grady was a good-looking young man, and people endeavored to be kind to him. That endeavor led to liking
for him, so he enjoyed his dinner at the Perry home and
regretted being called away early in the evening.

Openly, his hosts listened to his side of the telephone
conversation. "Oh, yes, I can come. All right. I'll be
there in about twenty minutes."

"You don't know how good that sounds to us," Mary
Margaret Perry told him as Grady expressed his thanks,
and his regret. "To have a doctor one may call. . . ."

"It's sleeting, Doc," said Joe from the doorstep.

"I know," said Grady, tucking in his scarf. "This is an
accident case. Somebody fell on icy steps. I think it's an
old lady."

He tugged his hat down on his head and went out to his
car. It *was* sleeting, and he was glad that he had his snow-
tires on. Though if he hit glare ice. . . . He'd try not
to hit any.

The patient was an old lady, more in shock, the doctor
thought, than really hurt. She had a badly bruised hip
and shoulder and Grady made a mental vow to start work
immediately on getting himself an X-ray outfit. One
would be needed, often.

He treated the patient and instructed her family as to
her care, urging them to call him at once if there were

certain changes. In the morning, he said, he would return and decide then if it was necessary to send her for X-rays. "We could really use a unit here," he dropped the first seed.

He went home, replenished the dressings in his bag and checked with the telephone operator. With Frank Seddens' help, he had made arrangements for his calls to be relayed. It was one of the problems of his present practice which had not been foreseen. In the city there were call services, or a man's family, sometimes his hospital, took care of such things.

Here there were many problems other than telephone service to be solved. It was, Grady thought, something like trying to establish modern medical procedures in a primitive country. For instance, there was the matter of whole blood. Hospital-trained doctors had learned to use it—well, not exactly like water—but to count on its being readily available and to use it for the many therapeutic purposes lately discovered.

But Dr. Grady Barton was entirely without a blood supply. He had nothing but plasma.

And the next day . . .

He was conducting office hours and talking to a young mother who wanted her children to be given the immunization shots and regular check-ups which she knew were advisable. She had, she confessed, not been able to take three little ones to a distant doctor as often as should have been done.

That day she had brought the oldest child with her, and Grady was examining him. "This is a telephone," he said to the child. "I'll listen to your tummy, and then you can listen to mine."

The four-year-old regarded him with suspicious blue eyes. "Steth-scope!" he corrected flatly.

"Excuse *me!*" laughed Grady. "My error."

As he bent over the child, the phone rang, and he shook his head in protest at the noise and the interruption. He would *have* to get himself some sort of office assistant! And right away. Because the call was from an excited woman. A child had been burned. Should they bring her to the office? Or . . .

"I'll come at once," said the doctor. "Don't handle her."

He looked at the woman and the child in his examination room. There were four people still in the waiting room.

"I have to go out on an emergency call," he told the young mother. He was putting rolls of gauze, a bottle of saline solution, some tetanus toxoid into his open bag. "Would you please tell the others in the waiting room? I may be back in an hour if they want to wait." He changed his white coat for his windbreaker, explaining what the emergency was. A burned child—over at Neighbors—at the edge of town.

"I can stay here for an hour," offered the young mother —her name was Ball, and from that minute Grady considered her his friend. "I'll tell people who come or call."

Even as he said thank you, Grady was out and into his car. He had studied a map and pretty well memorized the local neighborhood and the street names. That day he found the proper house without too much difficulty. There were a couple of women on the porch to flag him down, several more were gathered in the living room. In an adjoining bedroom, a child sobbed with pain and fright, and a comforting voice soothed it.

Grady shrugged out of his jacket and rubbed his hands together to warm them as he went swiftly in to his patient.

At his approach a tall, blonde woman moved away from the bed on which lay the little girl—she was about five— and her clothing had been cut or torn away from the badly burned areas of her arms and upper body. Now she lay uncovered upon the sheeted mattress, and Grady nodded with relief. So often people would wrap a burned person in something fuzzy.

"Are you the mother?" he asked the blonde girl.

"No. I'm the sitter. *There's* the mother." She nodded toward a dark-haired young woman who stood terrified at the foot of the bed.

"Tell me what happened." Grady was opening his bag; he asked for a clean bowl or basin. He went to the bathroom to scrub his hands—and the blonde girl told him what had happened.

"Help her, Doctor!" the mother kept saying over and over. "She's *suffering* . . ."

"I'll help her," the doctor promised, listening to the sitter.

It seemed that she was the sitter, really, for the people next door. "My name is Pearl. I was taking care of the kids over there—they have a baby, and Debby. Today was Debby's birthday, so we asked Judy—that's Judy—" she indicated the weeping child on the bed "—to come over and have a piece of cake. She did, and then the kids put on their wraps and went out to play in the yard. Judy has a cold . . ."

"Oh, fine!" groaned the doctor, going back to his patient, swabbing out the basin with antiseptic, pouring his saline solution into it, breaking open a pack of sponges.

"Go on," he instructed this Pearl, who was a fine, big girl. Very blonde.

"Well, somehow, the kids got hold of some matches and they lit 'em. Judy had this big handkerchief pinned to her dress—to blow her nose, you know—and it caught on fire. The fire went to her coat and her dress. She began to scream and to run. I heard the racket and went out. I caught her and brought her inside—here in her own house. I didn't rightly know what to do, but I dumped her in the bathtub and turned on the water. I tore off her clothes and splashed the water on her—"

"Pearl's dress was burned," said the mother.

"Not bad," Pearl tossed away that consideration. "People came. Somebody called you—it all happened so fast, Doc."

"You're very much a heroine, Pearl," said Dr. Barton, putting on dark-rimmed glasses and bending over the child on the bed. He put a thermometer into Judy's mouth and examined the burned surface, closely studying the puckered, whitened flesh; there was the usual sickening smell—he had had quite a lot of second and third degree burns—both arms, the child's chest and her right side. Judy's sobs came in gasps now and were fainter. . . .

He considered his supply of dressings and nodded. Yes. He had enough. But he wanted some blood—some was probably available, but he'd have to type. Well, the first thing was to apply the pressure dressings, administer toxoid and then, probably, send the child to a blood supply. She was going into shock. He tied on a mask and put on gloves.

"Will you help me, Pearl?" he asked.

"Oh, sure. What . . . ?"

"I'll tell you what to do." He glanced at the mother and the women clustered in the doorway. "Could we have the room?" he asked courteously. "We could use a little more air in here." They began to leave. . . .

Together, he and Pearl applied the bandages, the doctor's hands swift and firm, with relief instant to the child. He hung a bottle and started plasma dripping into the vein, then he went out to talk to the mother—and to the father who had come home from the school where he taught.

"I think we must take Judy to the nearest hospital," he said, explaining about the need for transfusions and the matter of blood cross-typing.

"She seems quiet now," said the mother anxiously.

"She's somewhat relieved," the doctor agreed. "But she needs the transfusions. You know, I suppose, that Pearl saved her life."

"Oh, yes, Doc—we know that. Our little girl . . ." The mother began to weep again.

"I wish you'd send for that ambulance at once," said Grady to the father, and he went back to his patient.

Within five minutes the ambulance was at the door, and
Judy was carried out to it; the doctor phoned the hospital
and told the surgeon there what he had already done for
the child.

"Are you going to attend her, Doctor?" asked the distant voice.

"Why—yes. I'll come right away."

So, now, he would have hospital-affiliation. He packed
his bag, phoned to his office and told Mrs. Ball to send
the patients home. He paused long enough to give her
an account of his emergency. In a community like the
Hollies, news was not necessarily gossip. "Just set the
latch and close the door behind you—and thank you very
much, Mrs. Ball!"

"Why, Doctor, I was only too glad to help you. It's
wonderful that we have someone for children when they're
hurt." He thanked her again and located himself to the
telephone operator.

Judy's parents had gone with the child in the ambulance. Now the doctor asked Pearl if she would like to
ride along with him.

"I'm hired to stay with the kids next door . . ."

But one of the neighbors said that she'd take over until
the mother got home—and Pearl gratefully got into the
doctor's car. "I sure love kids," she told him earnestly.

He smiled at her. He liked the big blonde. She was a
pretty girl, some of the time. Especially when her face
was in repose. When she talked or laughed, her mouth
was too large and her teeth too prominent. Her name,
she said, was Pearl Broni—and she liked baby sittin' bet-

ter'n she liked table-waitin'. She did cleanin', too, for
certain folks.

"Would you do cleaning for me?" the doctor asked.

"You need somebody?"

"Both in my home and in the office. I also need someone to answer the phone and do other things in the office."

"Why, Doc, I guess I'd like that work. The cleanin'.
I'm too dumb for the office work."

"You could try it and see."

"No," she said firmly. "Better stop at the cleanin'. Besides I got regular folks who count on me to sit."

Loyalty, too. That was good. "We can arrange matters,
I'm sure," said the doctor.

Impulsively, Pearl squeezed his arm. "Gee, Doc, I'm
glad you're here!"

He smiled at her. "So am I, Pearl," he assured her.

And thereon began a beautiful friendship.

Their destination was a small hospital in a town of
20,000 people situated halfway between the Hollies and
Madison. The Elmore Memorial Hospital, Grady found,
was administered by a board consisting of members of
the family who had put up half the money and citizens of
the town which had contributed the rest. The hospital
staff was made up of three local doctors, with attending
privileges to men like Grady Barton who brought cases
to it.

The building was new. The lab was small, but suffi-
cient. They had X-ray service—and the whole thing was
thirty-five miles from Grady's office.

He saw Judy installed, and the first transfusion under way. A newspaper reporter came with a camera to take the child's picture with Pearl at her bedside.

On the way home, Grady bought Pearl some barbecued ribs and pie at a diner, further arranged for her to help him, and dropped her at the house where he'd first seen this girl who more and more reminded him of a fine, but lumbering, Newfoundland pup.

At the house, people still clustered in Judy's home began the first stanza of the song which was going to be sung to him and about him for the next few days. Together, he and Pearl had saved Judy's life—they were sure grateful to have Dr. Barton.

The tune was pleasant enough. It was fine to know that the people of the Hollies approved of him and spoke well of him.

Life was settling down into a very pleasant pattern. He had a comfortable home; he had patients; some of them paid their fees as they left his office. And now he had Pearl to keep him clean and comfortable. He had friends.

And, finally, he met "the girl."

He had been in the Hollies for a full two weeks when he was invited to dinner at Judge Cowan's home. Pearl, who lived near the roots of the grapevine, tipped him off that this would be what she called a "swell" party.

"You won't get thrown out if you don't wear a tux, but I know good and well the judge'll have one on. You got one, Doc?"

"You know I have."

"Yeah," she agreed. "I dusted out the closet."

Grady, with the street address in mind, had decided that the judge must live in the big yellow brick mansion on Lake Street—with the "girl's" home two wide lawns lakeward from it. He was mistaken.

That night, he found cars lined up before the white picket fence, and lights burning beside the front door of the identical white house which he had studied and admired on his first walk about Green Holly—and which he had fruitlessly driven past a score of times since.

His cheeks hot, his pulse thudding, Grady parked his car, went in through the gate, up the walk, up the steps and across the verandah.

His hat and coat and gloves were taken by a white-jacketed houseman who was a dead ringer for the Seddenses' John. Standing in the wide hall, Grady could look into a gracious living room, see a white marble fireplace, pink roses in a Wedgwood bowl—and the girl who stood beside Judge Cowan. *The* girl! Judge Cowan's daughter, June.

Tonight she was dressed formally in a frock of some thin stuff over a multitude of frilly petticoats. The costume gave the general impression of being blue—a soft, muted blue, threaded with silver in a plaid pattern. Her throat and upper shoulders were bare; there was a pink rose fastened into the clustering brown curls. And she was utterly young and pretty and sweet. She was everything a man would want in a girl—everything Grady wanted.

From his first sight of her upon the beach, on that autumn day when she had raked leaves and scolded her dog, and again tonight, he had known that here was a girl whom he could love. Through school, through his war service, even through the disillusions of his marriage she was what he had waited to find.

But now, he had found her—and . . .

Sick at heart, he made his feet take him into the living room, made his voice greet Judge Cowan and acknowledge the introduction to "my daughter, June." He was *speaking* to her and *touching* her hand, standing *beside* her to speak to the Perrys, then leaving her to assist Miss Nellie when she came in.

Other guests arrived, but only June mattered to Grady. He talked, and hoped that he made sense. He accepted a cocktail without its spilling from his unnerved hand; he listened again to praise for his care of Judy Nolan. He brought in Pearl's name to share the limelight and the compliments; he even managed to tell a humorous anecdote about the girl.

In turn these others told him about Pearl. When the girl was sixteen her mother had remarried—a widower with four small children. Pearl had walked out of the house. "She said," told June with a gay laugh, "that if she was going to baby-tend, she'd do it where she'd be paid. And she's been on her own ever since. You're lucky to have her, Dr. Barton."

"I know my luck, but I wonder if I have her or if she has me."

"She'll be boss," June told him, "and you'll like it."

Then she turned, smiling, to greet the last guest. Mo Chronister.

Mo came in on a high wind of cordiality and good will to all. He greeted the men jovially and kissed all the women—Miss Nellie who tittered, Mrs. Perry who stood unresponsive and June, who blushed.

"How's my best girl?" demanded Mo, and kept his hand upon the sash at her slender waist when he turned to speak to the new doctor.

Grady stood ready to say, "I've met Mr. Chronister." As he had, of course, at the invitational meeting of the committee and later upon his examination table. But a glint in Chronister's blue eye warned him not to bring up the matter of the surgical session. The eye was still a pale mauve, beneath a careful dusting of talcum.

So Grady contented himself with an extended hand and a brief, "How are you, Chronister?"

The prosecuting attorney was an entirely charming rascal. If rascal he was. He warmly returned Grady's handshake, assured the doctor that he was *glad* to meet him again and went on to say, "We'll do a lot of work together, I expect. Police cases, you know—posts . . ."

Grady drew down his mouth, and Judge Cowan laughed. "Mo's overselling the place, Grady. You mustn't expect too much of anything unusual or exciting."

"That suits me just fine," said the doctor. "I don't *want* things to be unusual or exciting."

They soon went in to dinner, where Chronister dominated the general table talk, telling various anecdotes in a jargon of crime and underworld usage. His talk of *hoods* and *choppers* and *molls* was somewhat amusing to the man who had for years held Grady's job in Chicago.

Grady was seated beside June Cowan and would have preferred talking exclusively to her, and letting her talk to him, but the table was small enough—there were twelve people present—for Mo to prevent this, whether that was his intent or not.

Probably there was no actual intent. Mo Chronister, Grady decided, was a spoiled young man, popular and well used to being the center of interest. He probably felt it his duty as a guest to entertain the judge's party. Eventually Grady relaxed into a decision to take Chronister for what he seemed to be and now concentrate on his being near June tonight, able to speak to her in the course of general conversation and certainly able to look at her. Closely.

She was a very pretty girl. Her skin was clear and fine, her pretty brown hair clung in ringlets to her cheek and to the back of her neck. Her hands were short, square—capable. Her arms were slender and round.

Her voice was clear and her laughter musical. During the meal Grady managed to discover that she had been graduated from college only last summer and was keeping house for her father and "Candy, our dog."

Grady told that he'd seen her with the dog.

"He's an absolute fool," said June cheerfully. "But we love him, and he loves us."

She explained about her father's semiretirement. "He's off the bench, but he keeps an office. Takes cases that amuse him."

"Some even pay me a little money," put in the judge, catching a word of their talk. "Others are fun." He then gave a hilarious account of a recent case—conducted during the past summer—where a native woodsman had been arrested and charged with trapping out of season. A large and overripe muskrat had featured as the "corpus delicti," and the case had concluded in triumph lest the defense bring in too much evidence. . . .

The judge, as the well-told story demonstrated, was a clever man; his reputation in town said he was a brilliant lawyer.

The judge's home was comfortable and gracious. The appointments of his dinner table, the meal served, told of good taste and wealth.

The judge's daughter . . .

Grady let himself become enfolded by a warm and rosy cloud of thoughts, shot through with exciting impressions and plans and dreams—all dissipated, pleasantly, by the touch of June's hand upon his arm. Her smiling eyes indicated that Mo had spoken to him, had asked him a question and now awaited his reply.

"I'm sorry," Grady apologized. "I was thinking."

"I asked if you already belonged to any service club," said Mo with a grin. He was a very big man, Elmo Chronister, prosecuting attorney, with yellow-blond hair cut into a somewhat long crew cut, very blue eyes and a big mouth that smiled widely over clenched white teeth. When he smiled, two creases deeply bracketed his mouth. Grady, who had become somewhat skilled in reading a man's character by his mouth, thought that Mo Chronister, possibly, was a sadistic man, cruel—though perhaps only heedless. But, certainly, those watching, unsmiling eyes and

that toothy grin did not indicate actual good humor—or
good will.

He gave himself a shake. Mentally. He wouldn't like
any man so possessive of lovely June Cowan. And now
he'd better just answer the guy's question.

He did answer it, in the negative, explaining that the
admissions doctor of a big-city hospital had little free
time for good will luncheons or other activities.

"Well, then," said Mo enthusiastically, "I think you be-
long in the Lions. Rotary's made up of older men." He
glanced at the judge and across at Frank Seddens. "I'd
like to propose your name to our group, Doc."

"Why, that's very kind."

"It's a thing you should do," Mo insisted. "We're a
service club and particularly interested in civic matters.
We work hard and we do a lot of good. We buy glasses
for a child, we nag the town council to repair a bad spot
in the street, we help with the polio drive, distribute the
Salvation Army Christmas baskets—and we have a hell of
a lot of fun! Excuse me, Miss Nellie."

"Goodness, I don't mind," Miss Nellie assured him. "It's
only old ladies who get shocked."

Warm laughter greeted this sally, and Mo leaned closer
toward Grady. "You'd get a real bang out of a stunt soon
coming up, Doc. We do it annually. It gets our towns
known pretty well roundabout. You see, with the co-operation of the highway patrol—they have reasons to be obliging to *me*—we select a certain day or night, not known
except to the committee—in advance, I mean—so some
joker can't flash a CW to his friend in the next state—and

on that night we flag down a car with a couple in it.
Arrest them, you see. We bring them to the hall where
a dinner is being held—complete with our wives and our
best girls and all—and then we shower that couple with
gifts, put 'em up in a good motel for the night, service
their car; they have a whale of a time and go off to spread
the good word about the hospitality which they've known
at the Hollies.

"That's the sort of thing we do!" He leaned back to
await Grady's capitulation, evidently sure that he had
completely explained the activities, and the worthwhile
aspects, of membership in the Lions.

Grady, to date out of touch with such goings-on, sat
somewhat dismayed. He wanted friends and to become a
part of the towns, but . . .

Mo was not one to submit to cautious consideration of
anything which he'd proposed.

"Look, Barton," he said insistently, "a chap just about
has to join something of the sort, in a town this size. It's
about the only way to make friends. For a stranger, I
mean."

"I suppose," said Grady. "Where I came from, that was
accomplished through the church." June's blue eyes
smiled at him, and she nodded, as if pleased. "And of
course in college the medium was the fraternity."

"Were you a frat man?" asked Mo, with quickened interest.

"Yes," said Grady, "I was."

He saw Joe Perry smile at Judge Cowan.

"And," he continued, "I can see the merits of membership in your club. . . ."

"O.K.," said Mo. "I'll advance your name. Pronto."

"You'll like it," June's soft voice encouraged Grady.
"They do have fun—and manage to do a lot of good. Then,
as Mo says, it will establish you among friends."

"You make it sound like everything I want," Grady told
her.

After dinner, tables of bridge were set up, with Mo
assuming that he'd start, at least, paired off with June.
He assumed all sorts of privileges with the girl, told of
things they had done together, mentioned others that he,
at least, planned to do with her. It was evident, from his
manner, that he considered June his girl, though she wore
no ring, and when Grady drove home after the pleasant
evening, it was with the decision that Chronister could
not have her.

Not without some competition from the new doctor.

Who, of course, was "married."

Though now, definitely, there was another woman.
And Grady should lose no time "divorcing his wife." Or
announcing that his wife had divorced him.

CHAPTER *four*

THE DAYS slipped by, busy and happy. Contented. Grady liked the Hollies, and the people of the towns liked him. He enjoyed their friendship, liked being known and himself able to call everyone he met by name—almost everyone. After years in the city, he especially enjoyed that sort of friendliness.

He was busy in his office, but on most days he had time for a walk, and he exulted in the sharp winter air, the snowy woods with the tree branches black and stark against the sky, and in brilliant contrast, the pine needles, richly green, sharply pungent. Tall and dark, the evergreens cast long shadows upon the untracked snow, though the small tracks of furry beasts soon would interlace that white expanse. Grady liked the smell of the woods, the silence broken only by the soft *plop* of snow from a branch. He liked, too, to walk along the lake edge, to watch the slow inward roll of the water or its lacy spray before a wind.

One day he walked in the fall of a soft, feathery snow and met June with Candy. After that, usually, he went around to Lake street to "borrow" company for his walk.

June confessed that keeping house for the judge, what with a cook and a houseman-gardener, did not keep her really busy. She walked well and seemed able to share Grady's periods of silent thought, just as she was ready to share the other occasions when he would discuss almost anything with her, local gossip or world politics, women's fashions and the Negro question. . . .

On these walks, they became great friends, Grady and June. People in town mentioned seeing them together, and not only as that rarity of human beings on foot when wheels were available. The ebullient Candy made a poor chaperone against gossip.

So, Grady Barton was busy, he was happy, he was content. Pearl Broni gave him a few hours each day, and he was doing well both domestically and professionally. His first important case, little Judy Nolan, had come along fine.

It was a break, he knew, that this early case should have turned out so dramatically well. It made people talk about him, perhaps with an exaggeration of his ability; but that exaggeration would temper with time, and it was a good thing with which to start his work. People liked to dramatize a doctor's ability, his skill. They wanted excessive powers for the man to whom they would trust their lives.

Meanwhile he was liked, too, and could like his neighbors, in turn. He tried to serve them in many ways. He conducted health examinations at the schools, he started a well-baby clinic to be held once a month. He did the usual thing in advising the children's parents, in coaxing them. Before the PTA, he gave a talk on the value of proper diet. In general, the results of these efforts were encouraging, and he was happy about them.

He had, in six weeks, become a popular man; he was frequently invited out, not only by his initial group of friends among those on the committee which had brought him to the Hollies, but by others whom he came to know. Holly Neighbors had a rather gay set of young married people, and he was often included in their parties. Miss Nellie still kept him under her wing, and he ate a meal at their house about once a week. He had other invitations of various sorts.

But he was also busy as a doctor. Of course his main time and effort was taken up with the usual run of colds and digestive upsets, headaches and minor injuries, but he had a fair number of extraordinary cases too, to test his ability as a doctor, and sometimes to cause him to break out his books.

There was a case of plumbism which was interesting; he had an amusing case—amusing to tell about later.

"The mother telephoned me that her baby had 'swallowed an automobile.' He had, too. I took him to Branter, and the X-ray showed that the limousine—a de luxe model, an inch by an inch and a half—had traveled without detour through the stomach and into the bowels. A very good place for it to be. There was no pain, and it was out by night. As cars go, it was a good traveler."

It was a good story; his kindness with the frantic mother had established a good patient-relationship. There were two other children in the family, a husband and a grandmother. Grady had firmly acquired the household members as steady, recurrent callers upon his services.

The town told admiringly about the night at the movies when a man had had a heart attack, and the doctor had saved his life—right there at the head of the aisle! Calm as anything, he had just taken a little box out of his inside coat pocket, asked the usher to hold his flashlight on the man—it was Bob Miller, you know. He's had a bad heart for years. Well, Doc was there all ready to give him a shot when he needed it, but *bad*. I don't know what we ever *did* without Doc. . . .

Grady knew, or guessed. He knew that his carrying amylnitrite ampoules was a wise thing and helpful to Bob Miller. He'd needed a stimulant right then, otherwise his already weakened heart might not have made it. Grady supposed his performance at the movie had seemed dramatic, and he himself had considered it a lucky break that a routine treatment could have been given under such circumstances.

He wanted people to know him, to like him and to rely on him. There would be—there were!—other cases and other decisions which he must make and which, probably, would not be so popular or so acclaimed. Already he had had to handle the case of a young girl, a member of a good family, who was brought to him by an anxious mother because the daughter had a "nervous stomach." The girl proved to be pregnant, and it had required all of Grady's tact and patience to persuade the mother that this condition was a fact and also that the doctor could not "do something about it."

He discussed these problems of differing appreciation with Judge Cowan on one of the frequent visits which the judge made to Grady—dropping in for an hour, or for ten minutes, to talk, to evaluate just such matters.

"A doctor must have a lot of difficult decisions to make," concluded the lawyer.

"No. He doesn't," said Grady. "A doctor must heal and cure—if he can and how he can. There is no other decision ever for him to make."

The judge leaned back to look at the big, stern-faced man. "You're not one for compromise, are you?"

"I'm not. But other people . . ." Grady smiled and shrugged.

After six weeks, the clinic equipment was pretty well complete. Grady had found a high school girl who would come in every afternoon to help him with the laboratory work; he would need to teach her everything from scratch, but eventually she would be a real help.

He still wanted an X-ray machine, but he had a good supply now of other equipment and he thought he could hope for the X-ray within a few years. His office hours were well taken up; his house calls were sometimes more than he really enjoyed pushing into the time available. Of course the richer people of the community still went to Mayo's and to Madison—some of them. He himself sometimes sent patients to those medical centers.

The factory at Holly Neighbors used him on a contract basis. He did physical examinations for them and was on call for accidents to the personnel, also to check on such illnesses as were covered by the insurance carried.

With 200 men and women employed, this gave Grady
a firm and steady income which was a comfortable thing
for a doctor starting out in private practice.

That he was generally popular was an unacknowl-
edged break for the towns, because they hadn't much
choice when it came to medical attendance. The only
other doctor was a doctor of osteopathy who, Grady reluctantly decided, happened also to be a quack of the
first water.

This man rather fascinated Grady, who had come to
know him during his first week in Green Holly. Dr. Cellaburl Stone had paid a call upon Dr. Barton, to offer him
"co-operation." At the time, he had talked extensively
about himself.

A man of forty, he had once been a tool and die maker,
but he wanted social preference and so had studied for a
degree in osteopathy. He was, he admitted, something of
a screwball; he hated children and old people. He called
babies "monsters," and old folk "nuisances." He invited
Grady to come see his offices, he had a really fascinating
electromagnetic diathermy machine. It was supposed to
do wonders for headaches—and other ailments.

Grady had not yet accepted the invitation. He sometimes saw Dr. Stone on the street. The man dressed like
an intern all the time, putting an overcoat on over his
white ducks if the weather required it. He always greeted
Dr. Barton with a fevered account of "an interesting case
I had last night, Doc. Almost had to call on you for help."

To date he had not called on Grady; when he did would

be time enough for Dr. Barton to decide upon his response.

To patients inclined to tell him what Stone had done—
or had not done—his stock reply was, "That was his
method. Now we'll see what mine can do for you."

According to his habit of evaluating a situation, Grady
decided that he had just enough competition, just enough
adverse opinion available to keep him on his toes and
just enough busy-ness and enough leisure-time diversion to
keep him content and happy. He took his walks, he fished
a little, he played some golf and joined the Lions, where
indeed he did make friends.

He saw June Cowan often, both by chance and by
design. They had their walks together; he often met her
by accident on the street or at parties.

She had, after the dinner at their house, stopped in at
his office one day to ask him if he would sing in the church
choir. On their first walk together, she had repeated the
invitation, rather insisting that he do this, and suggesting
that he come by for her on the next Wednesday evening
and go with her to choir practice. They would let their
organist decide if he had a voice or not.

Actually, Grady had a good, firm baritone, and the
Wednesday night date became an established thing.
Grady would drive to the Cowans' home, pick up June,
then go on with her for her girl friend, Virginia Spencer,
and Virginia's fiancé, Henry Preston, whom Grady also
knew through the Lions. After choir practice, the foursome would have a snack either at Payne's drugstore or in
one of the girls' homes. It was a pleasant arrangement.

Mo Chronister couldn't carry a tune in a bucket. He said so himself. He didn't go to church very often either. The new doctor did. People approved of that.

The week before Christmas, June found that Grady was not planning to spend Christmas with his wife. When she had asked him, and he had answered somewhat grimly, "No, I don't think I'll try that," she smilingly invited him to eat Christmas dinner with her and the judge. And Grady gladly accepted.

Generally, he thought, people were beginning to wonder about his wife. . . . Pearl did. She must have. There were no signs of a woman in Grady's home. No clothing or feminine fripperies. Pearl decided that Doc's wife had "left him," because, maybe, he'd chosen to move from the city to a small-town practice.

Such gossip as there was about Grady's personal affairs liked Pearl's story—it explained many things. Doc naturally wouldn't talk about a woman who'd treated him so. And certainly Doc scarcely ever spoke of his wife. When she was inquired for, his face always took on a sort of tight look—as if he were angry about something.

He was angry, of course. That he had not told the whole truth in the first place, that he still had not told it.

That year Christmas was not, as his well-meaning friends feared it would be, a lonely time for Grady. He was used to spending the day "alone," so far as family was concerned. This year, on Christmas Eve, he was privileged to escort June home from the midnight service, and then go on to his warm home, rich with the spicy perfume of all the cookies and fruitcakes and candies which patients and friends had bestowed upon him, bright with the houseplants which Miss Nellie had put upon his window sills, and—he thought wryly—made even brighter by virtue of the grateful-patient ties which had been given to him. He'd have to wear those ties, too. Their donors were not only grateful, they were patients who saw him constantly.

Christmas dinner was to be at four, June had told him. A compromise between her father's customary evening dinner hour, and the traditional noontime dinner of Christmas Day. Grady had the florist take red carnations to the Cowan home, and that afternoon when he had kicked the snow from his heels enough to go into the hall, the house was spicy with their fragrance.

With a smile and a pleasant wish for Christmas, Aaron, the houseman, took his hat and coat; Grady went on to the white-paneled living room where a fire burned upon the hearth, and June rose from a corner of the curved sofa to greet him. Judge Cowan came down the stairs to add his greeting to his daughter's.

"I asked Virginia and Hank," June explained, "but Hank . . ."

"Has virus pneumonia," Grady completed. "He had the flu and went out too soon."

"Is he very ill?" asked June, bringing one of the carnations to thread into the buttonhole of his brown coat. She patted the flower softly. "Thanks," she said, smiling up into his eyes.

Grady nodded. "Of course he's ill. Judge, what's the chance of getting legislation on the confinement of people with colds?"

"None, as you well know. Sit down, my boy. And give some thought to the cocktail or highball you want before dinner."

"If there's going to be your brandy afterward . . ." began Grady, then a thought struck him. "Virginia isn't sitting beside Hank, is she?" he asked sharply.

June looked anxious. "She said she thought she ought to stay and keep him company."

Grady stood up. "May I use your telephone?" He was already into the hall, and soon speaking firmly to someone in the Preston home. June and her father smiled at each other.

"Seems that you'll need more than one bit of legislation, doctor," said the judge when Grady returned to the living room.

"There are things I'd welcome more happily," the doctor assured him, "than an epidemic of virus pneumonia."

"Be good for business."

"Too good. But, as you know, doctors and lawyers strive for less business, not more."

At exactly four, Aaron came to the door, an inquiring look in his eye.

"We'll wait five minutes for Mr. Chronister," June said to him with a conciliatory smile.

"A gesture, purely," commented her father. "He's no more apt to be here then than now."

"I know. But—we'll wait five minutes."

"The thing to do with that young man," fumed the judge, taking off his glasses and polishing them, "is for someone firmly to forget that he is Mo Chronister."

But fuming and smiling patience, alike, were ineffective. Grady and June and the judge went in to dinner without Mo, and the turkey had been carved before that young man burst in through the front door, full of Christmas cheer of various sorts. Still wearing his overcoat, scarf and galoshes, he came to the dining room and bent over June, intent on kissing her. Grady prevented this by offering to help him out of his big coat.

Judge Cowan stood coldly at the side of his chair, a frown between his eyes.

"Bring some coffee *now* for Mr. Chronister," he said, coldly clear, to Aaron as the men sat down.

"I'm a little spiffed," agreed Mo. "You know how it is, Judge. Everyone you meet asks you to have a snort, and you do—and—" He shrugged and smiled. "How'ya, Doc?" he saluted Grady, as if seeing him only then.

Grady laughed. "I'm fine, thank you."

The meal was resumed, with Mo—as usual—taking over the conversation. He told, interestingly enough, of his Christmas Day activities. Very early that morning he had ridden the patrol car and picked up a half-dozen unsavory characters on the "levee" at Neighbors. Five men and a woman—"in the tank, all of 'em drunk and down. I promised the citizens I'd clean up that levee," he said earnestly, "and I'm gonna do it."

The judge looked doubtful.

"You think I won't?" demanded Mo.

"I think you'll think you've tried."

Mo frowned in an effort to understand. "Now, whadya mean by that, sir?"

The judge smiled. "Oh, you'll pick up a handful of vagrants now and then, put them in jail and/or start them out of town. In between, the levee will go on about its business as usual."

"Now, Judge, I don't consider that fair." Mo was stiff with affronted dignity.

The judge shot Grady a look. "I didn't expect you to."

"What would *you* do?"

"If I were prosecuting attorney? Or if I wanted to clean up the levee?"

"Well—both!"

"They're not the same, Mo. If I were in your shoes, prosecuting attorney and thirty-five years old, with a political career ahead of me, I'd make the same gestures as you are making. But to clean up that levee—I'd take away the liquor licenses which are being violated, close your so-called hotels, shut up the lunchrooms that allow gambling and bookmaking in the back rooms and I'd crack down on the drugstores that sell forbidden narcotics and joy-pills. That would give me a *start*."

Mo leaned back to look at his host, dismay widening his eyes. "Well—gosh—Judge . . ."

The judge laughed. "I'm sorry, Mo. It's hell to get old and wise."

"But—I thought—well—that I could make an example of these men, and . . ." His face brightened. "I did something else today, too."

"You did? What was that?"

"I—we—raided the Moose Hall this afternoon and confiscated the slot machines they have up there."

The judge leaned forward in dismay. "Oh, you didn't!"

"Sure did. I went up the front stairs, the chief went up the back, and we caught 'em all red-handed."

"But it's well-known they have those slot-machines!"

"They're not legal!"

"Well, perhaps not. But—"

"Now, Judge, you know there's no such thing as a perhaps-legal operation. It'd be like Doc here saying somebody was perhaps-dead. They are or they aren't. Isn't that right, Doc?"

"Well, I'm not sure, Mo. I sometimes make a qualified statement."

With a reproving glance at her father and at Grady, June came to the young lawyer's assistance. "Tell me about the raid, Mo," she said earnestly. "Was it exciting?"

It was, he assured her with enthusiasm.

The Christmas pudding was brought in, aflame, and served. Eaten. Nuts and candies, cigars and the promised brandy took its place—and Mo still told about the raid, with a deal of noisy swagger and some genuine humor.

The police chief had not wanted to do the job on Christmas. "He said it seemed a shame to spoil anybody's fun on Christmas. But I knew there was to be this party—"

"For children, Mo?" asked the judge sharply.

"No, sir. Of course not. They had their children's party last Sunday. No, this was for members, and I knew it

would be a ball. Was, too. You never heard such a
helluva racket! Dancing and bingo games and the slots
going full steam ahead. The men kissin' the women an'
the women slappin' 'em back. A keg of beer on tap, and
food and stuff set out on a long table. Hot as Hades up
there—it's on the third floor, you know. *I* know, because
we had to keep old man Carstarphen from jumpin' out
the window.

"Well, like I say, I came up the front steps and I looked
the place over—they had these three machines, with someone workin' each one—then I said, loud as I could . . ."

"Which would be plenty loud," murmured Judge
Cowan.

"Yes, 'twas, Judge," agreed Mo, heartily. "I said, 'Hold
it, everybody! This is a raid.'

"And people just stood there, with their jaws hangin'
open—then they all sort of exploded into motion at once.
The women squealed and ran, the men yelled—some broke
for the back way and got stopped there by the chief—this
man Carstarphen bolted for a window. After that, they
kinda milled about, and pretty soon they got to fightin'
among themselves. Seems some of the members, and
especially the wives, hadn't wanted the slots ever brought
in. And they fell to callin' names—Denstetter picked up
a bung starter and made to break up a machine. I had
to stop that! So he took out after me with his weapon, and,
Lord, you never heard such a row in all your born days!
It was a toss-up whether they were madder at me than at
each other. They called names and brought up old grievances . . ."

His voice rose to such volume that Aaron had to touch Grady's shoulder to get his attention. "You're wanted on the phone, Doctor."

Grady glanced at June, rose and went into the hall. Within five minutes he came back to say, "I'll have to go out to the Kopp farm. A visiting grandchild there seems to have the croup."

There were the properly expressed regrets. The judge asked if he knew how to get to Kopp's.

"Oh, yes. I've been past there often."

"Well, be careful. There are slick spots on those roads."

Grady said thank you for the dinner, that he was sorry to be called away—and went back to the hall. Soon they heard the front door close.

"Doc to the rescue!" drawled Mo.

June whirled on him. "If you stage a raid on the Moose Christmas party," she accused, "it's important and dramatic. But Grady—children choke to death with the croup, Mo!"

"Oh, sweetheart," drawled Mo. "It's just another five-dollar house call."

June's flashing eyes appealed to her father. The calm in his face quieted her. She was able to rise and suggest quietly that they move into the living room.

Oren Kopp was, nominally, a farmer. He also, Grady had come to know, dealt in farm property, buying it, selling it, swapping it—lending money on farm land and farm equipment. He was, as such things go, considered a successful man. Grady had not liked him much, from the first. He was an ignorant man, not so much unschooled —which he was—as a person who considered himself smart enough not to need book-learnin'. He was a large and lumbering man, dark skinned, with thinning dark hair.

He seemed to challenge one to disapprove of his habits and say something about them! Of course few did say anything. But Oren Kopp was not a popular man.

He was a member of the committee which had brought Grady to the Hollies, probably selected as one who would represent the rural, the farm, people of the community. He actually was a farmer. His farm was a large and rather well-tended place on the state road three miles north of Green Holly. Its great red barns and silo were visible for miles. He still had and used horses, which was notable in these days of machinery. His home was a small, white-painted house set fifty feet back from the highway. As Grady had told the judge, he was familiar with the Kopp farm.

On this Christmas night, the doctor turned his car into the drive of the place, took his small bag and went up on the porch. At his step, the front door was opened for him.

Behind him at the Cowans', Grady had left beauty and graciousness, pleasure for every sense. A small, glittering Christmas tree, ribbon-tied holly and mistletoe, a dinner table sparkling with crystal and silver, the perfume of flowers, of spices and of the wood fire which burned upon the polished andirons on the marble hearth. He had left the sound of low-pitched voices, and Mo's louder one, his laughter of uncomplicated delight. . . .

At Kopp's—

A doctor becomes used to contrast; he learns to consider few things except his patient and require only such conveniences to his professional attention as hot water, clean towels and fresh air.

But, still . . .

The front door of the farmhouse was opened by Oren Kopp himself, and Grady went into a narrow and chilly hall, unlighted except for lamplight which streamed through an open door at the far end of the passage.

Here too were appeals to the senses—the smell of wet wool and recently cooked cabbage, the sight of a child's small tricycle, and a red crepe paper wreath which bobbed and twisted under the drop light in the dining room into which Grady was ushered. There was the sound of a baby's labored breathing, and the comforting sounds made to the child by Mrs. Kopp.

Grady's attention sharpened. He had never met Kopp's wife before. She was a small, dark-eyed woman, bent almost double with some spine-affliction, perhaps arthritis. It was pitiful to see her so afflicted and trying to care for the child in the crib.

After a swift glance at the baby and while listening to Kopp's explanation of his trouble, Grady warmed his hands at the oil-burning stove and set his bag upon the table, then opened it.

The baby, he was told, was a grandchild. His parents had brought him for Christmas from Detroit and had left Gregory there because he had this cold. They would return on the week end after New Year's to get him.

"How old is he?" asked the doctor, touching Mrs. Kopp's shoulder to get her to move away from the crib.

"He's eighteen months, doctor," said the woman.

Grady bent over the crib, picked up the child and the blanket and carried him to the table under the light. The baby was crying now, along with that choking sound which he had been making ever since Grady had entered the house. The doctor adjusted a forehead mirror, took his flashlight and a tongue blade and bent over the child. Then his fingers explored the outside of his throat; he listened to his chest. . . .

The baby stopped crying to watch him, but his breathing was still heavy and grating.

"How long has he been like this?" asked the doctor.

"Since—well, noon, I guess. Not so bad. Croup always gets worse at night." Oren Kopp had taken over the matter of dealing with the doctor. The grandmother had retreated to a corner.

Grady held a thermometer under the child's arm—and stood thinking. "You say the parents have gone to Detroit?"

"Yeah—left about five. My son-in-law works for Chrysler. They're young—like a good time. We'll take care of the kid, I told 'em."

"I see. Did they give you full responsibility?"

"Like to spank him, you mean?"

"No. I didn't mean that." The doctor withdrew the thermometer, read it, wiped it with a bit of cotton and put it into its case. He still frowned.

He wrapped the baby in the blanket and took him back

to his crib; the child's fingers held the tongue blade and he began to cough.

Grady watched him, his frown deepening. Kopp moved to the head of the crib and the grandmother began to pluck at her apron.

"You think a croup kettle . . . ?" she ventured.

"No," said Grady kindly. "I don't think the baby has the croup, Mrs. Kopp. I believe there is a foreign body—" He caught himself up short. "I mean, I think he's swallowed something. I think whatever it was has lodged in the windpipe, perhaps in his lungs—"

"He ain't swallered *nuthin!*" cried Kopp.

"Not necessarily today, sir, or even yesterday; but I think there definitely is some obstruction, some object which has lodged and is interfering with his breathing. It seems to have set up an infection, too—not as yet acute— but I would like to take the child, tonight, for X-rays and probably an examination by bronchoscope."

"Agh, you doctors! Big words. X-rays. Examinations! The kid's got croup. All kids get croup!"

"All children do not get croup! And I am certain that this child doesn't have it."

"He's chokin', ain't he? An' spittin' green phlegm?"

Grady nodded. "Yes, I'm afraid he is. That's why I want him taken to Madison . . ."

"*Madison!*"

"I believe it is the closest we'd find a bronchoscope. But I'm sure that Dr. Messmer there will have one. He's a very fine surgeon, specializing in diseases of the throat and thorax."

Kopp thrust his ugly face toward Grady. "You're gonna choke yourself, Doc," he said unpleasantly, "on one of them big words!"

Grady stepped back, slipped off his head band, dropped it into his bag and reached his hand for his suit coat which he'd hung over the knob of a chair. June's red carnation still glowed in the buttonhole. Kopp glared at the flower.

"Suppose you treat the kid for croup, Doc," he said roughly. "That's what I got you out here to do. We wanted take our ailments to Madison, we wouldn't-a needed to put up money to git a doctor in here!"

Kopp, Grady knew, owned eight shares in the medical project. He had risked $200. But . . .

Meticulously careful, the doctor repacked his bag. Fear was a cobweb, building strand by strand about him. On leaving his house, Judge Cowan had urged Grady to "be careful." He had not, entirely, been speaking of the snow-patched road.

Slowly, thoughtfully, the doctor zipped the bag, then turned to look again at the sick child. He glanced at the grandmother who still pleated and folded the hem of her apron. Poor wretch; she too needed expert medical care. Grady straightened and turned back to Oren Kopp.

"Obviously," he said in a cold, tight voice, the line deep between his nose and upper lip, "you know what to do for croup. That is not my diagnosis for the case, and I would be doing additional harm to the child should I treat him for that. If you will not assume the responsibility which the custody of this child imposes upon you and follow my advice to take him to a hospital . . ."

"Oh, now, look here, Barton!" Kopp broke in gruffly. "We brought you here to the Hollies to doctor, not to preach. Why can't you just give us a prescription for somethin' to cut the phlegm? Surely you know enough to do that! We need a doctor here, but maybe you should remember that the ones that brought you to the Hollies can send you away again!"

It was incredible, thought Grady, how ignorant this man was, how incredibly stupid!

"I have a contract with the committee, Mr. Kopp," the doctor said quietly. "The terms of it do not include any statement requiring me to accept the medical diagnosis of a layman and to act upon it. I feel sure that I know what is wrong with the child here in your home. I am afraid he is due to become dangerously ill if you do not act upon my advice."

"Now that I called you, it will be your fault, won't it, if he gets dangerously sick?"

"No, Mr. Kopp. You called me in professionally; I have made my diagnosis and given my advice. If you refuse to follow it, my connection with the case ends, here and now."

"Let it end, then!" shouted Kopp. "I can promise that you'll not be called back here very soon!"

Numb with the need to control his rage, Grady put on his hat, his gloves, picked up his bag and let himself out of the house. He got into his car, backed it out to the road, turned into it and drove for perhaps a mile toward town. He was angry. He had been *very* angry back in that farmhouse. Now his hands still shook with the effects of that tremendous anger. He was in bad shape to drive. He pulled the car into a path which led toward a pasture gate and sat for a minute leaning forward upon the wheel, trying to think. He rolled down the window, hoping that the cold, brittle air would clear from his brain the web of fear which was threatening to engulf him.

Along the far side of this road ran a small river, and after a week of twenty-degree weather—tonight was close to zero—ice covered the swift little stream, and in the silence its voice was added to that of the wind through the hemlocks. Grady removed the key, turned up his coat collar and stepped out of the car, his feet crunching crisply upon the packed snow. In a conscious effort to relax, he would walk along the road—not too far. The sky blazed with stars, and the world was a beauty of black and white stillness. The peace of Christmas again touched his nerves.

And yet, it soon became apparent, the night was not really still at all, for the voice of winter itself was singing in his ears, and brought an instant tingle to his cheeks. The snow whined under his feet, the wind moaned in the tree branches and the ice upon the river groaned aloud.

Like all childhood memories, it seemed to Grady that the snow had whined even more shrilly under his boots when he was twelve and plodding along toward school. He could remember the deep cello notes of it under the runners of a sleigh; but tonight there was a pleasant enough hum of snow underfoot, and the music of the wind in the evergreens was very soothing.

The sound of the ice was more ominous than peaceful;

now it sounded like distant thunder, now it fell into flinty mutterings. Ice crystal upon ice crystal creaked and complained; water turned steel-hard grated upon itself under the stress and strain of its own grinding.

The surface of the ice became a sounding board for its own growls and mumblings and so filled the air with crystal shards of sound that fell away, then echoed again into the wailing sound of water, never more full of voice than when winter gave it a tongue of ice.

The cold night, the frost-shimmering air, the sound of the wind and the ice, became a baffle against which Grady's thoughts shouted and repeated themselves, not diminishing.

Kopp—and his threats, his stupidity. Coupled with stubbornness, a stupid man could be an actual menace.

The baby—so small, so ill, for all his imposing name of Gregory—so much in danger and so helpless against that danger. . . .

The crippled, neglected woman back in that farmhouse. . . .

And Grady Barton's anger, red behind his eyes, clenched tight in his muscles, fogging his brain. . . .

Desperately seeking relief from that anger, escape from that fog of fear, Grady threw his head back on his neck and gazed up at the clean stars, as if their distance might give him perspective from which to consider his present plight and his problem.

Never far from that consideration these days, his thoughts picked up June. A swift, vivid picture of the girl came before him, her clear, honest blue eyes, her gentle voice and ways . . .

And again he groaned aloud. For the thought of June brought its own strands to be added to the web which already tied Grady Barton, hand and foot.

There was that monstrous lie which he had told. It kept him from June and would continue to keep him from her. A useless lie it had been, a silly one. Whatever had made him do it?

Kopp.

Kopp had been the one seemingly to offer objections to Grady's coming to the Hollies.

But only seemingly.

There was nothing in the contract he had signed which required that the doctor be married.

But Grady had said he *was* married; knowing that they did so, he had let the committee assume that his marriage was in good standing, and so his own statement had accomplished the fact. Which was a lie.

Now that lie stood against him. With June, with the people of the towns who liked him and had welcomed him, with Kopp. . . .

Should Grady, say, follow his angry impulse and go to the court to demand adequate care for Gregory, the lie would come out, and by itself would make the doctor's position shaky. He had, of himself, built his professional standing here in the community upon such quicksand, upon such quavering ground. A man who would lie to get a job was not to be trusted in other respects.

As angry as he was tonight at Kopp, as frightened as he

was about the child, he knew he was right in his diagnosis.
At least to the point that a bronchoscope should be used.
He still realized that any insistence to Kopp, any effort to
bring the health authorities into the matter, would expose
Grady as a doctor who would lie, who would come to the
Hollies by virtue of a lie.

Before he froze his cheeks and his toes, Dr. Barton
took himself home, but that same Dr. Barton slept very
little on that Christmas night. And when he slept, he
dreamed. . . .

It was a familiar dream, and one he had come to
dread. Just as he had dreaded a recurrence of the experience on which the dream was based.

As medical officer attached to the airborne troops, Capt.
Grady Barton had been required to learn to jump—and to
jump. He had never really liked it. Some men did, he
thought. They found it exhilarating—some of them.
They'd taken it all ways; some had shown their tension
in wise cracks, some stood stony faced, some had gone
green—but all had jumped, just the same.

Grady had not liked it. But a man scarcely ever went
to war and into combat to *like* the things he had to do.
So, one of the tense and quiet men, Grady had taken his
place in the line, his gear in place and checked. He
watched the doors of the plane open; he felt the wash of
air—he saw the earth undulating against the sky—brown
fields—black trees—a farmhouse—the spire of a church—
and fields again . . .

Along both sides of the big plane's belly stood the young

men, bundled into their equipment and harness, their young faces standing out like pale moons, their young voices shouting in rhythm.

"Six O.K.!"

"Five O.K.!"

"Four O.K.!" Very loud.

"Three O.K." Three's voice cracked, and the sergeant and the M.O. looked at him sharply. Three grinned.

The count went on.

"Two O.K.!"

"One O.K.!"

"Is everybody O.K.?"

And the answering roar, in mighty unison.

"*O.K.!*"

Then— "*Hit the silk!*"

And they were out and away, dropping in pairs, down from the opposite doors—the M.O. jumped simultaneously with a T5 named Williams.

And on that one day—that memorable day—Williams's chute had become entangled with the suspension lines of Grady's chute. Williams was thrown into free fall . . .

Not more than three seconds out of the box car, Grady found himself engulfed in folds of nylon and knew that a man below him was in trouble. . . .

He clutched and grabbed and held on to an armful of the canopy just before the full weight of Williams's falling body hit the end of his own suspension lines.

Williams had yelled and screamed and shouted at Grady.

"Hang on, Doc! Hang on, for Christ's sake!"

Later Grady would know that the T5's arms had been entangled in the lines above his head so that he couldn't reach or pull the cord on his emergency chute.

They had landed without injury, Grady having been able to support the weight of the two men in the continuing descent.

Those had not been pleasant minutes to live through at the time.

They were not pleasant to dream about afterward. But Grady did sometimes dream about them.

On that Christmas night he dreamed of them again. Twice he got out of bed and walked about, found a book and read, hoping that he might go to sleep and not dream . . .

And each time he slept again—and dreamed.

"Five O.K.!"

"Three O.K.!"

"Is everybody O.K.?"

"*O.K.!*"

"*Hit the silk!*"

The next morning, Grady was depressed and worried. It showed in his face, though he exerted every effort to keep his voice and manner free of his mood.

After he had eaten his lunch and made a couple of house calls, he decided that he had a free hour before office hours and would do well to get some exercise in the open air.

As had become his habit, he cut across the side street to the Cowan yard and whistled for Candy. The dog came

lumbering, an ecstatic grin above his whiskers. The day
was clear and cold, and in the direct sun the snow was
dissolving into watery sponge. Grady struck off toward
the hills, the dog at his side, behind him, ahead of him,
woofing and sniffing in a fine imitation of a hunting dog.

Grady glanced at his watch, ready to follow his usual
practice of walking for half the time available and allowing the rest for the return trip. He was disappointed that
June had not popped out of the house. . . .

Man and dog stuck to the road rather than cutting out
across country. That is, Grady stayed on the road. Candy
was all over the face of the earth. Soon little ice balls
weighted his whiskers, and he came twice to his friend
to have a ball of snow dug from his foot pads.

"Really rugged, you are!" Grady laughed, growlingly.

Candy licked his face, then with a *yip* of recognition
and a wild waving of tail and ears, he bounded away toward a distant red figure—Grady followed him as gladly,
if not so swiftly.

"A lady needs a little time to get into her snowsuit,"
June informed him when he came within hearing. "You
two just ran out on me!"

"You could have waved your hand from your tower window."

She glanced up, laughing. "So I could. What'd I do?
Get here in time for the return trip?"

"Within five minutes," said Grady, warmly pleased that
his habits had become familiar to this girl. She looked
half her age in that red suit and cap; her cheeks were

scarlet, curls peeked from the tight hood, and her eyes were sparkling blue.

She regarded him as critically.

"I don't think," he was saying, "that I properly made my manners on leaving your house yesterday, June. But I do want you to know how much I appreciated being asked for Christmas dinner. And of course I was sorry to be called away."

She nodded, her eyes still intent on his face. "Is something worrying you, Grady?"

For a minute he didn't answer her, and she walked along beside him, not speaking further.

"I'm not much of a poker player," he said then.

"I don't suppose I could help you, but—" Her mitten lay upon his coat sleeve. "I'd do what I could . . ."

He paused, standing for a minute to gaze out across the hills and the fields—at the snow and the trees—at a house beside the road—at the blue sky overhead.

Then, without looking at his watch, he touched June's elbow and they turned back toward town, Candy close at their heels.

"Maybe you can help me, June," he said slowly. "You're right—I do have a problem. And while of course it is not my custom to discuss cases, I find that I need some light thrown on the personalities concerned in this particular case."

Then, concisely, impersonally, much as he might have stated a case to a class of medical students, he told of the problem which had arisen the night before. He described the visiting grandchild, the symptoms, voiced his own opinion that there was some foreign body obstructing the bronchi, and he detailed the signs of a developing infection; he told of the family diagnosis of croup. Finally he stated his professional position . . .

"I don't feel that I should accept a lay diagnosis and act upon it, but of course there is that baby—completely dependent upon the judgment—and the mistakes—of its elders."

"No wonder you're worried!" cried June. "That must be old Kopp you're talking about. And what a character! He's ignorant, and he's mean!"

"Yes. Yes, he is. Both of those things. And if I had him alone to deal with, I'd let his ignorance finish him off. But what should I do about that baby? Not two years old—and helpless."

She was warmly sympathetic. Grady was definitely in a spot! And she was sensible. "Could it be croup, Grady?"

He looked at her, then nodded. "Yes. It could be."

"You specifically told him what you thought should be done?"

"Oh, yes!"

"But you're helpless to make him do what you advised?"

He nodded, his eyes watchful.

"Well, then—since you're hopeless of being able to do anything about your own diagnosis, maybe we'd better just hope awful hard that they're right and that you're wrong."

"If hoping is all I'm asked to do," he agreed. "I couldn't treat that child for croup, I'm afraid."

"You won't get a chance, will you?"

"No. Kopp assured me of that. But, June, at least half
of this worry-load I'm carrying is regret that I should have
made a personal enemy so soon."

"Oh, Kopp!"

"You called him ignorant and mean, and that combi-
nation makes a dangerous enemy. But—if I could have my
druthers, I'd rather not have enemies of any kind here
in the Hollies. I'd like to be able to stay here and do good
work and have people like me."

"But, goodness, Grady . . ."

"I should have handled things differently. Yes."

"I don't see how you could. In this case."

"Well, I couldn't see either, at the time. But I should
have, just the same, because now—" He lifted his shoulders in a shrug.

"Can Kopp hurt you, Grady? I mean, he can't drive
you away, can he?"

"I don't know. I can take a lot of guff, if he stops at
guff. But he said something about the same men being
able to get rid of me as brought me here. And just maybe
he's right in that."

"They wouldn't!"

"But we don't know, June! They must have some way
to get rid of a doctor should he turn out to be unethical
or of bad moral character—they'd have to be protected."

Her pretty face was thoughtful. They walked for a hundred yards, automatically skirting the puddles, careful
not to slip on ice, but both thinking hard.

"Why don't you talk to Mo?" she asked then.

"Oh," said Grady swiftly, "I wouldn't want to do that!"

She looked at him, startled. "Why not?"

"Well—I might talk to your father. He's given me legal advice before and . . . But Mo—he's too—too—"

"I was thinking of him as a law enforcement officer. But I understand what you mean; as a lawyer, he'd grasp the legal points, but probably not get the personal angle. He's too young—and I'll grant he is rather brash. But, Grady, he is a brilliant man. Dad says he's a very smart lawyer."

"Mhmmn," said Grady. "Yes, I suppose he is, June." He'd known other "smart" lawyers he'd not want to lean on in times of trouble. "And I will say he's a brave one, too. To invade the Moose Hall on Christmas Day."

By then they had reached the edge of town and the corner where it would be "handiest" to part and go their separate ways.

For another minute they stood at this point, laughing together, remembering Mo's raid.

"That was a political gesture," June assured Grady.

"He won't get many Moose votes by it!"

"Oh, no, he won't. Good-by, Grady . . ."

" 'Bye. And thanks—it always helps to talk to you."

He had not promised to talk to Judge Cowan. Grady half-hoped that June herself might mention his predicament to her father, and the judge would then seek out Grady . . .

But he did not. So Grady did not talk to anyone about the matter. There really was nothing, he decided, to talk about. A difference of opinion concerning a diagnosis.

Doctors often gave advice which the patient chose not to follow. Surely this was no matter on which legal advice was needed. If the child did not respond to croup therapy, Kopp would take him to another doctor. Grady would be wise to shovel dirt over his impulse to charge Kopp with child neglect.

As for the matter of his contract, of Grady's status, any discussion of that point must bring the BIG LIE into consideration. . . . And unless Kopp made his threatened move, Grady had better not stick his own head into *that* noose. . . .

Through Pearl, he was able to keep close tab on the baby. The big blonde girl came in almost daily to clean for Grady and had earlier established the habit of reporting to the doctor on the health and general behavior of the children for whom she "sat."

As early as the day after Christmas, she said, she had been called out to Kopp's to stay with a grandchild who had a cold, and the grandmother wasn't well enough to attend him day and night without some relief.

"The kid's mom and pop," chattered Pearl, vigorously wiping up the kitchen floor, down on her knees for the job, "they went back to De-troit on Christmas Day—they're young and like a good time. You never saw such rhinestones as that woman wears! Kid's kinda pindly. 'Course he's got this cold."

"Is he getting any better?"

Pearl sat back on her heels and looked at Grady. "That's right—they called you for him, didn't they? Old man Kopp tried to tell me you didn't know what to do for croup. I said he was crazy . . ."

She reached again for her soapy rag. "The baby isn't doin' much good, Doc. He's still all choked up and don't eat good . . ."

CHAPTER *five*

ON TWELFTH NIGHT, there was a party at
the parish house: a square dance, which the choir planned
to attend in a body. It seemed natural for Grady to "go
with" June to this affair, for he regularly took her to choir
practice; there were many jokes and soft laughter over
the "choir robes" worn that evening. June's dress was of
red calico sprigged in yellow; the skirt was full, the bodice
fell away from her shoulders, and she had tied a yellow
ribbon in her hair. Grady wore tight jeans, a plaid shirt
and some half-boots which he'd acquired while with the
airborne.

As many as twenty couples circled and promenaded,
bowed and twirled, to the music of a record player. The
party was noisy, and lots of fun. "It's all a bit out of my
class," Grady panted after one dance, "but I'm learning a
lot." They'd brought in a somewhat professional caller
who offered to teach the Hollies dancers if they'd care
to plan regular sessions.

During supper, this idea was discussed with enthusiasm.
The Twelfth Night cake was cut, and Mo Chronister got

117

the thimble. There was great hilarity about that, and a little teasing of June, which Grady did not like, but could do nothing about. By now he was sure there was no engagement between Mo and June. He was all too familiar however with the way a small town could pair off couples as irrevocably as marriage. Such seemed to be the tendency here with the rich man's son and the judge's pretty daughter.

And Grady, a self-styled married man, was helpless to take a decisive step against it. Damn! He sat with brows beetled, and mouth tight.

As the evening progressed, the party got more rowdy than just noisy because some of the young men were making frequent trips out to certain cars for what was locally called a "pick-up." Everyone knew of this drinking, but because it was not done openly, no notice could be taken of it, and no effective protest made.

The rector disapproved and talked to Grady about the problem of bringing the town's young people to church affairs while excluding some of their friends, as well as those friends' doubtful habits. "A drunken brawl, however, would not be an adornment to these gatherings."

"And still, presumably, you want to reach the young people who drink."

"Yes. Oh, yes, indeed. And we have to overlook their drinking, hoping that we can eventually produce a substitute for it."

Grady discussed the rector's problem with June as the young people were forming three circles of twelve to learn a new figure from the caller. She laughed with him about

it, even as they both frowned a little at Mo's insistence that
he be in their circle. He hadn't a partner, and his face
was flushed, his hair in disarray. He was, as well, ex-
tremely noisy.

But the whole room was in confusion, and the caller,
not knowing a thing about local personalities, finally got
the dancers established in three circles of young people;
the gay bobbing skirts of the women were accented by the
dark-jeaned legs of the men. The music began, and the
circles began to turn.

The instructor started with familiar calls. *Swing* your
partner! Salute your lady—pick the cherries. . . . Take
a little peek! And *another* little peek!

Gradually the figures became more difficult—someone
faltered, a foot slipped, a girl laughed in shrill excitement—and Mo Chronister missed a figure so that he ended
up with June as his partner in the *Promenade All.*

"Hey!" cried Grady at his shoulder.

Mo grinned at him and winked.

The little blonde who had started as Mo's partner
tugged at his arm.

"You are wrong, Mo," June said to him softly.

"*I'm* wrong? What about that two-timin' quack who's
tryin' to get my place?"

Guitars thrummed, a piano thumped, a violin sawed
and the thirty-six young folks circled the hall, Mo's hold
tightening on June's hand and waist.

"Let's drop out, Baby . . ."

She glanced back at Grady, who nodded. And the four
did drop out, ruining their group, of course, so that the

whole thing immediately dissolved into confusion. Mo
was very pleased with himself and only a little abashed
by the firmness with which the other three refused to
follow his suggestion of going outside for a "snort."

He seemed quite ready to exchange this excursion for
a session of baiting Grady, but the doctor wanted no part
of that, and June's efforts at smoothing things over were
successful enough so that no further incident arose in the
remaining hour of the party.

Before the general break-up, Mo disappeared, and
Grady could take June out to his car without any sort of
argument. "I'm glad," sighed June. "Mo can be a little
hard to handle."

"I could handle him," said Grady, "but I'd much rather
not."

"He probably calls any doctor a 'quack' on occasion,"
murmured June.

"And would just as likely resent being called a shyster."

"Oh, yes! Turn about is never fair with Mo. He's rotten
spoiled."

As they turned into her street, Grady mentioned the
Lions' dinner coming up. He was on the committee for
the "stunt" of that night—the occasion of "hi-jacking" a
traveling couple for their dinner guests-of-honor. "Would
you enjoy being in on that brawl?" he asked June.

"I suppose they have lots of fun."

"Yes . . . It was my thought that having a couple of
women along might serve to mollify the lady in the case."

"Oh, it would, of course! You think of everything,
Grady!"

"Oh, I do not!" he retorted comically. Then, "Would you be my guest, June?"

She hesitated, but only for a second. "I'd love to!" she said then, and warmly.

Parking before the gate in the picket fence, he walked beside June up to the lighted porch and unlocked the front door for her, remembering just in time not to bend to her for the good night kiss he would have claimed from any other girl he liked as well and whom he dated as often. But Grady must remember that he was "a married man," and June had already been generous in overlooking his status. So he shook her hand, thanked her and sighed— went down to his car and, his face grim, drove toward his empty house.

As he made the right turn from the narrow cross street on to Maple, where he lived, a low, racy car roared toward him from the left, too close, deliberately too close. There was a crunching, grating sound along the side of Grady's car, and his hand went down heavily upon his horn.

The black and white sports car was into the next block before it stopped, and then backed swiftly. Grady, who was getting out to see what damage had been done, hastily closed the door. The crazy loon would hit anyone foolhardy enough to be standing unprotected on the street. But the big car stopped five feet away from him, bucking with the sudden application of its brakes.

Grady was quite ready for Mo Chronister when that young man came forward into the glare of his headlights. His blonde hair was tousled, his overcoat flapping and he grinned foolishly. "Hurt you, Doc?" he called loudly. Mo

had followed Grady's car to Cowans', had circled the
block twice, while Grady was saying good-by to June,
and then he had deliberately . . .

He'd put a deep crease into the left side of Grady's car—
fifty dollars would handle it, probably—and the doctor
would perhaps be prudent to let the matter ride.

Without speaking, Grady strode past Mo, unlocked the
door of his clinic and turned on the lights. In full view
of the street, he picked up the phone and called the police.

"Oh, now, look, Doc . . ." protested Mo, standing at
the open door.

"I understand that this is the advised procedure in any
accident," said Grady quietly, breaking off to make his
report to the man who had answered.

"D'you forget I'm the law myself?" Mo asked, as Grady
came out again to await the patrol car.

"Oh, no, I know very well who you are," said Grady
quietly, taking out a cigarette and his lighter.

"*Agggh!*" cried Mo, in disgust. "I'm goin' on home. Get
your tin can hammered smooth and send me the bill!"

Grady said nothing. But his eyes sparked; he just
wished the prosecuting attorney *would* leave the scene. . . .

But he did not. By then, a couple of cars had pulled
up behind Grady's, and a neighbor or two had come out
on their porches; others appeared at their windows.
Everyone in the district was familiar with Mo's car.

The police came, and Grady quietly told what had
happened, Mo leaning, sulky, against the side of the automobile.

"I made a right turn around the corner," said the doctor. "He came fast from behind me and his bumper-end creased my car. The driver was drunk, Officer."

The policeman tipped his cap back on his head, glanced over his shoulder, then leaned toward Grady. "But, Doc," he said urgently, "that's the prosecuting attorney."

Grady might have said that it was through no accident that the prosecuting attorney had creased the doctor's car. In which case he—the doctor—could claim assault.

But— "The important thing is that he is drunk," said the doctor coldly. "And while drunk he was driving a car involved in an accident. I can, if you like, prove that he is drunk."

"Well, Doc, you know . . ."

"If you bring him across to my office, I'll use a test commonly acceptable in your police court and prove that this driver is drunk." Grady was firm, he was logical, he was correct.

Mo, in his turn, was none of these things. He was noisy, he swaggered, he threatened, and when finally he did go with the policeman and Grady across to the clinic and breathed into the apparatus, he was also shown to be drunk.

The policeman wrote down the reading in his book and suggested, still warily, that maybe Mr. Chronister had better let somebody else drive his car home.

"I can drive . . ." declared Mo.

"Better ride along with me, sir," said the policeman.

"If he gives you any trouble," suggested Grady, "call your chief."

The patrolmen liked the idea of delegating responsibility, and brightened.

"I think he'll go with you," said Grady. "And you can send a garage man for his car—and mine."

"Look here, Doc," said Mo, coming over to Grady—though by then his movements were not so assured. "I'll pay for your damned old car."

"Yes, I know you will," said the doctor, waiting for a chance to turn off the lights and close up his office again.

With various incoherent, threatening promises, Mo finally got into the police car to be taken home. The garage man came, surveyed the damage to Grady's car. "You can keep it to use, Doc, till I get a chance to iron it out."

"Yes," said Grady, "I only wanted an early check on what damage had been done."

"Chronister's good for it. We pay our rent with the fenders and stuff he crumples."

Grady nodded and drove his car around to the garage. As he came out, the tow truck rounded the corner with Mo's car on the hook. The doctor went inside to bed. Would June know, too, that Mo had deliberately . . . ?

If she didn't know, Grady was going to seem stuffy and self-righteous in the part he would appear to play when the event was talked about. As of course it would be talked about.

For one thing, Grady had been told to appear in police court at nine the next morning. He dreaded that session while firmly intending to see the thing through. For one *could not* let a man go vengefully about with a weapon as dangerous as that heavy car. And still, he wished the thing had not happened.

Through sheer dread of it, Grady's imagination built up the police court session to such an extent that the actual event seemed like an anticlimax. For Mo showed up the next morning, sober and seemingly regretful. Yes, he conceded readily, he had been drunk. Happy drunk. Not down. And yes, sure, he'd side-swiped the doctor's car. "Those things happen, you know, Judge? Didn't you ever get your buggy wheels tangled up with another guy's, comin' home from a dance?"

The judge cackled in admission of his own youthful folly. Mo gracefully paid his fine, cracked a few more jokes, wittily and charmingly with the clerk—then he turned to Grady, his hand outstretched. At the minute, Grady's hands were busy with the scarf which he was adjusting.

"It's all right, Mo," he said almost indifferently. "I've been living in a big city, where one automatically calls the police in the event of an accident." Now he smiled and extended his hand. Somewhat warily, Mo took it. As Grady went around him and down the stairs to the street, Mo Chronister stood looking at the hand which Grady had shaken—when he wanted to.

But, for all of Mo's charm that morning, and his gracious acceptance of the penalty for his folly, Grady was well aware that he now had two enemies in the Hollies.

The doctor went on from the courtroom to make a house call and then he conducted morning office hours, with a continuing, heavy sense of failure in the back of his mind. A really tactful man could keep clear of these personal conflicts, he rebuked himself. And a doctor had better be tactful!

The matter was still a dark cloud upon his mental horizon when Grady walked downtown after lunch to go to the bank and attend to other small errands. In his preoccupation, he would have passed Oren Kopp without seeing him, but the burly man caught at his arm. "Hey, Doc!" he cried in his rasping voice. "Got a minute?"

Grady moved to the building-side of the pavement. "Certainly. What can I do for you?"

His question was evidently not just what Kopp had expected. He fumbled briefly, then came out with, "Thought you might want to know about the kid."

"Of course. How's he doing?"

Kopp, he decided, looked better in his working clothes of jeans and lined denim jacket than he did in a cheap store suit. If not cheap, it was at least ill-fitting. A light colored felt hat sat uneasily upon his shaggy head. "The kid," he was telling, "still had a little cold."

"Has he gone home to Detroit?" asked Grady, knowing better, but he had been hoping that another doctor called in would have passed upon his diagnosis, and Kopp's.

"Naw, he's still with us. His folks decided he shouldn't be taken out, with his cold and all."

"I see." Grady's eyes went beyond Kopp to the people who passed along the sidewalk, to the cars in the street and to the Baptist minister in a red Mackinaw, with a shotgun on his shoulder and a setter dog at his heels. A smile flicked about his lips.

"I ain't got a lot of time," said Kopp loudly. "Gotta drive forty mile this evening to jack up a man on a mortgage payment. They hunt you up when they want to borra the money, but I got to run 'em down to get my earnin's back. Guess you know how that is, Doc."

"I'm afraid not," said Grady courteously.

"I wondered, Doc," said Kopp, his small eyes searching Grady's face, "if—sence the kid ain't choked to death yet on that grain o' corn you thought he'd swallered, maybe you'd be willin' to give me a perscription for some cough medicine?"

Grady shook his head. "I'd not prescribe without seeing the child again—and I am sure that I'd still advise you to take him to Madison for examination."

As he spoke, he braced himself against the anger to be expected at his persistence, but a glance showed a conciliatory smile upon Kopp's face. "Now, listen, Doc," he said with a show of reasonableness, "you could be wrong, couldn't you?"

"Yes," said Grady at once. "I surely could be. The examination at Madison might prove that, but I'll say that I'd much rather have it prove me wrong, than that you were."

Now the anger rose to the surface, nasty and sneering. "D'you know what I think about you, Doc?"

"I'd be interested."

"*I* think you're too big for your britches, young man! You think you're damn smart because you worked in the

city. You think country folks don't know nuthin! Well,
I think you'd a-better stayed in the city—you had no right
to come here to work . . ."

"Mr. Kopp," said Grady, as patient as a human man
could be. "I shouldn't have to remind you that you were
one of the men here in the Hollies who particularly asked
me to come to your community and practice."

"I know I was," said Kopp, heavily. "And there, Doc,
I'll grant you, I made a big mistake!"

Grady's face remained impassively courteous and interested. "How is the child?" he asked in a firm voice.

Kopp frowned. "Oh, like I say, he has a cold—wheezy,
you know. Guess there's nuthin to worry about. But maybe some medicine would let him sleep a little easier. It's
hung on for a long time."

"You say his parents have been here?"

"Yeah. A week ago."

"Weren't they worried about him?"

"Ah, no! They know kids get colds—and like I say,
they's nuthin to worry about."

Grady stepped back to regard this man—as lumbering
and awkward as a black bear, his mean little eyes, his
strength which was that of muscle and bluster and insult.
Months ago, Grady had thought he would like to fight
Oren Kopp. Now he knew differently.

His gloved fingers tipped his hat. "I hope you are right,"
he said quietly, and he walked firmly down the street.
Kopp, he was thinking, had all the components of an old-
time melodrama villain. He foreclosed mortgages and
neglected children and—yes!—and abused his wife. Grady

did not smile. In deciding what made up a villain, those old-time playwrights had known what to portray.

During the afternoon, the day grew colder. By nine o'clock that night a man, snug in his warm home, could rightly grumble at a phone call that might take him out into the frosty night. Grady so grumbled when he got up to answer his ringing telephone.

It was Pearl calling, and at the sound of her voice the doctor's back straightened, and his head went up alertly.

She was out at Kopp's, she said, and the baby was sick. "Will you come out here quick as you can, Doc?"

"Is Mr. Kopp there?"

"No, that's why they asked me. Oh, Doc, come *on!* He's chokin'—and he looks *bad!*"

"Pearl . . ."

"You can't let him die, Doc!" She was sobbing.

No, Grady could not let a child die. He'd go out, and once there, he would make the necessary decisions about ethics and so on.

Moving swiftly, he put on heavy shoes, his leather jacket and a cap. He went over to the clinic to pick up such things as he might need, then crossed back to his car in the garage. Frost lay like diamond dust on every surface; out into the country each weed stalk knew its hour of beauty. The stars overhead snapped in the black cold, and Grady's step rang like iron upon the ground. It was a very cold night.

In the dark, Grady stumbled over a board and released some of his pressure by kicking the thing out of his way.

He was tight-lipped, and tension was zinging through his
brain as he stepped upon the porch. Fear? Sure. He
knew all about fear; he had learned that lesson completely
in the paratroops, had learned to expect it and how to
handle it. But never to enjoy it.

He opened the door and went into the narrow hall,
down its length toward the lighted transom. The hall was
icy cold, as it had been on Christmas night—and it smelled
of a hundred lingering odors, none of them pleasant.

In contrast, the dining room seemed hot. It *was* hot.
For the stove was going full blast, and the smell of menthol
was rancid in the steamy air. Pearl came toward him, her
blue eyes wide with terror, her big mouth gabbling a
dozen messages. She was alone—Oh, Miz Kopp—but she
wasn't no good—and the baby was bad—old man Kopp
was away—*and do something, Doc! Do somethin' quick!*

The doctor knew for himself that he must do something,
and quick, for the sound of the child's breathing, his
efforts to breathe, filled the dining room and the small bedroom adjoining. Grady set his bag on the table under the
swinging light bulb, he shucked out of his jacket, put on
his forehead mirror and nodded to Pearl who led the way
to the crib where the struggling child lay. In a dark corner of the room, Mrs. Kopp, the grandmother, sat huddled
into a low rocker, her fingers plucking at her apron, her
black eyes beady.

And the child . . .

With a low moan of protest, Grady gathered the child,
mattress, blanket and all, and took him out to the table.

He had sterile instruments. "Boiling water," he said to Pearl.

"Got a kettle full on the kitchen range. Doc . . . ?" Her voice shook with fear.

Grady nodded. "Where's Kopp?" he asked, as he reached for the tube which he had brought, and a scalpel.

"Oh, he went into the country about some propity he owns. Had me come out here—the old lady's no good . . ."

Only this afternoon Kopp had told Grady that the child "still had a cold."

While tonight . . . The baby was suffocating, his eyes were already rolled back in his head and his lips were blue.

"Get hold of Kopp," Grady barked directions to Pearl. "Or the parents in Detroit. Tell the operator; she'll find them. I want their consent for surgery."

A moving shadow at the door attracted his attention. With his one hand massaging the baby's throat and chest, Grady turned. "Mrs. Kopp," he said in a clear voice, speaking slowly, "will you agree to my doing such surgery as I might find necessary to save this child's life?"

Mrs. Kopp stared at the doctor. Grady glanced at Pearl, and she repeated the doctor's request. The woman's lips parted, closed—then she spoke slowly, falteringly, as one speaks after long, long silence. "Can't take no stand," she said, "without—the—mister."

This effort seemed to endue her with some courage; she crept toward the table. "Could you—maybe—" her gnarled forefinger crooked toward Grady—"run your finger down his throat—bring up—the stuff?"

Grady shook his head. It was too late—much too late!
—for that sort of attempt. The baby's limbs had stiffened,
and he picked up his knife. His fingers moved so swiftly
that it was not until the sound of air whistled through the
inserted tube that Pearl realized what he meant to do,
what he had done.

She gazed at him adoringly. "Oh, Doc!" she sobbed.
"Oh, *Doc!*"

Grady lifted his hand for silence. He was using his
stethoscope. Dramatic as its result was, tonight a tracheotomy would not be enough.

He straightened and told Pearl that a little more surgery
was needed. "We've got to clear away the obstruction—
whatever it is."

"Oh, Doc . . ." she whispered, frightened again.

"It's his only chance, Pearl. Now straighten up, I'll need
your help."

"I'm too excited . . ." Her hands clenched, and she
looked at him imploringly.

"So am I excited," said Grady, spreading a towel and
setting out the instruments he would need. "Did you tell
the operator?"

She went to the phone, talked briskly to the operator
and came back to the table, still excited—her cheeks were
as red as flannel—but she was by then ready to be helpful,
too.

Her excitement took the form of talk, and she chattered
like a magpie. "Gee, you're wonderful, Doc." "So quick!"
"Know just where!" and a dozen like phrases, exploding
like small, harmless balloons about Grady's head. He paid

no heed to them. The overhead bulb brought blue and green lights from his auburn hair, his strong-featured face was intent on the work of his gloved hands. The only time he made a sound was when he brought out the quarter which had been there all the time, now dark and slick and unpleasant to see, to handle. But doctors being the creatures they are, Grady was delighted to get that quarter.

Of course by now the thing had made its trouble. The child's lungs were conjested, the bronchi involved—the doctor could do only the best he could—while ten days ago . . .   He kept thinking of that! Ten days ago the coin could have been detected, removed and within twenty-four hours the baby would have been as good as new. But tonight . . .

He worked for an hour, then he took the child to his crib and erected the oxygen tent which he had brought with him, adjusted the small tank.

It was too late. Grady was sure that it was too late. Everything he had done was too late—and yet a doctor did what he could, when allowed. . . .

A few minutes before midnight, Kopp came in, banging into the kitchen, his voice rasping against the ears of the silent man who sat beside the baby's crib.

As Kopp reached the bedroom door, Grady turned his head. "Put away your cigar . . ." he said sharply. So sharply that Kopp did step back and lay his cigar upon the stove in the dining room. Then he came charging into the bedroom, his jaw pushed forward belligerently.

"What goes on here?" he demanded loudly. Grady felt

a surge of pity. Kopp was scared, and fear expressed
itself for him in bluster and noise. He came over to the
crib and squatted to peer through the tent's window.

"Who called you?" he demanded of Grady. "And who
in God's name told you to cut? By God . . ."

Grady was on his feet. "Get out of my way!" he said,
bending over the crib, a syringe in his hand.

It was no good. All he had done was no good. In that
same minute, little Gregory died, even as they watched
him. "I'm sorry," sighed the doctor. "I'm sorry."

For a moment there was no sound at all in the room,
in the house, then all at once, sound burst out every-
where. Kopp cursed and roared, blaming everyone, de-
manding punishment for everyone, vowing vengeance . . .

Pearl sobbed aloud. "The poor baby! Oh, the poor
baby!"

Mrs. Kopp, throwing her apron over her face, keened
wordlessly, like a dog howling at the moon.

Only Grady was silent. He folded the oxygen tent, set
it and the tank to one side. He straightened the small,
convulsed limbs, closed the eyelids, spread the blanket
smoothly and turned to leave the room.

Now his hands—his fingers—trembled as he repacked
his surgical bag, zipped it and carried it across the room
to put it with the rest of his equipment. Moving deliberately, unhurriedly, he came back to the table where the
unshaded light bulb threw its circle of radiance and cast
the corners of the room into brown shadow. Death was
ugly in this home, without dignity. Loss and heartbreak
were voiced in angry recrimination.

"He was my only grandson, and ya had to kill him, Doc!"

With a real effort, Grady lifted his head. "I tried to warn you, Mr. Kopp." On a piece of gauze lay the quarter, black with tarnish. Grady turned to pick it up, but Kopp's hand caught at his shoulder.

"You dassed me, Doc!" he screamed in frenzy. "You dassed me, and I took your dass! Then, first chance you get, you come out here and kill that boy! You knew I'd be gone—I told you I was goin' off when I seen you this afternoon. Never dreamin' that you'd come out here and kill that *baby*. But you did—and I'll git you for it if it's the last thing I ever do!"

For a long moment Grady stood looking at this bitter, this ignorant man. For that moment, sunk as he was into the depths of his own disappointment and frustration, he considered means and words by which to state his side, to tell what he had done, as well as what he might have done if he'd been allowed.

But without speaking at all, he sighed, lifted his shoulders and let them drop. It would be no use. Later perhaps he could talk to Kopp. But now—he went over to the telephone and called the undertaker, speaking gravely to the man.

Gravely he went back to the table, pulled up a chair, sat down and made out the certificate of death. Death by suffocation. As he signed his name, he paused to consider the shadow of his hand, black upon the form. He sighed again and carefully wrote it out.

Grady Barton, M.D.

Then, with a few words to Pearl, a concerned glance at the grandmother huddled in her chair, he put on his jacket and cap, gathered up his gear and let himself out of the house. Kopp, he supposed, still stood beside the baby's crib. Poor guy.

CHAPTER *Six*

THE NEXT MORNING was a glorious one of a pink and blue sunrise glowing upon last night's frost. Grady smiled as he picked up the paper from the front porch, remembering a neighbor back east who had disapproved of the term "hoar frost." It didn't sound nice, she had said, primly.

"Hi!"

He straightened, looked, then looked again.

"Well, *hello*," he said in amazement. "You're out early."

She was; it was only minutes past seven.

"I get up early," said June. "May I come in?"

Grady stepped aside and indicated the open door. "You certainly may." He could think of nothing more pleasant than June Cowan in his front hall. At any hour.

She slipped out of her dark plaid coat. "Father asked me to bring you a message," she explained, with a glance around. She shook her head to settle her hair into place. And smiled at Grady. "He didn't want to use the phone— in this town—just at this time. Your house is nice . . ."

"Nicest I ever saw it," said Grady warmly. "Would you . . . ?"

"Father said to tell you," June interrupted, "that while he is somewhat retired from court practice, he will be available for your defense to any degree that you may need."

"But—" Grady stared at her.

"Let me say it before I forget it," she urged. "Father has drilled into me that the wording of a phrase or sentence can make a big difference."

"That's true, but—" Grady smoothed his hand up and back over his hair.

"He said," June continued, "that he feels . . . let me see if I can quote. 'I feel that since I brought that man into the Hollies, and didn't tell him what he was facing, I now owe him all the help I can give.' Does that make sense to you, Grady?" She leaned toward him, her vivid face eager.

Grady's mouth was grim. It was beginning to make sense—he feared.

"He said he knew the 'boy'—that's you, Grady—thought he was coming here only as a doctor."

Grady rolled the string from around the newspaper, unrolled it and gazed unseeing at the headlines. His thoughts were entirely upon June's outpouring of words. His fingertips tingled with apprehension—but even so, he was still in the dark as to what, exactly, she meant, as to what precise danger portended.

"What's this all about?" he asked the girl. "Your father must know something that I don't."

"But you'll find out. That's why I came over here before breakfast. Father wanted you to know *ahead of time* that you've a friend or two here in town."

"Well, that's good! And speaking of breakfast, how about having yours with me?"

"Oh, no!" She stepped back, shaking her head.

"I'm a good cook."

"I'm sure you are. And I'd love to do it, Grady. But—well—probably not this morning. You seem to be in trouble enough without that sort of gossip."

Grady chuckled. "I'd admire to share a scandal with you!"

"Oh, I don't doubt that, young man! But I do doubt, and very much, if your wife would like the experience."

She was putting on her coat again, then she turned to hold out her hand. "Remember what Dad said," she told him and went to the door, opened it and went out.

Grady just stood there, dumb-struck, trying to recover even speech after the unexpected blow which she had dealt him.

By the time he had recovered, she was gone. Grady, left alone, moved on to the kitchen, where, his mind at least preoccupied, he prepared his breakfast, sat down and ate it, then rose again to clear it away.

Her father's message and its promises of—unpleasantness—had been completely overshadowed by her mention of a scandal between June and Grady, a married man. *A married man.* Had he been free, known to be free, this nice, modern girl would have thought nothing—and the town little—of her staying to eat breakfast with him.

But married . . .

Grady looked around him at the kitchen, at the tea kettle, the coffee maker, the dishes, the chairs. He looked at all these familiar things, then went on to consider, mentally, the rest of his home as it must appear to the town, as they saw it or were told about it. Surely they must try to place a wife into his household. Did they have trouble doing that? And what did they make of that trouble?

Again caught up into what was becoming an all-too-familiar beehive of regretful thoughts, twinges of conscience, protest at circumstances, Grady tidied the kitchen, put on his suit coat, locked his house and went over to his office. He had a little correspondence to attend to, the lab to be set in readiness for the day, some sterilizing of instruments to do, the setting out of fresh drape-sheets and towels in the examination room. He had a house call or so to make, but they could be handled at noon.

While he was performing these tasks, he was thinking, thinking—of things he should do, things he wished he had not done at all or wished he had done differently.

". . . might think I was a habitual criminal," he growled at himself.

At nine, the doctor, in a fresh white coat, was seated at his desk, a book open before him, with his mind at Kopp's farm. He was reviewing every step he had taken out there, each thing he had said and done. If, as he suspected, Judge Cowan's message to him foretold trouble with Kopp, he must be prepared to give a clear and logical account of that matter to his attorney. He wished he had brought that quarter with him—of course he had witnesses. Pearl. And Mrs. Kopp, who would be worse than useless.

Well—these things happened to doctors. Grady had attended classes in medical school designed to prepare him for such events, or to prevent their happening. The one mistake he'd made, perhaps, was going out to Kopp's last night on Pearl's call. But she'd been left in charge . . .

A draft of cold air announced a visitor, and Grady got up to see who it would be at this early hour. He recognized the man who had come into his waiting room as someone he'd seen on the street; he could not have called his name.

"Yes?" he asked.

The man fished into the inside pocket of the fleece overcoat which he wore and brought out a folded paper. He thrust this toward Grady. "You Dr. Barton?" he demanded.

Grady nodded. "What is this, a summons?" He took the paper, not looking at it.

"I'm deppity," said the stranger. "Jim Hawkins. *Christ,* it's cold this morning!"

"Is it?" asked the doctor, pleasantly.

"Close to zero. P.A. issued that warrant—after his steno got on the job—and he asked me to bring it over to you."

"Are you arresting me for something?"

"Oh, no, Doc. It's jest a summons to appear in magistrate's court on a charge of criminal malpractice."

"Aagh!" Grady stared at the man, who shrugged.

"I don't know nuthin about it, Doc. I'm only doin' my job."

"Yes, of course. I was—just—startled."

"Don't blame you, Doc. Things I ben hearin'—you ain't that kind of man."

"I'd better hope that others will agree with you," said Grady, fingering the folded paper. He watched the deputy leave, then went back to his desk. He studied the paper and reached his hand for the telephone.

Mo's secretary said yes, of course, Dr. Barton could talk to Mr. Chronister.

Mo's big voice answered at once.

"Chronister, this is Barton. I just got your *billet doux* and thought you might be inclined to add a little information as to what goes on."

"It's down on the paper, boy."

"In legal terms, yes. But I thought you could fill me in."

"Simple charge. Man came in here and filed it. I had to serve you with a summons to appear. If you're there— and you'd better be—you'll find out all you need to know."

"Yes, but it strikes me that a lawyer could—and would— have told Kopp that he had no case."

"Now, Doc," Mo's voice was as bland as cream, "maybe you need to get things straightened out a bit. I have a public office to fill and uphold. There aren't any personalities involved in this. It's just as if you were back in the city, with the due processes of law enforcement going on as they would there."

Grady rolled his eyes to the ceiling. He might have known that Mo would seize this chance to get even for that car business. "But your paper indicates a suit for criminal malpractice, and you know damn good and well there's no grounds."

"That'll all come out in the hearing, boy." Grady could fairly *see* Mo's familiar smile. The triangle of gleaming white teeth, his mouth bracketed by the deep lines in his cheeks. And no humor at all to warm his blue eyes. "All I know is that Oren Kopp got me out of bed this morning to make a complaint that you'd let his grandson die."

"*Let him* . . . Look, Mo! Do you know what a tracheotomy is?"

"Well . . ."

"Yes," said the doctor. "It's an emergency measure. And as for that malpractice thing, I could much more readily prove a charge of child-neglect. I told Kopp ten days ago—almost two weeks—that his grandchild needed a specialist's care. And he refused to provide it."

"You mean he refused surgery?"

"I mean he refused my professional advice completely. He refused to do anything for the child but treat him for croup."

"Well, Doc, that's when you should have brought your neglect charge."

"Yes. Yes, I should have. I could have. But—I didn't."

"He says you performed surgery without his consent."

"A doctor," said Grady coldly, "is allowed to operate without permission in order to save a life."

"Yeah, but sometimes there's a difference of opinion, isn't there, as to the degree of danger?"

"Oh, oh!" said Grady to himself. But he made not a sound to Mo Chronister.

"Well, it's this way, Doc," said the prosecuting attorney. "There's a blue alarm out for you. Maybe I should have brought you in to be charged—and held—or released on

bail. But it so happens that the magistrate is out of town
for a day or two. We won't need to return that warrant
until he gets back. Then—well—I'd hate to think we're going to be able to pin a homicide charge on you."

"Yes, you'd hate it," thought Grady, bitterly. *"Your
heart bleeds!"* An honest lawyer, or prosecuting attorney
would not express his personal vindictiveness in this way,
to let Kopp file a charge without grounds. . . .

"Of course," Mo was saying in a reasonable manner,
"we'll have the body posted, and—"

Grady sat tight-lipped. "Perhaps you'll ask me to do it!"

"Would you, Doc?" asked Mo brashly.

"I don't need to do an autopsy. I know that child died
of suffocation due to lung congestion. I found a coin
which he had swallowed and which had stuck in his
trachea. Who's going to take my word on a p.m., if they
won't trust me in the simplest processes of medical practice?"

"Well, now," drawled Mo, "maybe you've got something
there, Doc."

"Good-by!" said Grady furiously. "I'm sorry I bothered
you."

"I was glad to talk it over with you, Doc. And I'm
sorry I can't offer you any legal assistance."

"Oh, I don't need that. You may have forgotten, but
Judge Cowan is my lawyer." Grady slammed down the
phone. That would hold Mo for a second. Or two.

In the city the hearing would have been held at once.
Here in the Hollies—the magistrate had gone hunting or

fishing. Maybe both. He'd be back next week. Meanwhile the doctor, under a charge of criminal malpractice, could go on dressing cut foreheads, delivering babies and prescribing for colds.

Grady did go on doing those things, beginning five minutes after he hung up on Mo. At noon, he went to confer for two hours with Judge Cowan; in the afternoon his patients were asking him about the trouble, and Grady was following his lawyer's advice to "Be careful how you talk, son."

The town as a whole, of course, was swept up into a perfect storm of talk and exaggeration and side-taking. The city newspapers picked up the story on exchange, and on the second day Dr. Barton had a long distance call from Dr. Messmer at Madison, who was, precisely, the surgeon whom Grady had mentioned to Kopp as being the specialist to treat Gregory.

"Wha' hoppened, Doctor?" asked this man.

And Grady told him.

"Why didn't they take it to the Medical Society Grievance Committee?"

Grady gave then a brief character sketch of Kopp, mentioning his fear and his ignorance. He also spoke of their local prosecuting attorney as an eager beaver.

"But doesn't he realize how this sort of court wrassle can hurt you?"

"He realizes," said Grady tightly.

Dr. Messmer made a whistling sound of disbelief. "Well, look, son, maybe I should give your story to the *Capitol Times* here. Would you agree?"

It was tempting. "My lawyer says not to tell my side just yet," said Grady, laughing wryly at this belated memory of the judge's advice.

Dr. Messmer understood his reason for laughing and chuckled, too. "Well," he said in a heartening tone of warm sincerity, "if you want to walk out on 'em, come over here. Our door is wide open for a man of your experience."

"And reputation?" asked Grady sourly.

"I'm serious, Barton."

"You think I'm not?"

"Heck, boy," the older doctor soothed, "you can clear yourself. A frenzied parent—or grandparent—gets funny ideas. We doctors are all exposed to 'em. Always have been, and these days I guess one doctor out of thirty is fighting some sort of suit for malpractice. Not the doctors' fault—they're as ethical and skilled as ever. But the populace seems to think we promise miracles. And sues when we don't produce. . . ."

"This is a criminal charge, doctor."

"Yes, yes. And that's bad. But it won't stick, Barton. I'm sure it won't."

"I hope you're right," said Grady. He thanked Dr. Messmer and hung up.

Perhaps he should brief the judge on the A.M.A. method of handling malpractice charges. . . .

He did tell the judge; he talked several times to that wise and clever man, and eventually, as time passed, Grady was able to calm down, somewhat.

The magistrate returned on the twelfth, and the hearing

was set for ten o'clock on the thirteenth. That morning, Grady picked up Judge Cowan and drove over to Holly Neighbors where the courtroom was located above the laundry and the newspaper office. It was a cheerless room, with sun streaming in through the winter-browned windows. An oil stove heated it, and the curved benches, which had been bought from a church undergoing modernization, were that morning well-filled with eager spectators. To the right were a dozen chairs usually occupied by "cases" and their attorneys. In front of these chairs, and directly below the magistrate's raised desk, was a long, scarred pine table. Here Mo Chronister sat, and Judge Cowan led Grady to a chair at the far end of it. Mo spoke to them both in the friendliest fashion. After they were seated, Oren Kopp came in and seated himself in the corner of the front bench. He glared at Grady who appeared to ignore him, though he could feel tension building up within him. Cowan gave him a warning glance, then nodded to see only tight impassivity in the doctor's face. Grady's was the second case called, and he rose quietly to go up to the magistrate's bench. Judge Cowan went with him.

The magistrate read the charge, Grady identified himself and affirmed his innocence of the charge as filed.

That, Oliver Cowan had told him, would be almost all he would have to say or do. "You let me handle Mo," he'd advised.

It became evident almost at once that Judge Cowan was well able to do this. Well-bred, elegant of speech and manner, humorous at chosen times, sharply stern when

needed, he was in frequent clashes with the prosecuting
attorney, and each time came out the victor.

The audience of local people seemed to expect this sort
of show; they exchanged knowing smiles, and once burst
into applause which the magistrate quickly silenced. Mo's
color rose—evidently he was determined to top the judge
as a skirmishing trial lawyer.

As things progressed, Grady almost forgot how deeply
concerned he was in the excitement of watching a fine
legal mind at work. Once, however, he did glance at
Kopp to see how that man would be taking all this. Kopp
still looked like a bear, watchful, waiting. He'd filed a
charge, he wanted the man arrested and punished. He
could wait upon that development. Other things didn't
matter.

Grady turned back to the sword play going on before
the magistrate's dais.

Chronister now was talking. And expressing a wish to
be reasonable. He would, he said, hope for as much from
the defendant's attorney. "Now, Mr. Cowan," he was saying, "you surely are not going to claim that you think
every surgeon can operate at will, regardless of a family's
wish or judgment."

"You're right, Mr. Chronister. I am not going to claim
such a thing. However, I am going to point out to you,
and to this court, certain aspects of this case which justified the defendant's act. Which required him to act. Here
we had a child as a patient. A child unable to speak for
himself, a child needing someone to defend his right—
which is the right of all of us!—yours and mine, and his

own grandfather's—a right to the *chance* for life, for living. Failing all else, as all else did fail that baby, the doctor had no choice but to defend that right himself, to give the infant the one chance in a million which he had for life.

"The odds were too great—and the baby died. I am certain you would not claim, Mr. Prosecuting Attorney, that the doctor here accused set up those tremendous odds against Gregory Kopp Lohr. The odds of delay and neglect, of stubborn ignorance—"

"Can you prove those charges, Judge Cowan?"

"I could, but I'll confine my efforts to proving that the doctor in question acted according to accepted medical practice. That there was no criminal *malpractice* involved."

Judge Cowan had prepared a much more thorough case than had the P.A. Even Grady, who had worked with his attorney, was amazed at the man's knowledge and the skill with which he now used that knowledge.

Maintaining his air of fastidious courtesy, the judge thoroughly discussed the matter of legal claims of medical malpractice. He mentioned that they were increasing in number.

Mo brightened.

"The *claims*," said Judge Cowan, "the *number* of lawsuits. There has been no demonstrable increase in *actual* malpractice, just as there has been no increase in the number of inefficient and uncapable doctors. But the suits have increased. For various reasons, one of which I am sure is being demonstrated at this hearing.

"Now—" the judge paced the length of open floor, "medical malpractice is not a vague concept. It occurs."

Kopp looked pleased. Mo vigorously nodded his leonine head.

"It occurs," said Judge Cowan's suave voice, "when the physician does something that the ordinary, reputable physician would not do, or when he fails to do something that the ordinary reputable physician would do.

"Had my client treated the Kopp infant for croup, without detecting or seeking to remove the coin later found in his windpipe, he would have been liable to a suit for malpractice on the first charge. When he found that child convulsed and choking to death, had he failed to take his scalpel and open that clogged windpipe—he would have been guilty on the second charge."

Judge Cowan continued, and too swiftly for Mo to speak. "Now many patients think that a doctor should be able to guarantee results. Actually, all any doctor can do is to treat a patient with his best care and professional ability. There has been, I'll agree, lately a great advance in medical knowledge. But there still is no implied contract or warranty that a cure or even benefit will result from any course of treatment.

"There are many diagnostic and therapeutic techniques—"

Here Kopp leaned toward Mo and whispered loudly. Mo nodded and rose to suggest to the magistrate that the judge speak in simpler terms. That the court so order him.

"I don't believe," said Judge Cowan gently, "that the

court finds it difficult to understand me. But should you feel the need of a dictionary, Mr. Prosecuting Attorney, I'll gladly agree to a recess until one is made available to you."

The magistrate rapped his desk for order. Mo chewed his lower lip.

"Then," said Judge Cowan, his face as grave as that on a coin, "I shall continue. I was saying that there are many medical techniques in which the calculated risk is considerable. X-ray therapy for cancer destroys healthy tissue as well as that diseased. Certain wonder-working drugs have toxic results. The attending physician must exercise his best judgment as to the method to use and the risk to run. In an emergency, a doctor cannot lengthily study a case—as lawyers do or as an engineer can figure on stress and strain. In an emergency, a doctor must take immediate action, applying his highly trained and specialized knowledge as to the proper treatment to use.

"It is my contention that no patient has any moral or legal right to accuse the doctor because of the poor result of a treatment.

"It is also my contention that our young, and earnest, prosecuting attorney did not properly advise the plaintiff in this charge as to the available processes for examining this situation. He should have told Mr. Kopp—what he surely knew—that the State Medical Society has an established, and available, panel of specialists on whom Mr. Kopp—or Mr. Chronister—could have called for an examination of this case and who would have been prepared to testify in court."

"Did the lawyer for the defense so consult?" asked Mo coldly.

"He did," said Judge Cowan tersely. "And should this charge ever become a matter of trial, I should ask that panel to investigate further and to testify in my client's behalf."

"A loaded panel, you mean, made up of the defendant's colleagues?"

"I'd have no trouble establishing that such a panel would not be 'loaded.' It has become a recognized thing for medical societies to work actively to prevent or reduce suits for malpractice by setting up rigid standards of practice, by constantly bringing up to date the requirements of good practice.

"Those panels remember, as we should remember, that the human body is not a machine. Certain results can be expected of certain medical and surgical treatments, but they cannot be guaranteed.

"When results are bad—as they were in this case—they and you should carefully consider what happened, and they would—you *should*—obtain expert opinion on the matter before filing any charge of criminal malpractice.

"Your charge that a medical society grievance committee would be—what was your phrase?—*loaded*, indicates to me that you did not seek or obtain such expert opinion."

"I've said what I think about your panels," said Mo stubbornly.

"Yes. So you have. Not even knowing that there have been occasions when such a committee has recommended the expulsion of the physician charged, thus allowing the case to become solely one of civil malpractice."

"Our charge," said Mo, "is that this case is one of *criminal* malpractice."

"And my opinion is that it is not. A contention which I can prove and will prove. Just as I shall prove that my client acted under a circumstance of emergency according to his best medical judgment—*and* according to accepted medical practice for the circumstances presented to him."

For the next half hour, Judge Cowan did establish such proof. He read from various books—a Navy Corpsman's Handbook on first aid measures. Textbooks in use by well-known medical schools. He produced a colored chart diagramming the matter of tracheotomy. Finally he took a clipping from his wallet; he carefully read the newspaper's name, the dateline.

CHICAGO, ILL.   SEPT 27.   AP

A two-day-old infant whose breathing is obstructed by a tissue obstruction was rushed from Danville, Ill. to Chicago by plane today and placed in an oxygen tent.

The patient, David Long, who is breathing through a tube placed in his throat by a physican of Danville, was accompanied . . ."

Judge Cowan broke off, and his long forefinger stroked his cheek. "A *physician* of Danville . . ." he repeated thoughtfully.

Then he turned to Grady. "Would that tube indicate a tracheotomy, Doctor?"

"Yes, sir."

"You need not be a *surgeon* to perform one?"

"No, sir. I once knew a Boy Scout who performed a tracheotomy. The purpose is to prevent strangling, to relieve choking."

"Is it a curative measure?"

"No, sir. It is an emergency device, purely."

"You did something of the sort for the Kopp child?"

"Yes, sir. Because he was choking to death."

"But you *are* a surgeon," Mo challenged.

"Yes, I am. But the operation which I performed you could have done with your own pocket knife."

"Only I wouldn't."

"Wouldn't you?"

Judge Cowan smiled gently.

Then he turned to the magistrate. "I would like to call a witness," he said.

The magistrate nodded. "Sure. If you've got one . . ."

"I have. I would like to call Miss Pearl Broni to the stand."

There was a little stir of recognition and excitement as Pearl made her way down the aisle. She was wearing her familiar woolly coat, and a gay scarf was tied under her chin. Pearl called it her *babushka,* and it was very becoming. She took the oath, smiled, sat down and looked about her—removed the scarf.

Judge Cowan stepped toward her. "Miss Broni . . ." he began.

"Oh, now, Judge, you always call me Pearl."

"Yes. Yes, I do."

"Everybody in the Hollies calls me that."

"You're very well known. And, I might add, well liked."

Mo was on his feet, insisting that Judge Cowan's feeling toward the witness might be prejudiced but scarcely significant to the question in hand.

"I like Pearl, too," said the magistrate mildly. "A fine, hard-working girl. Sit down, Mo, and let Cowan get on with his witness."

The people in the courtroom exchanged pleased glances. Grady took a deep breath.

"Now, Pearl," said Judge Cowan, "will you tell the court where you were on the night of January 7?"

"Why, Judge, you know where I was! I was sittin' out at Kopps'. The baby was sick, and Mr. Kopp had to go away. He asked me to come and stay the night—his wife ain't strong, you know."

"He *called* you and *asked* you to do those things?"

"Oh, yes, sir."

"Had you stayed with his grandchild before?"

"Yes, sir, two or three times since he got sick. Maybe as many as six times."

"Did Mr. Kopp pay you for this service?"

"He sure did," said Pearl, with an emphasis which made laughter ripple again across the room. Pearl was not trying to be funny, and she took no evident pride in achieving that effect. She was honest and sincere in her efforts to answer the questions put to her.

"You say you'd been there frequently while the baby was ill?"

"Like I say, Miz Kopp ain't strong."

"How long was the baby ill?"

"Sick, you mean? Well, it began about Christmas. Yeah, on Christmas Day itself, and he died on the seventh —that's two weeks, ain't it?"

"And you were there every other day or so?"

"About that, yes, sir. Kopp'd come get me. Mr. Kopp."

"Could you tell us, in your own words, how the baby was ill? And the changes, if any, in his condition over those two weeks."

"Oh, sure. Well—first it seemed like he had a cold. All choked up and breathin' hard. Real hard—you could hear him all over the house. He spit up green stuff—an' that got worse. Sometimes there was blood. He wouldn't eat— not even when they gave him milk in a bottle—and he got thin. He couldn't sleep good on account of it bein' so hard to breathe. He was an awful sick baby. Mr. Kopp told me to rub his chest and give him syrup—an' we fixed a homemade croup kettle. Finally he brought a regular one from the store—so I know he was worried. He's a close man with a dime."

The magistrate pounded for silence, but the people went on laughing, with Mo shouting objections and the gavel pounding—and Kopp himself red-cheeked with anger.

"But he didn't call a doctor?"

"Oh, yes, sir, he did. On Christmas he called Dr. Barton, and the doctor wanted to take little Greg to Madison, and

Kopp wouldn't. An' about a week later, Kopp had Doc Stone out, and he gave a prescription, but of course it didn't do no good. I kept beggin' Kopp to do what Dr. Barton said, but he jest told me to shut up. He's as stubborn a man as I *ever* knew! I think he was worried, but—well, he was more stubborn than he was worried.

"Dr. Barton was worried, too. He kep' askin' me how the kid was doin'—and you could see him bein' sorry. He's a fine man, Dr. Barton is. The way he saved Judy Nolan when she got burned . . ."

Here Mo intervened, and this time his objection was upheld.

"Well, he is fine," Pearl restated, when allowed to continue. "Considerate and nice about the house. I clean for him, you know. But he's real tidy himself. Never so much as drops a dirty sock and leaves it lay."

Even Grady laughed now, and then covered his face with his open hand.

"Now, Pearl," said Judge Cowan, delighted with his witness, "will you please tell the court about the night of January seventh? What happened? You were called out there, you said . . ."

"Kopp asked me to go. He came into town after me and said he might be away all night. That the baby was doin' no good and his wife was wore out. He wanted me to come and stay with Gregory so she could rest."

"Do you stay with Mrs. Kopp at other times when Mr. Kopp is away?"

"Oh, no, sir, he leaves her alone. It was on account of the baby . . ."

"You were particularly asked to go out there and take care of the child?"

"Well, yes, sure!"

"Go on, please. What happened?"

"Well, I don't rightly remember what time it was. It was well after supper, I'd washed up the dishes and all. Miz Kopp had gone to bed, when I saw that Gregory was worse. He had a convulsion-like. Got stiff and his back kinda bowed up . . ."

Her hand indicated the arching of the child's spine.

"He didn't seem to be breathin' for as long as a minute at a time. And, well, I got scared and I thought the hell with these men and their stubborn ideas, so I go to the phone and I called Dr. Barton and I told him to come out there, whether he wanted to or not, that he couldn't let a kid die . . ."

"He didn't want to come?"

"Oh, it wasn't a matter of *want*. But Kopp had said he wouldn't call him. But he's the only doctor we got, and I just *made* him come. And he did come, too. Within the half-hour."

"Can you remember just what the doctor did?"

"I won't forget it to the last day I live," said Pearl solemnly, her blue eyes pale with earnestness. "He come in and took off his wraps; he warmed his hands and he went in to the baby's room. He said somethin' under his breath, then he picked the baby up on the crib mattress and he brought the whole thing out to the dinin' room table. He had a bag full of instruments and he reached into it and brought out that little knife—a real little blade it had, don't think it would even peel a bu-tata—but he held it like it was another finger, and the kid strugglin' to get its breath, turning a funny dark color, and the doctor put his two fingers on his throat—" Pearl demonstrated with the second and third finger of her left hand "—and then he stuck that little knife in with his right hand. He spread the cut with his other hand and he put in a piece of red tubing, and all of a sudden the kid breathed—whistlin'—like this—"

Her big mouth made a rhythmic, whistling sound. The people on the benches leaned forward to watch her, and their opened lips let their breath too pass in and out, in fascinated cadence with hers.

Judge Cowan turned to Grady. "*That* was a tracheotomy, Dr. Barton?"

"What I did then, yes, sir."

"And an emergency measure," said Mo Chronister nastily.

"It was that," Grady repeated his agreement.

"Had you," Judge Cowan asked, "personally ever done that sort of operation before?"

Grady looked at him in amazement, then he laughed a little and shook his head. "I was admissions physician at a big city hospital, Judge Cowan, for several years. Since children get diphtheria and strep throat and swallow everything in reach, I would safely estimate that I have done, personally, as many as 250 tracheotomies."

"Were they all fatal?" asked Mo Chronister. "Or many of them?"

"No, sir. Some of the children died. As Gregory Kopp

died. But not from the effects of the emergency surgery."

"That's your opinion."

"Yes, sir, it is. I might add, that given the same set of circumstances, I would repeat the exact medical procedure I used for the Kopp child. Though, another time, I would myself go to court to enforce medical care for the child early enough to save his life."

"As your dramatic tracheotomy did not do," said Mo.

"No, Mr. Chronister, it did not. I saw at once that it would not. To Pearl, I suppose, his breathing seemed dramatically relieved. But there was so much lung congestion that I had to exert further effort and seek to remove the obstruction which, from the first, had caused his trouble. I did find that obstruction—a quarter which the child had swallowed, perhaps on Christmas Day, perhaps earlier. There was extensive infection caused by its long presence; the lung and bronchi were completely involved—and the baby died. I'm sorry; I did what I could. Which is about all any doctor can do."

"It sure wasn't enough!" cried Kopp, jumping to his feet.

Judge Cowan stepped forward. "Please?" he said to the magistrate.

Order was restored, and the attorney asked a few more questions of Pearl—defining the fact that the doctor now accused had been called to the house by a person delegated to be in charge of the sick child.

Then he turned to Mo Chronister. "Now, we could waste a lot of time, sir," he said, "in establishing Dr. Barton's medical license . . ."

"I know as well as you do that his license is in order."

"Yes, of course you do. So, I'd think this case could be dismissed as showing no evidence of malpractice—unless you are trying to prove that Dr. Barton went out to Kopp's farm with the intent of doing murder. In which case you'd also have to establish his motive."

Mo began to gather up the papers on the table.

"Can you establish such a motive, Mr. Prosecuting Attorney?"

Mo's lips twitched, but he said nothing.

"No," said Judge Cowan silkily. "You cannot. You could not. Therefore," he turned to the magistrate, "Your Honor, I ask that this charge of criminal malpractice be dismissed for lack of supporting evidence."

The magistrate leaned toward Mo. "D'you have any witnesses or stuff to support the charge as it stands, Mr. Prosecuting Attorney?"

"The case speaks for itself!" snapped Mo.

The case was dismissed for lack of evidence to support the charge of criminal malpractice or intent on the part of Grady Barton, M.D. The matter was to be dropped.

So far as court procedure went. . . .

As for Kopp . . .   Down on the sidewalk, as the doctor prepared to step into his car, Kopp's hand fell heavily upon Grady's shoulder.

"Just a minute, Doc," he rasped, his breath unpleasant in Grady's face. The doctor stepped back, his distaste evident. "I just want to tell you," said Kopp angrily, "that here and now I'm promisin' to run you out o' this town. And no smart lawyer's gonna stop me!"

Grady made no reply; he got into his car and drove Judge Cowan home; he would go on to his office and any patients that might be waiting, determined not to discuss the Kopp case with anyone. Nor the man's threat. He made that promise to Judge Cowan, who nodded.

"But I can't help wishing that Kopp had put his energy to work in that child's behalf instead of expending it on you."

"This morning, sir," said Grady morosely, "I was cleared of only one crime. The other one—I knew what to do in the case of a neglected child. We got lots of them in Chicago. The court would have stepped in . . ."

"Our court might not have," interrupted his attorney.

Grady stared at him. "The law isn't any simpler to practice than medicine," said the judge kindly. "You'd better keep in touch with me, Grady. And don't say or do one thing to Kopp. Or let him do much of anything to you."

"No, sir. I'll be careful. Thanks a lot."

"Enjoyed it," said Judge Cowan. "Now I must make a good story for June. I wouldn't let her come this morning—and she'll be waiting for me."

"What if you hadn't got a dismissal?"

"Couldn't have come home! I had to get one."

Grady watched the slender man go in through his gate and up toward the house. "I should feel good . . ." he told himself as he drove away. "I don't." He suspected that Cowan didn't feel "good" either. Oh, he'd defended his client successfully against a charge inspired by various emotional circumstances, none of them legally sound.

But the whole thing left a brown, ugly taste in a man's

mouth. Kopp was still blind-angry, and the new doctor
had got off on the wrong foot.

Well, not exactly "off." For a time, there at first, things
had seemed to be going well.

His brow furrowed with consideration of his choice of
the word "seemed," Grady went into the clinic.

The patients who came to his office that afternoon
knew all about the hearing and about Kopp's threat, too.
"You're not going to let him run you out of town, are
you, Doctor?" asked Mrs. Ball.

"I hope not," said Grady.

"I wish someone would point out to that man how much
we need you."

Which was heartening to hear, but Grady well knew
that any doctor's usefulness to his patients depended exactly upon their trust in him. He had come to the Hollies
because the citizens had "seemed" to need him. Now—if
they *showed* they wanted him to leave . . .

On the third day after the hearing, Grady went to dinner with the Seddenses. This had become a somewhat
fixed habit, but Miss Nellie made a point of calling him
that day to remind him of his "date with them."

Grady assured her that he would be there and he went
to the house that evening, taking Miss Nellie a ribboned
box of candy, which pleased the little old lady enormously.

"Oh, Grady," she blurted, "that awful Kopp *can't* run
you out of town, can he?"

Grady folded his scarf and laid it on a chair with his
overcoat.

"I know he's going around threatening you," said his hostess, "but Brother needs you so, and . . ."

Grady patted her shoulder. "Let's not worry about it tonight," he advised.

In the living room he greeted Mr. Seddens, and through the first part of dinner they talked of various local happenings. But with dessert, Miss Nellie again voiced her worry about Grady's possible departure from the Hollies.

"Nellie!" said Mr. Seddens, as sharply as his exquisite manners would allow him to speak to anyone. "I've told you to forget that!"

"How can I forget it? That awful man is going around with his threats and his stories! Grady's worried about it, aren't you, Grady?"

"I—" He glanced at his host. "I must remember, sir, that Mr. Kopp was on the committee which brought me to the Hollies."

"Yes," Frank Seddens agreed, "he was. He is. But unless you become informed of some action by the committee, Grady, I don't think you'd need be concerned about the notions of one member."

Grady's mouth twisted wryly. "I would like the sponsoring group to be unanimous in its feeling about me," he confessed. "Those men represent the towns, and I had hoped—perhaps too rosily—that the towns would like me and trust me."

"But did you count on *everyone* . . . ?"

"Yes, sir," said Grady. "I'm afraid I did. Why not?"

Frank Seddens shook his head. "You know human nature better than that, I'm sure."

Grady sighed and lifted his hand in a gesture of conceded defeat.

"The only thing I want to know," said the indomitable
Miss Nellie, "is, *can* he make Grady leave?"

That essentially was what Grady wanted to know, too.
The hearing itself, the fact that he could be charged with
malpractice seriously enough to require a hearing, followed by Kopp's threat of persecution, had just about
convinced him of his need to leave. He would like to
fight the thing, but a man couldn't "doctor" people against
their will; he might be ready to spend a small part of his
time in court answering charges of malpractice, but certainly the nervous tension of working under such opposi-
tion was not what he had hoped to get in the Hollies.

On the other hand, Mrs. Ball had said he "must not
leave." Miss Nellie questioned Kopp's ability to run him
out. Frank Seddens was not worried about one man's
opinion.

Perhaps Grady could fight through this situation . . .

The next day he took his contract and went to see
Judge Cowan. Could Kopp, he asked, force him to leave
town?

The judge made a show of reading the contract, which
of course he well knew. "Has he bothered you?" he
asked. "Since that morning?"

"No. People keep quoting his threats to me."

"I see." The judge folded the paper and laid it on the
desk. "Legally, your position is firm, Grady. The court
said you had committed no fault." He sat looking at
Grady, but not smiling.

"But . . ." prompted his client.

Judge Cowan nodded. "Actually—" His shoulders lifted.

"What I'd like to persuade myself," said Grady, "is that the dismissal of the charge indicates that no one really believes I would hurt a child."

Cowan said nothing.

"It doesn't mean that, you think?"

"I don't know, Grady. The facts are there—you were charged, and the charges were dismissed. But meanings—they change with the weather, with a person's disposition. Kopp is definitely being vindictive. He may talk himself out. Or he may get others to believe him. People are odd, you know. If enough people listen to Kopp, things could be difficult here for you. Not in a legal sense, but really—actually."

"Yes," Grady admitted, "I see what you mean. It's a funny thing, sir—when I took routine care of Judy Nolan, I was praised far beyond my merit. Then, when I took just as routine care of Gregory Kopp, I find myself threatened with destruction."

Cowan's blue eyes twinkled. "You call that 'funny'?"

"Peculiar," amended Grady. "Strange."

"And unfair. But, Grady . . ."

"Yes, sir?"

"You're a thoughtful young man. You must have given some consideration as to why rural communities—places like the Hollies—don't attract, and keep, young doctors."

"Well . . ."

"The work isn't too hard. And I think you've found out,

once established to a modest extent, that a man can make a living."

"Yes, sir."

"Granted," said Judge Cowan, seeming to go off at a tangent, "that young men don't always choose the medical profession for high ethical reasons of noble self-sacrifice and so on—it must be in the mind of most doctors that they should be allowed to practice the art of healing unhandicapped by the effects of personal prejudice and vindictiveness."

Grady leaned forward in his chair. "That's just it, sir," he said eagerly.

"Small towns give a clear field to personalities, Grady. In the city you can escape them or cover over such bruising experiences as occur. But in a place like the Hollies— what one man says and does and thinks is loudly evident. Eh?"

"You're saying that a shortage occurs because most doctors won't be bothered to fight for a right to practice."

"Some in small town practice," said his friend, "are too incompetent to make a good thing of practice in the city. Some can bring themselves to compromise with the Kopps.

"And a few of them—a very few—are ready to fight the Kopps. Some even think it's worth doing." Judge Cowan lifted an eyebrow at his visitor.

Grady stood up. "I don't know if the fight's worth doing, sir," he said firmly, "but I'm ready to give it a try."

Judge Cowan nodded. "That's what I thought," he said quietly, "when I agreed to be on the committee ask-

ing you to come here and practice. I thought you were
that kind of man."

On that high note of resolve, it was rather deflating to
have it seem for a time that the fight was not going to be
a very tough one. Though Grady realized that his own
busy-ness might have blunted his awareness of adverse
currents.

He was busy, and the town certainly needed a doctor
during the epidemic of measles then running among the
children of the town, and the wave of flu sweeping
through the ranks of all ages. For two weeks Grady had
so many house calls to make that he could scarcely keep
office hours. For one week he didn't get to the Seddenses
home as usual, and he began to warn his fellow Lions
that he might not be able to serve on the committee for
their stunt-night dinner.

He decided to wait, however, until a day or so before
the event before releasing June from her date with him
for that affair. He'd had only glimpses of her during these
two weeks, and as sure as he'd tell her he couldn't make
the dinner, Mo would take over her entertainment. That
Grady hoped to prevent.

The stunt and dinner was planned for the last Friday
in January, their regular meeting night, and on Wednesday of that week, Grady could say he thought he might
make it. On Thursday he talked to June and confirmed
their date. They made a few plans.

The group would go first to the Junction filling station
where a police car would assist the Lions in choosing their

guests for the evening entertainment. The committee consisted of Grady, Norvell Lee and Mo Chronister.

"Virginia is going with Mo, I think," June broke in.

"Oh?" What was Henry Preston saying to that? He and Virginia . . .

"She often helps Mo out," June went on to explain.

"It isn't necessary that he drag a date."

"No, but—well, I think this sort of arrangement will work out, Grady. Considering everything . . ."

Grady's free hand clenched upon his desk blotter. "Considering that Dr. Barton was a married man," was what June had left unsaid. Virginia, "as good as engaged" to Henry Preston, would make a chaperone-type second girl in their foursome. And those matters had to be thought of, for everyone's sake.

Grady concluded the arrangements, put the phone down and sat frowning at it. As soon as he possibly could, he *must* set things straight here in the Hollies about his status as a divorced man. He only hoped he could do it before Kopp, or some character like him, began ugly questionings about the doctor's wife.

The simplest way to handle the matter would be to go to the committee, state that he'd not told the whole story —in his anxiety to come to the Hollies as their doctor— admit that he shouldn't have done this, say that he was sorry, and . . .

Yes, and Kopp would ask what other lies he had told? Or would tell?

Grady groaned aloud. But he still meant to "do something," and as early as the next week. Meanwhile the

Friday night stunt had to be gone through, and with as much fun as possible. For everyone.

He did the things required of him as chairman of the "stunt" committee. He contacted the highway police, the filling station attendants—he briefed the young people who would be on the welcoming committee with him, and checked with the chairman of the dinner committee to be sure their plans meshed.

Friday turned out to be a cold evening, but clear, with the roads open. A huge moon hung in the eastern sky, and the young people waiting at the junction were in good spirits. They were a well-dressed group, the girls in furs; Grady's Homburg and Lee's western-style Stetson lent an air of respectability—or so Mo announced. It was only ten minutes after six when the police radio announced that they were bringing in a car.

"Honeymooners, I'll bet my britches," commented the officer.

Everyone was delighted!

That would be better, declared Mo, than any previous year's haul!

The welcoming committee buttoned into their wraps and went out upon the lighted apron of the junction station.

Mo picked up the florist's box, and when the red car pulled up behind the police car he was the one to step forward and greet the somewhat apprehensive young couple.

They could be honeymooners. The girl was no more

than twenty, the young man older, but both were considerably flustered.

Mo welcomed them effusively, turning on all his charm. His teeth flashed, his dimples sparkled, his voice boomed. . . .

"We represent the Hollies Lions Club," he announced to all concerned. "Tonight is our annual stunt dinner, and you have been selected to be our guests, not only for the banquet, but to stay overnight and accept the gifts which we have for you. As an earnest of what we have in mind, it is my pleasure and honor to present the little lady with this orchid."

He bowed and held out the box. The girl took it, after a glance at the young man to see if he approved. "Why," she said faintly, "thank you very much. I—"

But Mo was going on to list the entertainment in store for the young people. A de luxe cabin at the motel, breakfast in bed, their car serviced, oil and gasoline supplied—and a long list of "gadgets and things to be presented at the banquet, with appropriate plugs for the donors . . ."

"I thought you were chairman," June murmured to Grady.

"I am. But you know Mo—and let him alone. He's doing all right."

Mo was doing all right. Now he was making a production of introducing the Lions, and their ladies—listening only briefly when their guests offered to identify themselves.

"I'm Fred Reynolds . . ." the pleasant-faced young man began.

"And this is your blushing bride!" boomed Mo. "Oh, yes!" he continued, "ten miles down the road, we spotted you. Our powerful radar took up a trail of rice and rose petals . . ."

Again the young people exchanged glances.

"That's some radar you have," drawled the young woman. She was a small, slender girl, with black hair cut urchin style.

"I'll pay a dime for every grain of rice you find in our car," offered Fred Reynolds.

"What are you quoting on blushes?" asked the irrepressible Mo.

"They'll bring a quarter."

"If they are honeymooners," Grady heard Ruth Norvell say to June, "they are making a good job of not admitting it." His own eyes began to shine.

"Let's get this show on the road, Mo," he said, going up to that noisy young man. And within ten minutes the doctor's car was following the red one of their guests, Mo and Virginia now riding with the strangers.

On the way to the Masonic Temple where the dinner would be served, June and the Norvells and Grady summed up what little information they had concerning the Fred Reynoldses. The girl's name was Julia—they came from Minneapolis, or near by—and June suggested to Grady that the girl might want to change her clothes before being photographed as their guest of the evening.

"She looks all right," said Lee Norvell.

"She does look all right," agreed June. The girl was

wearing a camel's hair coat over a knitted dress of dull green.

"We'll give her a chance to change if she wants it," Grady agreed. "There always is some cheerful drinking beforehand. Or so I've been told."

They pulled up at the Temple and saw that Mo was already marshaling his guests indoors, flash guns popping. "I'm still going to ask her," said June, moving with speed and determination.

It turned out that Julia Reynolds definitely did want to change, and June sent Grady for her toilet kit and wardrobe case, giving him the keys to the red car so that he could bring in those things.

"It won't take long. I'll help her," June said when he brought the two bags to the door of the lounge.

It didn't take long. Within ten minutes, Julia appeared in a smart costume of brown and gold, her orchid on her shoulder, her short hair brushed into a black satin cap. "*Now*," she said, "you can take my picture!"

Dinners of this size and importance were served by the ladies of the Masonic Lodge as money-making projects. Alcoholic beverages were certainly not provided, and Grady had at previous affairs been amused by the devious ways in which pre-dinner stimulation was achieved. Tonight half the overcoats came in sagging on the right side, and the coke machine did a thriving business in the lobby of the lodge hall. It must, he thought, take a deal of preoccupied concentration on the part of the serving ladies to ignore the smell which hung like a fine mist over

the crowd of well-dressed dinner guests, also not to hear
the rising noise of excited joviality.

Fred Reynolds was plied from all sides with paper cups
of "coke." He would, he said firmly, wait for Julia.

So Julia's appearance was greeted with loud cheers.
She looked startled, and Mo noisily, and wittily, told of
the drought which her appearance had ended.

She laughed, said she was sorry—and that she was a little
parched herself! Could she please have a drink?

The members and their guests crowded delightedly
around the two strangers, Mo still acting as master of
ceremonies.

"Isn't your tongue tired?" asked June, coming up to
where Grady leaned against the wall, watching what went
on.

He looked down at her questioningly.

"Move it to the other cheek, or it'll get cramped."

He grinned. "Entertaining an idea . . ." he murmured.

"Can I help?"

"You'd do better to keep out of this kind of idea—but,
yes, you can help."

"Well . . . ?"

He stood looking at her for a long minute. She was
such a pretty girl—tonight she wore a shiny sort of white
dress; it had a demure jacket held snug with twinkly but-
tons, and a stiff, flaring skirt. There was pleased ani-
mation in her pretty face, and genuine interest. He sighed.
"Tell me," he asked, "that dress Julia is wearing—is it
rather sophisticated for a bride's trousseau?"

June turned and stood on tiptoe to look again at the

guest of the evening; she was in a group of people now going through the opened doors into the dining room. About all she could see was the back of their honor-guest's cropped head, her bare shoulders and arms.

"It's an Indian print," she told Grady. "Copper on black—very handsome—and yes, *sophisticated* is the word. But brides could, I suppose, have such clothes."

He laughed. "My notions of such garments are rose-colored and floaty."

"I always suspected that you were a sentimentalist," June told him, laughing, and going along with him to the dining room.

The guests of honor would be seated with the club officers at the head table. Grady's committee job was just about over and done, except to read the list of gifts to be showered upon the young couple. Mo bustled up to suggest that he should sit at the head table to do this . . . Grady demurred. The seating was all arranged; he was near by . . .

"You got that list?" Mo demanded. He'd probably had one paper cup too many, thought Grady.

"I have the list," said Grady, "though what your honeymooners will make of a dozen diapers. . . ."

"Nobody's got 'em to admit they are honeymooners," said Mo loudly. "Hey! That gives me an idea. Watch me have some fun."

The tables were set to form an extending E from the head table, Grady's committee sat at the one forming the middle prong. Now Mo could turn and by lifting his voice get the attention of their young guests. "Hey, Reynolds!" he called, "how many kids do you and the missis have?"

"Oh, now, look . . ." cried Reynolds, good-naturedly. But red flamed into Julia's face and throat, a painful, hurting blush.

"Let them alone, Mo," June urged the big man.

"Only havin' fun," he excused himself.

They must all be silent then for the blessing, and after that everyone was seated with a great scraping of chairs, and the food was brought in, hot and savory.

"That blush tied it," declared Mo. "You should get a big *boffo* out of the diapers, Doc. They're honeymooners, all right."

Grady's gaze went to the side table which was piled with the gifts to be presented. Diapers—canned goods— toilet articles—a toaster . . .

"If they're married at all," he murmured, then tasted his sherbet.

"What do you mean, Doc?" demanded Mo, leaning across the table toward him.

"Nothing, maybe." Grady seemed ready to talk to June rather than pursue the subject which he had dropped like a chunk of ice down the back of Mo's awareness.

"But you said—"

"Oh, it was only a guess, Mo. I suppose these affairs present some risk. Unless you begin by asking for marriage certificates and identifications of respectability . . . and we don't. At least, we didn't tonight."

Mo leaned back to look at Grady across the spread ferns and the pink carnations.

June too looked curiously at the doctor beside her. Was he serious? Or joking? Grady had a poker face, she knew. He *sounded* serious.

And Mo sounded upset. "Now, look here, Doc . . ."

"I know," agreed Grady, "the patrolman said he thought they were honeymooners—and we carried it on. But from the first Reynolds has denied this . . ."

"Julia has," corrected Virginia. Lee and his Ruth were leaning forward, too. Was their committee in trouble?

"They could be honeymooners," Grady went on logically. "Though the girl's dress looks more—well—and of course they could be old married folk, a year or so old. And then there's the chance that maybe Reynolds is just a man out for the week end with a babe."

Mo choked. Ruth squealed a little, and Lee silenced her, his own face concerned. "That's right," Grady approved his gesture. "No use getting everyone excited. But I did notice when I got out Julia's bags that her things were marked with different initials from his."

That was enough for Mo, who was in no condition to reason. In rising panic, he was on his feet. "Got to stop those pictures . . ." he said in a choked voice as he ran out of the dining room.

Within five minutes he came back, even more wild-eyed than when he left. "Newspaper wouldn't listen to me . . ." he told Grady excitedly. "Actually laughed when I reminded 'em I was prosecuting attorney."

"I suppose news is news," said Grady quietly.

"Yeah, but this kind . . . What we goin' to *do*, Doc? We'll be the laughing stock of the county."

Lee and Grady exchanged resigned glances and shrugs. "I don't see that we can do anything," Grady began.

"Well, I sure as hell will try!" Mo evidently meant to make it a noble try. With the appearance of scrambling in all directions at once—he went to the head table and asked Reynolds and Julia if they would please step into the lobby for a minute? Thinking this part of the stunt, they agreed, Julia taking her coffee cup with her and laughing as she walked the length of the long room.

With the door firmly closed upon them, Mo turned to face the assembled Lions and Lionesses.

Before this, Grady Barton had noticed that Mo Chronister's face could look much the same whether he laughed with humor or grinned with malicious intent. In both cases, his lips drew back from his strong white teeth, his cheeks were furrowed deeply with lines which bracketed that smiling mouth and his blue eyes shone. Tonight they glittered.

"Gentlemen," he said solemnly, "we're in trouble."

A stir of interest, and questioning concern, rippled around the room.

Mo nodded portentously. "Just luck we didn't run into trouble the two years before when you pulled this trick. Tonight, looks like we've had it. And I just hope to Pete that we can hush the thing up, get those two out of town without . . . Why, a little precaution, Barton, like getting the patrol to check would have avoided all this embarrassment!"

Grady sat quietly, his face immobile, his fingers turning the stem of his water glass.

"What's happened?" asked a dozen voices at once. "What's wrong?"

Mo undertook to answer. "You got any proof those two are man and wife? You got any proof the name's even Reynolds? I tell you, the committee shoulda been more careful. Yes, and the president should appoint his committees more carefully. Crazy business, just bringin' anyone in here, without some kind of check.

"Tourist court romances—could be criminals on the lam for all we know—certainly this couple isn't what we'd like to think they are, and I move here and now that Dr. Barton go out and tell 'em we made a mistake—tell 'em anything, just so we get rid of 'em . . ."

Grady stood up, but it was Norvell Lee who said in the stunnned silence of the room. "*You* tell 'em, Mo. You were the one to take the Reynolds over from the patrol; *you* accepted them, *you* made them welcome. Yes, and you introduced them to the president as the chosen guests."

He turned to that president. "Am I right?"

He was right. The club knew Mo. The club was unanimous in thinking that he should be the one to straighten out this matter.

As all this developed, Grady had been dropping short comments into June's ear. Now he said, "A simple question would do it."

She laughed and pressed his arm.

Well . . . Mo finally agreed, he guessed he could go out and . . .

"Bring them in here," called Lee Norvell. "When you

get through with them, we probably will owe them some
sort of an apology."

So a somewhat puzzled Julia and Fred were admitted
to the dining room, and a red-faced, angry-seeming Mo
Chronister made a clumsy attempt at an explanation and
apology for the Lions Club. He had, he said, no wish
to embarrass Julia and Fred—if the whole thing rested
on him, as a private individual, he'd let 'em stay and
be entertained, whatever their status. Mo, by his own admission, had been around! *He* knew how these things
went. . . .

But after all they were a national organization with a
reputation to uphold . . . The whole trouble began
with the committee, he said, their plans had not been well
made, and they'd managed to foul the whole thing up.
Of course the element of surprise was important, but they
should have asked for some sort of identification. They
hadn't, and now, well, he only hoped the Reynoldses
understood? And no offense?

Fred Reynolds looked more and more bewildered.

"As well he might," murmured Grady to June when she
noted this.

It was Julia who took over their reply, stepping forward, one hand tugging at her earring, the other reaching back for Fred's hand. "I don't completely understand
what your trouble is, Mr. Chronister," she said with dignity. "It's pretty clear though that there's been some
mistake about choosing us, and of course we're sorry. We
liked getting into this party because, you see, we had
only this week-end for our honeymoon, and we don't have

any money. We were trying to keep where we were a secret, but we couldn't go far enough to be safe.

"You see, Fred is a university professor—associate—and I'm a student. A senior. And the student body—well, we tried to keep our trip a secret from their idea of a joke. It began to look as if your stunt were going to give us a memorable honeymoon, but—well—as I say, we're sorry about whatever mistake there has been."

She released Fred's hand, and unpinned the orchid, regretfully held it toward the stunned and befuddled Mo.

His lips moved, but no sound came. He wiped his face with a very large white handkerchief and tried again to speak. June and Grady, Lee and Ruth and Virginia smiled, and then began to laugh.

Finally Mo's voice came, though in a strange squeak. "You're *married?*"

"Of course we're married!" shouted Fred, beginning not to like all this horseplay. "At nine o'clock this morning. *And* in a church!"

"That's what you wanted, wasn't it?" asked Julia sweetly. "A married couple?"

"Yes . . ." agreed the dazed Mo Chronister. "Guess you're everything we wanted. Only . . ."

Deciding that he still might find a whipping boy, he flashed around on Grady. "Doc, you told me . . ."

His words were lost in a mighty roar of laughter. The whole club was laughing, loudly, boomingly, continuously. Doc had framed Mo, and good! This was going to be a very big evening.

It was, too.

With Julia telling how careful they had been not to look like newlyweds. "We stopped at the first filling station and I changed out of my pretty suit, sacrificed my flowers . . ."

But big evening though it was, and one long to be remembered, Mo was not soon going to forgive the man responsible for all this laughter at his expense. Grady knew that he'd done nothing to assure Mo's friendliness. The man was not the sort to accept this sort of beating.

CHAPTER *Seven*

LATER GRADY COULDN'T decide whether he was glad to have had that one last evening of fun and triumph, with his friends slapping him on the back, admiring him for the way he'd tricked old Mo.

That gay evening served to demonstrate what could have been his if the dice had fallen more favorably, and after its pleasure, it was doubly hard, as February progressed, to recognize the growth of a feeling throughout the Hollies which he at first suspected, then identified and finally, painfully, had to consider, to take.

Once recognized, he could trace the feeling; whatever the court had said about his not having been guilty of criminal malpractice, the town, and town talk, was still accusing Dr. Barton of the death of the Kopp grandchild. They were, in effect, calling him a murderer, which perhaps was to be expected from certain people, the ignorant, the uninformed, scattered through the community. But as the days went by he must recognize the growing extent of that talk, and the belief in it.

And now there was no definite way to defend himself.

183

With no formal charge made, he could not hire a lawyer to present his case, nor could he testify in his own behalf.

If once someone had said to him, "You killed that baby," he could have replied. But they said nothing to Grady.

The townspeople—some of them—looked at him askance; they talked to one another about him as he passed on the street or came into the barber shop. They—some of them—stopped calling him to their homes as a doctor and did not come to his office. At first he thought this defection was only a gradual letting-up from the spell of winter illnesses which had kept him so very busy for two weeks there in January. But as more and more appointments were canceled or simply not kept; when for one whole afternoon no one at all sat in his waiting room, Grady must consider what was going on.

"If that child had lived," his thinking summed up the matter, "I'd have been a hero. But—he didn't live."

He was hurt at this injustice, not a unique thing in the history of medical practice, but his for the first time. He gave the town one reason for not accusing him, or discussing the situation with him, because Grady himself retired into a shell of silence which amounted to brusqueness. He would not talk on the subject at all. Not to Pearl, who was as ready as a blundering pup to sympathize with Grady, to express her opinion of "folks." Pearl knew that people were talking; and she knew what they said—she wished Doc would do something about it! He wouldn't even discuss the matter.

Not with Pearl, nor with June when, innocently, she

asked, as they went to choir practice on Wednesday evening, how bad a break Bert Waller had suffered.

"And what made him fall down the steps, Grady? Did
he get dizzy or did he fail to turn on the light when he
got up at night?"

"He's not my patient," Grady said quietly, "so I don't
know."

June stopped short on the snowy street to lean toward
him, her face troubled. "But— *Grady!*"

He shrugged and smiled. "They took him to the hospital at Elmore. I'd have done the same, for X-rays."

A month ago, his thoughts ran, *I was planning on my
own X-ray outfit. Now it will be a matter of paying for
food and coal. Hoping I can.*

June was still trying to get him to say why Bert's family
should have failed to call Grady. Why, they were friends!
He'd been one of the men . . . "If your friends don't stand
by you at a time like this . . ." She was almost in tears.

*It was at times like this that a man found out who his
friends were.*

June stamped her foot. "Grady!" she cried. "Say something!"

"What do you want me to say?"

"You *know* people are acting—Grady, they're so *wrong!*
Surely you could make them know that they are wrong.
Why, it's awful, the way they are treating you. They
brought you here to practice—they need you! Bert Waller
falls down the stairs and breaks his ankle, and with a doctor as close as seven miles away, he calls the ambulance

and gets taken to Elmore. As if you weren't *here!* Grady, that's a ridiculous situation."

"It's a bad situation," he agreed soberly.

"What are you going to do about it?"

"Just now, I can't think of a thing."

"Aren't you worried?"

"Of course, but I don't think you should be."

"Well, I am," she said stanchly, "and even if you won't talk about it, I'm going to try to think of something to do."

He wouldn't talk about the matter to anyone. The situation existed, and it was hard to take—but he was determined to act as if nothing was wrong.

Until the day came when Oren Kopp, with Mo Chronister as his attorney, clapped on Grady Barton, M.D. a suit for $25,000 damages for the loss of his grandchild's pleasure and company.

That day, Judge Cowan came to see Grady. "I asked Mo if he'd completely blown his cork!" said that elegant gentleman, "and *he* talked to me of personalities. The gall of him! Telling me that I'd lived in a small town so long that I confused personal considerations with a man's legal rights."

Grady sat in his desk chair, shaking his head.

"As if he weren't being personally vindictive," Judge Cowan fumed. "For all his discourse to me about this being the sort of action a person would take in a large city against a doctor who was careless with ethical rules."

Grady sighed and told of the night when Mo had sideswiped his car and Grady had called the police. "The man was drunk . . ."

Judge Cowan nodded. "You did exactly the right thing. Had he contested his arrest, it would have gone against him."

"I wasn't very wise in making him my enemy."

"No," the judge agreed. He sat thoughtful. "I'll handle your case, of course, Grady," he said after a little.

"There can't be much money in the project," said Grady wryly. "Whether Kopp gets his judgment or not."

"He won't."

"No, I don't think he will, either, but the talk around town has already hurt me, and this lawsuit may finish me."

"What are you going to do about it?"

Grady smiled. "June asked me that last week. I told her I hadn't thought of anything yet."

"If people needed you badly enough . . ."

"Don't say that, sir! We want no disaster!"

"For the town, you mean."

Grady sighed. "I'll admit, in my low moments, that this seems pretty bad, sir. But—"

"Yes?"

"I hope I can hang on for a time. Maybe people will come to look at me and Kopp and Mo as we all really should appear in this. I'm sorry as hell for Kopp, if he really does think I'm responsible for that child's death; he must have loved the baby very much."

Judge Cowan looked surprised. "But, Grady," he protested, "a father—even a grandfather— Their grief doesn't express itself in wanting to hurt someone else. At such times, you beat your own head against the wall or you go into a numb silence. No, it's guilt or fear or remorse, maybe, that takes this sort of vindictive action. Kopp knows that his own stubbornness cost the child his life. Mo has persuaded him that he can blame you, publicly, and Kopp is agreeing in the hope that it will make his own sense of guilt less galling. You know that's how things are!"

"Yes, I know it and you know it. Maybe even Mo knows it. But I don't believe the town knows it enough to help my practice any, Judge."

"Not just now, I'm afraid," said his friend.

Grady thought it would be easier if he could hurry things to a conclusion, but the law moves slowly, and the days were made up of minutes that had to be passed. Soon Grady established a routine by which he lived. He continued to be available in his office at the hours designated in gold leaf upon his front window; he made the house calls on his list and filled the rest of the time as best he was able. Except for going to Seddenses' once a week, a habit which he'd built up since coming to the Hollies, he did little socially. Some people called him professionally, some came to his office, but not nearly so many as had been doing those things. His friends all might have been friendly, but Grady gave them little chance. He did continue to attend the Lions Club meetings—on other evenings, he read.

They had ten days of bitter cold weather, and one late afternoon he dug out his ice skates, anticipating a pleasure which had been his since childhood.

He was an excellent skater, and he thoroughly enjoyed the exercise in the crisply cold air—until it occurred to him that not one person had spoken to him, that he had

touched no friendly hand nor shared his pleasure with
anyone. That circumstance could have just happened,
but on a chance that it had not, he made a wide circle
to the bank where he sat on a log and changed his shoes.
He took his skates home, and having carefully wiped
them and oiled them, he put the things into their flannel
bag and into his trunk.

He was not a man to need effusive friendliness, but
since he was also not one to exist in a vacuum of polite
tolerance, he was going to have to do something about
his present circumstance.

What he did first, mistakenly perhaps, but naturally,
was to give up singing in the choir. He told June that he
meant to do this, and said he wished to "save the church
embarrassment."

"Has anyone said . . . ?"

"Oh, no. We're a very polite congregation."

"But we need you—and if ever *you* needed the
church . . ."

"I'll go to church."

He did go. Slipping in after the Processional to sit in
a rear pew. Of course there were many people around
him there; he'd have been more alone to come early and
sit up in front. Their little church was in constant danger
of sinking by the stern. But seated back there he could
slip out with the Recessional and not put his friends to the
strain of being polite to him should they be inclined
otherwise.

"You're oversensitive, Grady," protested Judge Cowan.

"I have a foolproof system of knowing who my friends are."

"Some of us aren't sick."

"That's good."

"Grady, we brought you here because we needed you—"

"I'm here, if I'm needed."

How could even an experienced trial lawyer argue with such a man? He was wrong—mistaken—but he was irrefutably right, too.

His friends—and whatever he thought, Grady still had friends—considered ways to help the doctor. A mass meeting? A campaign of personal visits to the people of the community? But in those first weeks, there wasn't much of anything to combat. Had those concerned friends been themselves afflicted with illness they probably would have called upon Grady's services. They were not ill, and so it seemed that he had little practice. Some people who did need a doctor went elsewhere—but that was their privilege.

Meanwhile, Dr. Barton's once-promising practice continued to dwindle. He made out bills as they came due, mailed them and without exception was paid in full.

Frank Seddens came in once a week for a check on his blood pressure—Grady had a maternity case due. A woman in her forties, her other children already into their teens. It could be a somewhat critical case, for the woman was very fat and afflicted with hypertension. Grady held himself ready to be called on that case. Until the morning when the local radio station announced the birth of the baby—in the Elmore Memorial Hospital.

Alone in his empty house, the big man rubbed his hand down over his face. Well—a safe delivery was the essential thing.

The next morning, only two mothers came to his monthly well-baby clinic, and when they were cared for, the doctor sat in his empty office and considered the future. He should, he supposed, leave the Hollies. Next month such minimum expenses as food and light and heat would make him draw money from his savings, which were not great in the first place. That would be justified if he thought time would clear up his present difficulty, but why should it? The Hollies had tried the new doctor, and the people were deciding that they didn't want Grady Barton. If Grady left, they'd get someone else in, someone who would not "let a child die."

The towns needed a doctor, and Grady should step out and let them get someone else. If they could.

Grady should—he must—give up the whole project so far as it concerned him as a doctor, and move on. But where and how would he make that move?

Perhaps he could go back to Chicago, perhaps the medical director still needed an assistant. But did he want one with a lawsuit for damages to a patient hanging around his neck?

There was Dr. Messmer at Madison. "If they don't want you, we can use a man of your training and experience." Could they also use Grady Barton with a lawsuit pending?

Grady would not apply in either place just now, he could not. It would only mean a refusal. He must wait until, as Judge Cowan promised, that suit should be dismissed. The judgment refused.

He must wait . . . and he guessed he could wait.

That afternoon he walked down the street, a tall, broad-shouldered man in a good overcoat and felt hat, his face overly grave. People greeted him and he replied—briefly in both cases. He stopped at the drugstore window to examine a display of art done in an adult education class. He moved on, and examined a sign in the fruit store window.

BOY WANTED, said the sign.

Grady was hardly a "boy" in the sense of that sign. Nick would be shocked, and—here it came again!—*embarrassed* should the doctor come in and apply for the job.

A doctor, a professional man, should not need work in that sense. But what did a doctor, a professional man do, when he *did* need work? In that sense.

Surely there was something . . .

The next day, Grady got out his car with which he was being economical, and drove over to the Neighbors and to the factory which was there.

This was a picturesque building of limestone—an old structure, sturdily built. Behind it ran a swift river which had originally supplied power for the industry. Back in the eighties it had been a woodworking factory. Today the factory made small electrical appliances, but the owners had wisely maintained the building as near to the original as possible. Concrete floors had been put down, and reinforcing beams—but the windows were the original small-paned ones, brick chimneys rose at each end of the long, gabled roof. Evergreens still stood handsomely upon the lawn, today their green pyramids dusted with snow. Behind the factory and across the river, the hills displayed a Grandma Moses scene of winter, with glimpses of red barns and white houses and a few children on sleds. Birch trees stood like silver wands, the bare-branched "popples" etched the sky—and always the evergreens. Over all was the blue sky, with sunlight dazzling upon the white snow.

Grady got out of his car and walked toward the factory. He knew it well, having been named the factory doctor, though it so happened that his services had not been called for lately, and he, in his thickening shell of protective withdrawal, had not yet made this month's visit of inspection.

Today he walked past the glass door marked with the name of his friend, Joe Perry. He hoped Joe was still his friend, but he would rather not put the matter to the test.

In the larger general office, he asked the receptionist if he might see the personnel manager. The girl knew him, and simply pointed her pencil toward the proper door.

The Holly Neighbors factory was a subsidiary of a large manufacturing concern, and their employees were sometimes shifted about. The personnel manager now at Holly Neighbors had come to them three weeks before from the Milwaukee office. He was, as Grady had heard Joe Perry tell, a time-cost expert.

His office door stood half-open, and knocking upon the door frame, Grady went inside. The man at the steel desk looked up inquiringly. He was a slender man, with a pale skin that might mean poor health, but probably only indicated a city man uninterested in outdoor exercise. A small sign on his desk announced that he was *Mr. William Brockman.*

This gentleman now tipped back in his chair and looked up at his visitor, seeing in his turn a big man with dark red hair, a strong face, good clothes—and a tense manner.

"Yes, sir?" he said receptively.

"I came to ask you about employment," Grady told him. "The employment office here in the Neighbors told me that you were hiring men for March first."

"Do you want to do factory work?" asked Mr. Brockman.

"I'm ready to take any sort of position you might have to offer. I need work, and I don't want to go out of town just now to seek it."

"I see."

Mr. Brockman opened his top desk drawer and took out a printed form. Any questions he might have asked would be answered on the form—it was the nature of personnel managers to depend on facts so set down.

"We are going to hire some men," he said pleasantly, "to begin work in March. If you fill that out, and think you could help us here, you must go to Dr. Grady Barton in Green Holly and bring back a physical-condition report from him."

Grady took the form and smiled gravely at Mr. Brockman.

"I am Dr. Barton," he said quietly. Without saying anything more, he took out his pen and began to fill in the form, conscious of Mr. Brockman's surprise, his dismay—and his bewilderment.

"What are you saying?" he finally demanded, sounding angry.

Grady glanced up, then sat back in his chair. "I'm not playing tricks, sir," he said with dignity. "I *am* Dr. Barton. Three months ago I came to the Hollies—as I suppose you know the two towns are called—to practice medicine. It was thought that the communities needed a doctor. Among other things, I was hired by the factory here to examine its workers, attend their sick and hurt—"

"Yes. Yes, I know that. We have a plant doctor in all our installations."

"You didn't for this plant until I came here."

"Is that so?"

"Yes. It was one of the circumstances which made it seem that the Hollies needed a doctor."

"I see."

Grady laughed. "I don't suppose you do, sir. But I can tell you, if you like."

"Oh, yes, I'd be interested to know why, if you're the doctor, you should want to operate a machine."

Grady took out cigarettes and offered one to Mr. Brockman, who took it, then thrust it toward Grady again. "I don't smoke!" he remembered. "But I'll swear I'm so befuddled . . ."

"There's no need. Even with what the factory pays me, I don't have enough work as a doctor to pay my expenses. So I came here to apply for work."

"But—I'd think—"

"Oh, there *is* medical work here, sir. But—well—I'll tell you briefly what has happened.

"I came here in November, and things looked very promising for me. I was busy and I thought I was making friends. I did some interesting medicine here, too. I liked the whole setup. It was the sort of place where I wanted to live, the kind of medicine I wanted to practice.

"And then—at Christmas—I had a little bad luck. A child whom I was attending died. The death in itself was regrettable. I felt that the family contributed to it by their refusal to follow my medical advice. *They* felt—feel—that certain emergency measures which I took at a time of crisis were the cause of the baby's death.

"To the best of my knowledge gained from good training and ten years' experience, I had followed acceptable practice. The child's grandfather, who was in charge, was ignorant of all medical procedure. When the baby died, this man charged me with criminal malpractice."

"Oh, dear!" said Mr. Brockman.

"It is a risk which doctors run, and against which most carry insurance. I do. But—fortunately, I thought—the preliminary hearing cleared me of the charge. In other words, the court said I had done nothing wrong."

"I see."

"I suspect that you don't, sir. The gentleman disagreed with the court to the point that he's bringing a civil suit against me for damages."

"He can't collect."

"So my attorney tells me. But—well—the original arrest

hurt me as a doctor, this lawsuit is hurting me still more. People want to trust the man who gives them medicine or in other ways manipulates their lives—and they should trust him. So—I am the first to say that people have a right to select the doctor they want to attend them.

"The people in the Hollies have decided that they don't want *me*."

"But you're the only doctor here, aren't you?"

"The only M.D. Yes, sir. But that isn't, and shouldn't be, an obligation upon the people of the Hollies. I do not endorse state medicine, or any of its aspects."

"But once that lawsuit is disposed of—"

"Yes, it might help. Especially if no damages are awarded. Gradually then I might build up my practice. But—meanwhile—I need to eat. That's why I came over here, why I have applied for a job with you. I can run one of your machines—if you will hire me to run it."

Mr. Brockman looked distressed. "I'd have to let you know—Dr. Barton, believe me, that is regular procedure!"

Grady stood up. "I know. I suppose you'll call me?"

"Yes. Yes, I'll call you."

CHAPTER *eight*

He won't call me, thought Grady, going out to his car. *I'll not hear from him.*

He had not made out the application form, and it was just as well. His pen had stopped short of a certain question.

Married
Single
Divorced
Widowed

How would he have answered that? With his other troubles, the lie which he had told on coming to the Hollies had grown tenfold. Grady must agree with O'Hara when he wrote, "There is one time in a man's life when he has a secret . . . he knows he will never be rid of."

Such a secret was Grady's. He might have better taken Kopp's accusations and attacks if he'd known that he could defend himself and his moral behavior in every detail.

But that lie . . . It had been a small thing when told. Or so it had seemed, even to a truthful man. Yet

199

in his troubled thinking since, the lie had grown and grown until the monster could not now be slain with a few words, with a laughing admission of his mistake, his error.

Now, here in the Hollies—and where else did anyone care if Grady Barton was honest, or not—such direct evidence of untrustworthiness would condemn him far more completely than could be accomplished in the courtroom.

In any attempt at confession, Grady would be saying, here in the Hollies, "I am a man who would lie to get this job as your doctor. So—I might also be a man who would . . ."

Over and over the treadmill went Grady's thoughts—explanation, justification, explanation—regret, explanation—and anger.

And he sat, discouraged, in his office by day, in his living room at night, or walked, still discouraged, across the snowy fields and woodlands.

He no longer went past Cowans' to pick up Candy to share his walks. The Cowans were his friends and very kind to him—but he feared to seem to monopolize their time. Leaning far, far in the other direction, he saw almost nothing of them.

So, when June wanted to talk to him, she must go in search of him. And she did just that on a certain cold Thursday afternoon. It was Grady's free half-day; he would not be in his office, and when Grady had free time, she knew that he often walked.

It was a cold, steel-gray day, with fine snow blowing like spume across the ground. In town, past snows had been shoveled into soiled ridges and heaps. Out in the country, in the woods, the old drifts still lay dead white and thick upon the ground. June put on her red snowsuit, her boots and mittens, and with Candy's leash in her hand, the dog leaping and bounding in all directions around her, she went first past Grady's office to be sure he was not there, then up the street and toward the woods.

She pretty well knew his habits, and so did Candy. Within the half-hour the dog stiffened, pointed, then took off with every hair a flag of joyous recognition.

Grady had got well into the pine woods, with the shadows of the tall trees lying blue across the snow. June perhaps would not have seen him except for Candy who was churning the snow into froth around his distant figure. When free of the leaping dog, Grady turned and waved to the girl upon the hillside.

They walked toward each other, their eyes and smiles acknowledging their gladness at this meeting.

"I've been tracking you," said June frankly. "How do you expect me to keep my girlish figure if you don't ask me to walk?"

"I was preoccupied in preserving my own," Grady retorted in kind.

"Where were you going?" asked June, falling in beside him, a lock of her hair blowing against her forehead.

Grady's arm made a half-circle. "I thought up into the woods a way, then around and down toward the lake."

"Fine," said June. "Candy, you leave the rabbits alone!"

The dog looked at her in shocked amazement, and Grady laughed. "He says the rabbits shouldn't worry."

"He found *you!*" June defended her dog.

"I don't have very long ears." His hand helped her across a small, ice-bound stream.

They walked for an hour, not talking much. It was cold; the pine woods were as still as an empty church and as soothing to the nerves. When they turned down toward the lake again, the wind whipped red into their cheeks, and their step hurried. Little white-edged waves ruffled the blue water, and the gray ice at the edge of the beach lifted and ground its teeth.

They were chilled through and tired—and content— when they approached the picket fence around the Cowan yard. Candy no longer raced and ran; he too looked forward to a warm corner in which to stretch and rest.

"Come on in," June told Grady. "I'll have Fanny make us some hot chocolate—unless you'd rather have coffee."

"This hungry man at your door will take what's offered, and like it!" Grady told her, going into the hall with renewed pleasure in its graciousness.

June disappeared toward the kitchen; Grady shucked out of his galoshes and leather jacket and cap. In corduroys and plaid shirt, he appreciated his incongruity in the handsome living room. A fire burned below the marble mantel; there were flowers upon the table beside the curved couch where June seated herself when she came downstairs, having put on a dress of blue just a shade darker than the painted walls.

Aaron brought mugs of hot chocolate and a plate of spicy cookies. Candy came in and stretched upon the hearth rug, sighing with pleasure. Grady leaned back in the blue arm chair and sighed, too. "This is all very wonderful to a man who is beginning to think he hasn't a friend in the world. I do thank you, June."

June had told Aaron not to light the lamps, and the rosy firelight sent shadows leaping up the walls, touching into color the pattern of the india-print curtains, the blue of June's eyes and the bronze shine of Grady's hair.

She sat gazing at the wavering profile of the man which the flames on the hearth cast upon the wall behind him. "You have friends, Grady," she said, almost dreamily, so softly did she speak. "My father—and me."

The shadow nodded. Grady's face was a good one for a silhouette, the features strong—his fine nose and firm-lipped mouth, his cleft chin . . . the crest of his hair.

"But I think probably that advice goes along with most friendships." Now she looked at the man himself.

"You have the privilege of advising me," he said quietly. "Though I might as well tell you that I have decided, and firmly, not to leave the Hollies. They are not going to drive me out!"

June's thick, curly lashes flew upward and back. "Oh, Grady, that wasn't my advice!" she cried. "I certainly wouldn't— Oh, no! But, well, it's this! And Father agrees with me. We both think you should send for your wife, Grady. We don't think you should be alone in this fight which you're being forced to make. Her place is with you, now."

Grady sat stunned. Cold, as he had not been out upon the wintry hillside nor beside the icy lake. Cold to his heart's core, cold to the marrow of his bones. He clasped

his hands hard together between his knees and remembered the companionship which he had known with this
girl on their walk that afternoon. A companionship so
close as not to need talk. He had thought June shared it.
And she *had!*

But, of course, she thought—

With a gesture of decision, he clapped his hand against
his knees, got to his feet and came across to sit beside
June. Turned toward her, he took her hand between his
two big ones, and with his eyes upon her sweet face, he
told her of the lie.

"I do not have a wife, June. I am not married. Oh,
I was when I first came to the Hollies—but—my wife—"
He said the word with difficulty, sat silent for a second,
then went on, his face pale. "My wife was in Reno then,
getting a divorce. She did get one—she was within days
of getting it when I came here to be interviewed. And,
well, I wanted to come here so much that when Kopp
said they must have a settled man, a married man, I just
said that I *was* married, without any sort of qualification.
And, so—well—it amounted to a lie.

"I know it was a crazy thing to do! I've regretted it ever
since! But there it was. I didn't tell the truth—and so—
I lied."

As he talked, June's eyes had clung to his face. "Oh,
no!" she moaned now.

He swallowed with difficulty. "There's more," he told
her. "I—I love you, June."

Slowly, she drew her hand from his and bent her head
away from his gaze. Grady watched her, with the same

tense feeling of life and death being a matter of this minute, of this second, which he had known in Belgium, and dreamed of since. He was in free fall, tumbling and plunging, down, down, down—thirty seconds was an eternity! Would his chute ever open? No, it had not, it would not— *Oh, God!* And then—dear God, sweet God, the shrouds tightened, the canopy snapped open above his head, and the harness straps jerked upon his body; above him the chute billowed and grew taut against the sky.

And here in the firelight, June lifted her head and smiled at him.

But when he would have touched her, she drew away. "Wait, Grady . . ." she urged. "I have to think."

"I'm sorry I told that lie, June."

She searched his face. "Does it mean that telling it makes—everything worse for you?"

"I'm afraid it does."

"Up to now, they haven't had much to go on. Father has said they haven't. Kopp, I mean, and Mo. He's jealous of you and resents you, but he hasn't had anything, really, to work on. But now . . ."

"Yes, when the lie is known . . . But I had to tell you, June!"

"I know. But still they'll use it as proof—what would Father call it?—corroborating evidence that you can be dishonest. Oh, it's the worst thing that's happened, Grady!"

She looked at him pleadingly, her eyes filled with tears.

"I know," he agreed. "I've gone around feeling like that old chap with the albatross."

Compassionately, she touched his hand. "Even your friends, even those who have been sorry for you and have resented Kopp's vindictive action against you, some of them, Grady, will stop now and wonder a little. About your honesty."

"But I'm not dishonest, June!" he protested. "I told a lie—but I am *not* dishonest!"

Neither he nor June recognized any absurdity in his claim. "No," she said slowly, "you're not, Grady. In fact you lean over backward to be honest. I remember how Father exploded that time you had Mo arrested for running into your car. He said, 'Does the guy *have* to be so damned honest and legal?'"

She smiled wanly at him, and he caught at her hands again, his tone roughening. "June," he cried, "tell me! Do you love me? Could you?"

She sat very still, not taking her hands away, but they became lifeless things in his grasp, and gently he released them. Then he looked so lost that impulsively she leaned her shoulder against his.

"Oh, Grady!" she cried. "I have to have a little time . . . I like you. I've always liked you! But love— You see, I've never thought of you as anything but a man with a wife. I've never let myself think of you as free."

He sighed. "I love you, June," he said gravely. "This afternoon, when I watched you come across the snow toward me, I felt—perhaps I can't put it into words, the way I felt about you. The way I feel now. I suppose it's the way I shall always feel, even if you decide . . .

"Of course you don't know if you love me, or could.

I don't know if I could expect you to love me, because I'm not sure that I know why a woman ever would love a man."

He sat for a long minute, his eyes upon the fire.

Then his face tightened, and he spoke firmly, his deep voice vibrating.

"But I know why I would love a woman!" he said. "It would be because I would want to give that woman a feeling of security and faith in life. Because I would want to do everything I could to fulfill that woman's hopes and passions. And more—I would want to perpetuate those things, to perpetuate that kind of world for the children my beloved would give me.

"That is the way I feel about you, June. I want to do those things for you, and so—I know that I love you."

She sat trembling against his arm, her emotions tumbling like the whirling snow which the wind blew against the windows. She was at once thrilled by what he had said to her and sorry for the man who had said it. She liked Grady, she had always liked him, and now she was swept upward in a surge of joy to know that he was free.

She turned a laughing face upward to him. "I've always been horribly jealous of your wife," she confessed. "I've criticized her bitterly for leaving you alone!"

He nodded. He saw that June was still not ready to accept his love.

After a bit, she lifted her eyes shyly. "Was she—" she began diffidently, then broke off to summon courage. "What was she like, Grady? What was her name? And—was she—pretty?"

He held her hand and smoothed the back of it with his fingertips. His face was grave, his eyes dark. "Her name was Gisela," he said in the quiet way one would describe an acquaintance. "I met her when I was a prisoner in Germany, and hurt. She was a nurse in the hospital. And —yes, she was beautiful. No! She was *handsome. You're* beautiful. Pretty."

Her eyes flew open. "Is that better?"

His smile answered her. "That's *best!*" he said firmly.

"Oh—Grady," she cried in a tone of helpless protest.

"I'm sorry," he agreed. "I wish—" For a moment he was silent. "I wish I had never *known* Gisela!"

She leaned against his arm. "Do you want to tell me about her?"

"I have to tell you!" he cried. "For the whole thing was not right, June!"

"Not ever, Grady?"

"Now I believe it wasn't—ever. It didn't work. Maybe it *couldn't* have worked. I don't know. I thought I was trying, but, anyway—

"It seemed that we hadn't anything in common. We didn't like or dislike the same things. We couldn't even talk happily together, let alone—" He coughed and rubbed the knuckles of his free hand across his lips. "She didn't want anything I was able to give her. At first, of course, things were strange for her in America. She'd thought that our women all lived in luxury and idleness. And, of course, going into civilian practice for the first time I hadn't much money and was very busy.

"Anyway, things didn't go well, and for a while I

thought it a matter of adjustment. She *hated* being a doctor's wife and taking second place to the calls of my profession."

"Selfish," murmured June, as softly as the snow whispered against the window.

"Well—yes. Very soon, I had to decide that she'd married me principally as a means of getting out of Europe. Still, I should have been able to make her happy. I thought."

"And you were not happy either?"

"No. No, I was not, June. I know that now. Though, at first, I thought I was trying. Lately, of course—for the past five years neither of us tried at all to make things work."

"But she stayed with you?"

"In a way she did. Yes. And I seemed to be the sort of man to feel obligated to support his wife and—" He sighed.

"When . . . ?"

"Last summer. She asked me to give her a divorce. It —shocked me, and I couldn't figure why it should, except to know definitely that I'd failed to do the job I'd taken on."

"Was there another man?"

He smiled. "A man who would marry her? Yes. There was."

For a long minute, both sat silent. "The way you said you could love a woman," June asked then, "did you . . . ?"

"No," he said firmly. "No, I never did, June. As I told you, things were *never* right in that marriage. It was—

well—like a man's getting on the wrong train, riding for miles and miles in the wrong direction and then, when the train finally stops, having to walk back. But I am back now, June, and— Oh, June . . ."

She looked up at him with shining eyes. "Welcome home," she said shyly. "We're glad you're here. We do like you a lot. I do—and Father—and liking is—well—a deeper thing. Different from being excited by a man's looks and his line."

Well, he'd hoped for too much; but he could not help showing his disappointment. "You don't leave me a lot . . ." he managed to say.

"Oh," cried June seriously, "you have a line, and looks, both, Grady. And more. Because you have strength and dependability . . ."

"There's even more to me than that!" he said wryly. "*I'm* a man without any visible source of income, and my professional standing is in complete disrepute. Who else could offer you so much, Miss Cowan?"

She patted his sleeve and rubbed her cheek against his shoulder. "Oh, I know, Grady," she sympathized. "It's been too tough on you! Maybe what you should do is to go away for a time—establish yourself as a doctor somewhere, and—"

"I was already established as a doctor," he reminded her, "when I came to the Hollies. *Here* I had hoped to establish myself as an individual."

She gazed at him wide-eyed, reminded that he was older than she; she recognized and admired his point of view as that of an older man, one more mature.

He was still talking. ". . . can't say the project has met with notable success. . . ."

He's really wonderful, she was thinking. *And not married . . .*

Suddenly, emotion threatened to catch her up, and, unused to the high winds of passion, she spoke from the top of her mind. "Well," she said, with a lightness that was almost heady, "I'm terribly sorry, Grady, but anyone could make the mistake you did . . ."

He turned, his face sharply inquiring.

She fluttered her hands. "I only meant," she said hastily, "the mistake you made in selecting the place to work—to practice—"

"Oh." He turned his gaze back to the fire. Feeling that, while his feet had finally touched ground, he still was scarcely on target.

"I've found," he said dispiritedly, "some very fine people here in the Hollies. I thought they were fine when I decided to come here and work. I still think they're fine—most of them—but—" He turned to face her. "As a doctor, I'm *needed* here, June! So, to save me, I can't understand why this town of fine people would let one man run me out!"

"One man can't do that!" she replied with spirit. "Unless that man would be Grady Barton!"

He smiled at her, but shook his head. "That won't do it," he told her. "For you know as well as I do that one man is working mighty hard against Grady Barton's staying here in the Hollies. I think you know *why* he is working so hard. I know, and it has given me a little hope—or it did until you began to suggest that I crown his efforts with the success of my going away. Which of course would leave you here with him, without competition. It's what he wants. Do *you* want that, too?"

She sat gazing at him, lovely color rising in her cheeks, then suffusing her whole face and throat. "Oh," she said softly, "you mean Mo."

He nodded. "I mean Mo. He calls you his girl—"

"I know," she agreed. "And if you had never come to the Hollies—maybe even if you left—I might *be* his girl. He can be utterly charming, Grady. You forget his faults when he tries to be charming."

"Not me," he assured her. "You, maybe—"

"Yes, me, maybe. I have been charmed by him—often—into overlooking things he has done. But, you see, Grady, he's a very brilliant man."

"Brilliant is a high-powered word, June."

"But I think it fits him as intelligent would not. No, he has this fine mind, he learns things easily, he has ideas that amount to strokes of genius. Of course he isn't a dependable person. For one thing, his parents are rich and have spoiled him outrageously. That element of brilliance in him got him things in school more easily than they came to other boys. He's big and he's handsome and I think girls—women—may often have made fools of themselves over him. But he does have a wonderful line, and I've thought that if some day he could love a woman—"

"And forget himself?"

"That's hard to imagine, isn't it?" she was laughing. "And Grady, I'll admit that he may be vindictive toward you or just wants to get rid of you—but isn't there a chance that he might think he's right in this case which he feels he has against you?"

"Do *you* think he's right?"

"No, but I don't think what I feel is important."

"It is to me."

Again she blushed. "Let me finish what I was saying about Mo. I know him pretty well—his faults and his good points. He has both. And I'm pretty sure, Grady, that he'd get old Kopp to drop that damage suit against you, if you would leave town."

With the damage suit withdrawn, Grady could leave. He could go to Madison and take Dr. Messmer's job . . .

He rubbed his knuckles against his teeth and his face was marble white. "Did Mo Chronister give you that message for me?" he demanded, frightened—and angry. "Or was it your own idea? In which case, can you tell me— *Are* you on Mo's side? And against me?"

Again she felt her youth as against a man's stern courage, and his direct approach to a question which must be solved . . . answered. Panic took hold of her, and so she could identify the panic which was Grady's, to think that she, too . . .

"Oh, darling," she cried softly, "I'm for *you*. Of course!"

He put his hands upon her shoulders, looked close into her eyes. "Then why do you try to send me away from you?"

"To protect you," she said bravely, her eyes smiling. "I suppose it's every woman's instinct to try to protect the man she loves."

Sighing, his hands drew her to him, his lips sought hers.

"I love you, June," he whispered against her soft hair. "I love you . . ."

"Oh, Grady," she breathed. "I—I never knew it would be like this . . ."

"Like what?" His cheek was against hers, his strong arm held her close.

"Like Christmas candles and Fourth of July sky rockets —and—and—"

Laughter rumbled in his deep chest. "Like candle-shine," he told her, "and moonlight . . ."

"Oh, sunrise!" she announced. "You know, the way it catches you by the throat—it's so beautiful."

"Yes, that says it. For me—" He held the slim girl, both ecstatic and humble. That this should have come to him! He did love June! He did love her! From his first sight of her.

With her warm and loving there in the circle of his arm, he told of that first sight he'd had of her. That was why he'd wanted so especially to come to the Hollies—because of the girl he'd seen upon the beach.

"But, *Grady!*"

"I know. You could have been—oh, almost anything! But the way you looked—I was right about you, too."

It brought tears to her eyes, for some feminine reason, and he must console her. "I'm silly," she told him.

"You're nothing of the kind. Or if you are, and it's a part of this, it's quite all right."

"*You're* not silly."

"I'm not so sure—for I have a feeling, which may be

foolish at least, that *now* I can do anything. I can stay in the Hollies. I can fight that lawsuit. I can marry you and make you happy! Yes! and I can practice medicine here, too."

"Why, of course you can," she said reasonably, "you—"

They heard the phone ring and drew apart in case Aaron should come into the room.

He did come; it was a call for the doctor, he said, from the factory at Neighbors. A man had been hurt.

"This is my day for miracles," Grady told June solemnly. "A promised bride—and a professional call."

Smiling as if she personally had invented this thing called love, June watched him bundle into his wraps. It would be as quick, he decided, to walk the three blocks to his office and medical bag as it would be for her to get out the car . . .

He dropped a kiss on her cheek, smiled at her gaily and took off, a new man, a strong man, a man with hope restored.

The case was a nasty one of shock. Grady found his man prostrate upon the factory's concrete floor, though someone had had the sense to cover him warmly and not try to handle him.

With various people telling him how the accident had happened—the chap had just collapsed at his machine— probably an electrical shock—a short of some kind—Grady made his examination. The blood pressure was down, the pulse was fast and weak. The man's hands and feet were icy, his mouth slack, his eyes glazed, and perspiration was beaded upon his face. The fingernails were blue.

The doctor applied restorative measures and told some-one to send for an ambulance. He would take the patient to Elmore; he supposed he still had attending privileges there at the hospital, but in any case. . . .

At Elmore Memorial, his presence was accepted as quite in order. Grady decided that he'd been somewhat overdramatizing his situation.

He renewed that decision the next day when he was called to Bob Miller's home—Miller had had another heart seizure. The guy was not going to make it . . .

On Saturday, two farm families came in to his office. The mother of one group was pregnant; two of the children in the other family had strep throats.

It began to look as if his practice might survive the law-suit, if Grady could also weather its effects.

And Grady could! With June's love—and his for her— he could level mountains!

CHAPTER *nine*

ON SUNDAY, Grady drove Judge Cowan and June to Madison where the judge would catch a plane for an extended trip to Washington and New York. On the way, Grady confessed his lie to June's father and went on to ask if their plans to marry met with approval.

The judge was not surprised at either development. He had, he said, made certain inquiries; he knew that Grady was divorced, and why.

"Did you tell the committee?" asked Grady, amazed.

"No. I was the only one with a daughter in whom you were interested."

Nor was the judge disturbed at what the revelation of Grady's falsehood might mean. "Let it alone," he told the young people. "Half the town has guessed the truth—and the rest don't much care."

As for their engagement. . . . "Maybe you'd better not announce it just now," he decided. "Though I am sure you two will make a go of it."

So June hung Grady's ring on a chain around her neck and was happy to cherish her new found love in her bosom, close and warm and secret. Grady would have shouted it aloud—except for the lawsuit. As always, he guessed the judge knew best.

Meanwhile he was working some and the conviction that things would improve persisted with him until the second Thursday in March. Grady was not exactly busy, but he did have a few steady patients, and he thought the number was increasing. The shock case at the factory was recovering nicely; the children with the strep throats had responded well to penicillin.

Grady's divorced state had not yet been declared to Green Holly, and this chafed. Once, when someone asked when his wife would be coming, he said shortly, "She's not coming!" and then wished he'd blurted that he no longer had a wife!

He saw June regularly, but not as often, nor as pleasantly as they might have enjoyed, had they been free to announce their engagement. Of course Grady knew that he could make no definite plans toward marriage until things looked more promising. And this time of trial would soon be over; the judge had said he thought the damage suit would be set for the spring term of court. With that disposed of . . .

But still things were seeming more hopeful than they had been on the morning when Grady sat at his desk and slit open the envelope from the secretary of the State Medical Society.

And read—

"*Oh, no!*" he groaned aloud.

Two weeks ago he would have numbly accepted this new blow. But now. . . .

No! No! No!

He beat his fists upon the desk edge, he clutched the letter into his hand, crumpled it into a ball, then slowly, slowly, he smoothed it and read again the words which were all too familiar to him with one reading.

". . . . notify Grady Barton, M.D. that the grievance committee of the State Medical Society at the instance of the Holly County prosecuting attorney has found it advisable to recommend the suspension of his license . . . pending the outcome of litigation . . ."

Grady spent thirty minutes thinking of things to do; he would go in person to the president of the society. He would knock Mo Chronister's block off! He would write a letter—he would write a dozen letters. He would stand out on the street and denounce those who had done this thing to him!

Someone came into his waiting room, but he still sat staring blankly at the wall of his inner office. That one patient—or Frank Seddens who came regularly—required that Grady, beginning at this very minute, must act upon this letter.

But he sat there in his chair like a man in a trance; his staring eyes saw nothing, the objects in the room were blurred in a red haze of hurt and anger and hatred. *They couldn't do this to him!*

And if they tried, he'd hurt back! The very strength of his limbs, and his size, was now a burden upon him. He

could hurt people. He could run and destroy—the effort
to keep from doing those things made his head spin and
his throat ache. He sobbed aloud and heard the noise
which he had made. And thought about it. He rubbed his
big hands down over his face and got painfully to his
feet; he walked about the room to restore circulation in
his limbs which ached from sitting so long, so still, so
stiff with anger.

After a minute he was enough in possession to take
deep breaths to quiet his heart and his zinging nerves.
He made his fingers unclench—and he changed his white
coat for the jacket of his suit, sick at the significance of
what he did.

Then he went out to his waiting room, appearing to be
a calm man.

It was Frank Seddens, neat as always, who looked up
at him, smiling. "Good morning, Grady. I'm early . . ."

Grady shook hands. "Yes, sir. I—" His tongue mois-
tened his lips. "I have to tell you, sir," he said quietly,
and then he did tell his benefactor of the letter which
he had received. "So I can't treat you any more, Mr.
Seddens. I—I'm sorry." He smiled wryly at this under-
statement.

Mr. Seddens jutted his small gray beard upward into
Grady's stony face. "You're still a doctor!" he cried.

"They say not—for the time being, at least."

"Aggh! I mean, you still know all you knew when I
came in here last week. Don't you?"

"Yes, sir. I do."

"Will you take my blood pressure?"

"Yes, I can do that."

"But you can't give me any advice. Is that it?"

"That's it."

Frank Seddens snorted. "When I have my stroke," he cried in disgust, "I won't know *whom* to blame!"

"I shall know," said Grady soberly.

The older man looked at him with keen blue eyes. "This has hit you hard, son?"

"I wouldn't want you to know how hard, sir."

"Can't you do anything?"

"I'll have to do a lot of things. None of them will change the fact as it now stands. That I'm under a legal suit for damages to a patient, that my medical license is suspended. If I win the suit, it will be restored. If I don't—" He shrugged.

Of course, given time, he got hold of himself and did the "many things" there were to do. He talked to Judge Cowan, to June—now he was glad that no one knew of their engagement; he assured June that he would and could make no claim upon her.

"I didn't fall in love with your medical license!" she told him.

"Sometimes I wonder what . . ."

"I'm not wasting our short minutes together in flattery."

He laughed, and it was the best thing to do just at the minute.

But he'd had a crushing blow. Against the advice of several members of the committee, he moved his personal belongings out of the house and closed the clinic build-

ing. He rented a room in the home of a woman whom
Pearl recommended to him. Pearl was not at any loss for
words to tell about what "they done to Doc!"

The newspaper carried a discreet news item; people of
both towns were as kind, as polite, to Dr. Barton as he
would allow them to be.

He had told June of his original application for a job at
the factory; at a word from her, Frank Seddens and the
rector went to see Joe Perry. If Grady came again asking for employment, they said they thought the company
should hire him.

Joe looked amazed. He had not known that Grady
had ever applied! Why, then he supposed . . .

"We'll stand behind him personally, Joe," said the rector.
"As to character—"

"I know Grady as well as you do," said the plant manager, with a smile.

"Well, this lawsuit business makes it seem extra important for his friends to go on record!" declared Mr.
Seddens. "Grady could surely run one of your machines."

"Or I might place him in the office," mused Joe.

"Somehow I think physical work would be better for
him," said the rector. "Grady's a big man; he needs an
outlet for his energy, needs to be tired when he goes to
bed at night."

Frank Seddens' beard was wagging up and down in
agreement.

"If he's already applied, I'd need only to send for him,"
said Joe. "I expect he'll be useful. At least he'll be on
hand if we need any first aid."

"But he won't doctor beyond that," Seddens warned. "That boy's almost too ethical . . ."

"We've given him a rough deal here in the Hollies," said Joe regretfully. "It's a little hard to figure just what became of our good intentions."

"We haven't been too good to ourselves," said the rector as he and Mr. Seddens walked through the factory and out to their car. The whine of metal upon metal, the whirr of belts, the clash of steel presses, played a dissonant symphony behind them. "Our two towns don't have a doctor now—and we need one."

"Yes," agreed his companion. "I know that better than anyone."

Early March had shown little promise of spring; frosty meadows and brown hillsides gave way reluctantly to grass slowly turning green; the lilacs put out a few cautious leaves and the apple trees were only faintly dappled with pale green and pink. The maples were a haze of half-open buds.

But then, on the last days of the month, heat came suddenly; the temperature climbed into the seventies, and spring opened her arms wide to smother the countryside with blossoms. Within a day's time, the maple trees showed leaves two inches across, and the apple trees became giant bouquets. This miracle of color and growth came to its fragrant climax on a Saturday, and Grady Barton, factory worker, could pick up June and Candy and go for a walk out toward the woods.

During the winter they'd followed the same path a

dozen times, noticed and commented upon. But on that warm spring day, it happened to be Oren Kopp who met them, passed them and looked back at them.

Then he went on into town to speak acidly of Judge Cowan's girl and that doctor—a married man and all— carryin' on together.

He dropped his word like soaked seeds into various fertile places, and the next day, after church, someone asked June about it. This person happened to be Virginia Spencer, June's best friend ever since their childhood. "People are talking, honey. I thought you should know."

June hung up her choir robe and took off the square black cap, shook out her hair. "I wish they'd let Grady alone."

"But, darling, it's just—he *is* a married man, and— Were you walking hand in hand with him?"

"Maybe. I don't know. You walk hand in hand with Henry sometimes. I've seen you, down on the beach."

"Henry is not a married man."

"Neither is Grady."

Virginia gasped. "Why, *June!*"

June's cheeks were scarlet. Virginia remembered that, afterward, and the way she refused to say anything, but, "He isn't married. I know him better than anyone, and he—isn't—married!"

She stalked out, leaving Virginia to shake her head in concern for her friend. Of course Grady Barton was married; that had been known since before he ever came to the Hollies, and now—even if he was getting a divorce, or something—or had got one—June should be a little careful. From her manner, it would seem that things had gone a bit beyond hand-holding in the woods. . . .

June, on her part, tilted her chin and decided that she would take no notice of gossip. She should have said nothing to Virginia. Now people would go about discussing whether he was married or not. And if not, why did he say that he was?

Why, indeed?

When Grady heard of the story which Kopp was telling —much embellished, of course, by Wednesday of the next week—discouragement swept over him with renewed force. He could not drag June into the mess he'd made of his life!

Her father knew the truth; June had his ring—worn secretly. But if this sort of thing could touch a girl like that, he'd better leave to avoid further danger to her. Now he must give in and go! To avoid hurting her, he must make immediate plans to leave the Hollies. This was the end!

But like other blows which had seemed final, he was to discover that this one was not. And then begin to wonder how much a man could take.

That same week a baby broke her leg. The distraught parents brought the child to Grady's boardinghouse—and he must hand her back to her mother. "I can't help you . . ."

Big-eyed, the woman searched his face. "We'd pay you, Doc."

He closed his own eyes in pain. "It isn't that. Just now, I am not legally permitted to help you." He tried

to explain, he gave explicit directions for their handling
the child, and he did fasten a splint of rolled newspaper
to the soft little limb—but then he sent the puzzled and
somewhat indignant parents off to Elmore.

At the end of the same week, he got a frantic telephone
call in the middle of the night. It was from the husband
of the farm woman who had come to him two months
previously, asking him to handle her pregnancy and confinement. This man said his wife was in convulsions. "Oh,
Doc, come at once!"

Instinct made him want to do just that—but he could
not, he must not. He picked up the phone again and told
Dr. Cellaburl Stone what was going on and what to do.

"Her blood pressure was 180 over 120 last month—I am
afraid of eclampsia. Give her some castor oil, doctor,
and then quinine to induce labor. I don't think you'll have
to use instruments. She isn't at term . . ."

Next morning, Stone reported to him. He had not used
instruments, but the baby had turned as blue as ink and
died. The mother would live.

"*You* probably coulda saved the baby, too, Doc."

"Oh, we don't know . . ." said Grady dispiritedly. Stone
with half of Grady's training, a third of his experience, had
done all he could.

With no training at all, with no medical license ever,
Grady as an unskilled citizen happening to be close by
could have helped that woman and her child.

But a doctor with his license restrained must stand back,
fold his hands behind him and do nothing. It was very
hard.

It was hard to walk past "his house" and to see his clinic dark and unused. It was hard to know that the town needed a doctor, needed him.

Surely if they could get another man, they would. It struck Grady that he might even be standing in the way of that solution of the town's need.

So that night, after supper, he came back to his room at Mrs. Schmieder's and got out paper, an envelope, a stamp—and he wrote a long letter to Stanley Tomyanovic in Chicago.

He had acted on impulse, so when he went out again to mail the letter, he decided that he'd better go around past Seddens' house and talk to his friend about the D.P. doctor. It was only 8:30. Mr. Frank and Miss Nellie would be still watching TV.

They were. Miss Nellie cozy in a quilted robe and soft slippers, for which she apologized. Grady ate popcorn and visited with the two old folk for a half-hour, then he talked to them about his friend. He told what sort of person "Tommy" was; he outlined the difficulties which a D.P. doctor faced in establishing himself in America. He told of the national requirements, and those which individual states demanded. He told what Tommy had done toward meeting those requirements; he'd passed the examinations, he'd started citizenship proceedings . . .

"But the nearest he's come to practicing medicine is the job I helped him get in the instrument room in the hospital where I worked before coming here. Now I've written this letter to him, thinking he might come here and help out—certainly while I'm restricted."

"A foreigner . . ." mused Frank Seddens.

"Yes," said Grady tightly. "D'you remember Kopp asking me if I was one?"

"Kopp's father was an immigrant."

"So were all our fathers—at various generations back."

"That's true, son, but—"

"Tommy's a good doctor, sir, and has a pleasant personality. I—well, I'd be here to help him—I don't mean professionally, but to know the people, and the people to know him."

"How can *I* help?" asked Mr. Seddens keenly.

"Back me up, sir. Indorse his application for a *locum* license. Speak in Tommy's behalf here in town should any question arise."

"Do you expect him to use your office?"

"That would be up to the committee. And of course dependent upon that locum license from the state society. But at least he'd be here in town—and the town desperately needs a doctor." He told of the baby with the broken leg and the confinement case which had not come out as happily as it might have . . . Dr. Stone had done as well as possible, he said, but there were new techniques which might have proved effective.

Miss Nellie clicked her tongue and said, *Oh, dear! Oh, my.*

And Mr. Frank looked keenly at Grady. The big man sat relaxed in the deep armchair. *He's a good doctor,* thought Frank Seddens. *All a doctor should be. He thinks of the welfare of his community.*

So he asked, somewhat brusquely. "But what about *you*, Barton?"

Grady looked up in surprise. "Oh, I'll go on working at the factory. They pay good wages, you know. I'll do that until, as I hope, I win that lawsuit and get my license back." His jaw tightened as he spoke.

"It's Chronister, behind Kopp, who is fighting you. You know that?"

"I know he's fighting me. But, Mr. Seddens, he isn't the only man in the Hollies, is he?"

"Brother . . ." prompted Miss Nellie, softly.

He smiled at her and nodded. "No," he said firmly. "No, Grady. He isn't the only man here. So—ask your friend to come."

Twenty minutes later, Grady left, walked to the post office and put his letter into the slot.

Ten days later, Dr. Stanley Tomyanovic arrived in Green Holly, dropping off the bus, retrieving his two heavy bags, his small medical one, and then smiling into the face of his friend, Grady Barton.

Grady looked him over. Tommy was still as thin as a pipestem and probably always would be. His black hair had had a fresh crew cut. His clothes were American, but Tommy's manner with a scarf, the way his hat sat squarely on his head, betrayed his foreign birth. That was all right; his first words would have given him away.

His smile was everything, and his manner. Grady took him to Mrs. Schmieder's and established him in a room next to his own. For the time, he had decided, this was the proper thing to do. He outlined, briefly, what had happened to him here in the Hollies.

"They're crazy!" declared Tommy.

"They're mistaken," Grady amended.

"What did you do?" asked Tommy keenly, "to make somebody so mad at you?"

Grady nodded and told him.

"You think I can work with people like that?"

"I don't know. I thought I'd give you the chance. It would accumulate experience for you—and you told me once that you were hungry to doctor. The work you have been doing—"

"Pfagh, no!" agreed his friend. "Within sight and smell of it, but what do I do? Check in hemostats, check out hemostats, so many forceps, so many syringes—and scalpels—and thermometers—and retractors—and—"

Grady laughed. "Come on. We'll go eat some lunch, then I'm going to take you to see the committee and you can ask for the job as locum doctor here in the Hollies."

"Asking for it isn't getting it," said Tommy in a reasonable tone.

"It's worth a try."

"Just by chance," she explained, Pearl was in Mrs. Schmieder's kitchen when the two doctors came downstairs. Grinning, Grady introduced Tommy to the tall, blonde girl. Tommy seemed pleased, and Pearl . . .

"Gee, Dr. Barton," she said in Grady's ear, as the men went out the side door to his car, "he's cute!"

Cute was not a word which Grady would have used

about the little man, and yet he could find many others
of praise for the way in which Tommy conducted himself that afternoon, and the next. Grady took him to see
each member of the committee and introduced Dr. Tomyanovic as one who would be willing to fill the position as
doctor for the Hollies if it should be offered him. Tommy
wanted the job, he asked for it, but as he did so he kept
his air of dignity and self-confidence.

Grady was proud of him. He even took the man out
to Kopp's, and Kopp's wife, looking scared to death, said
the "mister" was not home.

Finally, Grady took him to see Mo Chronister. Mo
was cordial, effusive and said, why, yes, he'd do all he
could for Dr.—er— What's-his-name.

"That man would poison your soup!" Tommy told Grady
as they left Mo's offices.

"He already has."

They went to see each one—the judge, where Tommy
met Candy and June, and smiled softly at his friend as
they left the big house, to the Seddenses', to the rector—
who begged Dr. Tomyanovic to persuade Grady to sing
again with the choir.

"The churches here put on a choral program at sunrise
on Easter," he told, "and we need Grady's big voice to
represent us."

"I'll be very bossy with him," Tommy promised.

Everyone seemed to like the friendly little man, and
with the exception of Kopp, the committee voted to indorse him as a doctor for the two towns.

"What about my license?" Tommy brought up, when Grady told him of the action.

"We'll fix that up. I'll call the secretary of the State Medical Society tomorrow morning and ask for a locum permit."

It took three days for that society to send word that it was against the present policy of their organization to recommend even temporary licensure for foreign-trained doctors.

So—there they were. The towns had two doctors, which were needed badly, but still the people of the towns lacked available medical help.

Before Grady could get himself squared around to handle this latest disappointment—Tommy took it with numbed familiarity—word came that Frank Seddens was ill. He'd had a stroke . . .

Grady went immediately to him, verified the diagnosis which Miss Nellie had made—she'd come upon "Brother," seated in his armchair, his face swollen and red, his eyes glazed, his limbs stiff.

There were things which a doctor—which *Grady*—might have done immediately. Things which Miss Nellie and Tommy begged him to do.

But— "Call an ambulance," Grady said stiff-lipped. The last person to want him to use a syringe, and thus complete his medical destruction, would have been Frank Seddens.

Stony-faced, Grady helped put his friend on the stretcher and into the ambulance. Stony-faced, he went back into the house to see what could be done for Miss

Nellie. Salt tears stung against his eyelids. Perhaps he
should have risked everything for his friend . . .

One thing was sure. Frank Seddens' stroke had finally
come to that fine old gentleman, and Grady at least knew
whom to blame.

He did blame that person.

CHAPTER *ten*

THE HOSPITAL at Elmore did everything for Frank Seddens that Grady would have done; procaine was injected, he was given dicumarin. Within a week his mind had cleared and his limbs relaxed. He would be all right—or almost. Grady went to see him and managed to appear cheerful before the sick man.

March had brought apple blossoms and summer warmth to the Hollies, but the first day of April brought a storm with driving rain and shrieking wind.

And that night, too, a wild-eyed man plunged into the brightly lit restaurant at the highway junction to demand help for his wife. She was about to have a baby, his car had broken down, and he was still thirty-five miles from the hospital. Oh, somebody get a doctor! *Somebody!*

Pearl Broni sat at the counter, eating a cheeseburger. She stepped down from the stool, calmly chewed the last morsel of this confection, tied her *babushka* firmly under her pink chin and went over to the distraught young man. "Come with me," she said firmly. "I will take your wife to the doctor. He won't come here."

Pearl drove a funny little old car—it was well known in the Hollies, the butt of many jokes. Pearl had herself painted the thing a coral pink; it rattled and shimmied when it went along the street—but the important thing tonight was that it would go. That it did go.

She helped the distraught young man get his burdened wife out of his car and into her own.

"We'll never make it . . ." the man kept saying.

"Her pains come quick now," agreed Pearl cheerfully. "But it isn't far."

"Thirty-five miles."

"Oh, no, it isn't that far. Not near that far." The little pink box of a car was already in motion. Pearl leaned forward over the steering wheel to see through the streaming rain; she turned one corner and then another, and she pulled up in front of a white frame house. A glance upward showed her two lighted windows on the second floor. The Docs were home . . .

"Help her inside," said Pearl. "Can you make it, dearie?"

The woman, grim-lipped, nodded her head. Pearl went on to alert Mrs. Schmieder, to shout up the stairs, "Hey, Doc! Come down. I got a baby for you—"

At once, the two men knew what they had. Grady had had too many imminent delivery cases come into receiving not to recognize the sounds and the sense of urgency in the bustle going on downstairs.

Tommy made an instant break for those same stairs, but Grady followed more deliberately. The woman, he saw at once, was in advanced labor.

"Take her to a bed—you can use mine," he said.

"I can't—get up—any stairs . . ." gasped the distressed woman. And indeed she could not.

Grady snatched a plastic cloth from the kitchen table, and spread it atop Mrs. Schmieder's own soft bed. He helped get the woman out of her heavy coat, he took off her shoes.

"This here's a Doc," announced Pearl at his shoulder.

Grady straightened and stepped to a place against the wall. Tommy came in and the two men looked at each other. They could hear Mrs. Schmieder advising the anguished father to stay in the living room. "I got two docs stayin' with me," she comforted him. "Your wife'll be fine."

And still her "two docs" stared at each other, beginning to realize the horror of their position. They could not, they must not, touch the woman upon the bed. To save a life, almost anyone could have helped deliver her child. A policeman, the druggist—Dr. Stone—Pearl or Mrs. Schmieder . . .

But not Grady Barton, M.D. Not Dr. Stanley Tomyanovic, D.P.

"Pearl!" said Grady in a loud voice. "I'll tell you and Mrs. Schmieder exactly what to do."

"But, Doc, you're here, and—"

"I'm here. And I'll help you. Now, do what I say, and it will be all right."

He did what he could. And things were all right. He sterilized scissors and string, he brought newspapers and carried them away again. It was a routine delivery, though accompanied by considerable pain. The doctor must sternly refuse all suggestion of "easing" the mother.

But finally, at ten o'clock, the baby was safely born. Pearl took charge of the infant, while Mrs. Schmieder, still following Grady's directions, cared for the mother. As a final act, Grady carried the woman upstairs to his own room and bed; he would, he said, move to the motel down the street for the night.

He talked to the father, particularly instructing him as to the registration of the baby's birth.

"But can't you tend to that, Doc?" asked the excited young man.

"No. I didn't deliver the child. It was done under emergency conditions—but the birth has to be registered. And, if I were you, I'd move them on to the hospital tomorrow. By ambulance."

"They're doin' all right, ain't they?"

"I sincerely hope so."

"Won't you go on taking care of them? I'll pay."

Grady shook his head and went out of the house.

He had brought his pajamas and toilet kit downstairs with him; now he got his car out and drove to the motel; he went into the small cabin allotted to him and sat down to consider the events of the stormy night. The place was warm enough, but he shivered as he sat in the armchair and looked at the somewhat spattered wall beyond the desk and its lamp. In the adjoining cabin, a man and a woman talked loudly; the rain slapped against the roof and the window. On the highway, headlights swooped

toward his window; twin red lights dwindled away from
it. . . .

Life went on. One did not question why. Though tonight Grady questioned it. Questioned why it should
seem so important for him to guard his behavior just
now, to keep his medical standing in good shape.

Tonight, would he have held his hand should instruments have been needed to save that young mother's life,
and the life of her baby? They had not been needed, but
the question still required an answer. The druggist could
have delivered the baby—the druggist could not have
used instruments.

But what would Grady Barton have done? Was his
M.D. so important to him that he would have held his
hand? He had, at the beginning of this nightmare, made
one strong vow: "I'll not give them any chance to add to
their phony case against me."

But wouldn't he—tonight—to save a life?

He had not yet answered his question when Pearl's
funny pink car clattered up and Tommy shouted Grady's
name. Grady opened his door; Tommy came in, and
Pearl drove away.

Tommy gazed after her admiringly.

"She's wonderful," he told Grady solemnly.

"Yes," said Grady. "Yes, she is. Why'd you come here?"

"I let the husband stay in my room—he take care his
wife." Tommy dropped his raincoat into the shower stall
and came back, grinning, then cast a look around their
quarters. Chocolate colored walls, chartreuse upholstery,
patterned draperies.

"No bed?" he asked.

Grady pointed to a door, and Tommy investigated, beaming. "Wonderful!"

"I hope you're right."

"Grady, my friend, what is wrong with you?"

Grady broke the match which he was trying to strike. "I've had a hard evening," he said dryly.

"I thought you would be feeling good, to know a baby can be born, and safely, without us. It is a nice baby boy, and the mother is doing excellently."

"Mhmmmn. But—well—I didn't especially enjoy watching them get along without us. Did you?"

"We might have had to watch them *not* get along."

Grady hunched forward in his chair. "Tommy, you've had this problem longer than I have. What would you do about refusing to give medical care if a life was at stake?"

"Once," said Tommy cheerfully, "I got myself very drunk."

"If the emergency was great enough—would they hold it against you?"

Tommy's face and shrug answered him, and Grady had that answer repeated the next day.

They might, had said Tommy.

And the next day Grady *knew* that they might.

Not knowing what better to do, Grady went to work the next morning, and about ten o'clock he looked up from his machine, aware that two men had come to a stop beside him. His gloved hand shut off the power, and he turned, tipping up his safety goggles.

He was wearing coveralls, as did the other men about him. But there was an air of reserve about this big, red-headed man that made him stand out from the other workers. His head erect, his face grave, his hands steady . . .

He waited for Mo Chronister to state his business. Beside him, Joe Perry looked distressed.

"Grady," he said, speaking only as loudly as was absolutely necessary to make himself heard above the din, "Mr. Chronister—"

Mo shouldered Joe out of the way. "I'll get it said, Joe," he said roughly.

All down the aisles of the big room, machines were being shut off and men stood still, listening. So Mo's big voice came out very loudly.

"As Prosecuting Attorney, Grady . . ." Joe was endeavoring to explain, "I had to let him—"

"It's all right, Joe. I understand. What is it now, Mo?" Grady was taking off his heavy gloves, not wanting to look into Mo's face. He knew just how the white teeth would be showing, the way the blue eyes would sparkle and the cheeks be creased—almost as if the man smiled.

He could feel anger building up within himself, a tight core.

"*This* time," Mo Chronister was saying, unpleasantly ready to tell about this time. "This time, it seems, Doc, that in spite of your license being revoked—"

Suspended, corrected Grady to himself.

"You not only delivered a baby, you had the unmitigated nerve to bring the patient to your own bedroom to

do it. Guess you didn't figure on the father's registering
the kid's birth so quick."

Oh, Lord, thought Grady, *could that fool guy have put
my name down as attending doctor? He should have
waited—the hospital would have made out the certificate—
an emergency birth—*

A red haze began to swirl through Grady's mind.

". . . amounts to an illegal operation . . ." Mo was
saying. "Seems you're everything, Barton, from a philan-
dering liar to a dishonest doctor . . . You—"

Grady took a step toward him.

Mo took a step back.

Grady looked around. Joe Perry's face was clay-colored.
All the workmen were leaning forward.

"If you'll step outside, Mr. Chronister," said Grady
tightly, "I'll get this matter straightened out for you. If
you won't step outside, you owe me an apology here and
now. Because you know damn well the exact circumstance of that baby's birth—and any little detail that isn't
known, I'm ready to knock into you."

For a moment, he thought regretfully that Mo was going to back down. By now, Grady wanted nothing so
much as to smash his fist into that smiling face, to knock
that crest of yellow hair into the dirt.

But a glance about him had changed Mo's mind.

"I guess with all these witnesses, I can afford to beat
your ears off, Doc," he said, swaggering toward the wide
doors which a half-dozen men sprang to open.

It was not raining, but the stone chips of the driveway
were dark with last night's rain. Mo took off his gabardine

raincoat and his suit coat; Grady handed his mask to one of the workmen.

A circle was immediately formed by the factory men, Joe Perry among them. Faces appeared at the windows of the second floor—quiet faces, watchful, neither friendly nor unfriendly—just ready to see these two men fight out the quarrel which all knew had been building between them throughout the winter. One or two voices called out.

"Give it to him, Doc!" cried a little rooster of a man, safely on the second floor of the factory.

"Knock him down and stomp him," yelled a bigger voice, which did not declare its owner's loyalty.

But largely the crowd was quiet, shoving a bit to get a place in the circle and to hold it, so that there was the scuffle of heavy shoes upon gravel.

"I hate to do this to you, Doc," said Mo, swinging his doubled fist at Grady's chin.

But the gleaming red head had jerked back; the fist fanned air, and Grady came in with a pretty left hook which sent Mo back on his heels. Then Mo would have grappled, but Grady put his two hands on his shoulders and pushed him away, coming in again with a swift right jab and another uppercut.

Blood began to run down Mo Chronister's chin. Angered at the taste of it, he bored in, by sheer weight knocking the breath from Grady's lungs. He stepped back, circling, watching, his face still, his hands ready. Mo, fists flailing, was beginning to talk, to shout, to threaten. Grady watched for his chance.

When Mo barged in, feet braced wide, Grady seized him, lightning swift, one hand on the back of his neck, the other on his leg—and to the mounting roar of the men about them, he lifted Mo Chronister above his head and instead of throwing him hard upon the stones he bore him to the ground, going down with him, his knee in his belly, his hands on his throat.

"Say *uncle!*" he cried, as he had used to cry when ten years old and in a schoolyard fight.

Joe Perry's hands tugged at Grady's arm. Grady swung his head like a bull. "He's gotta say it, Joe!"

Mo's eyes bulged, his mouth worked—only bubbly blood came from between his lips. The workmen pulled the doctor off. Breathing hard, Grady rubbed his hands together and stood looking down at Mo who was getting up, groggily, on one knee. The back of his white shirt was dirty and torn from the sharp rocks, blood was smeared upon his face—otherwise he was not hurt.

Grady smoothed his hair and shouldered his way between the men. "Let's get back to work," he said gruffly to one who wanted to shake his hand.

They fell in behind him. Admiringly. Some of them voiced that admiration.

"Doc's a good man," they told each other, and when Joe Perry came to Grady at the noon hour, the plant manager repeated the statement. "You're a good man, Doc."

Grady looked up from the cup he was filling from the vacuum bottle of coffee.

"I'm a good *Doc*, too, Joe," he said grimly.

"Nobody says you're not."

Grady laughed and shook his head.

"Your friends would like to do more for you, Grady, than you're letting us."

"I know. A lot of you have been swell. Of course I was still a pretty new friend to you—and—" He shrugged.

Then he looked up at Joe Perry. "Maybe it's time," he said, slowly. "Maybe it's *more* than time for somebody to get busy and say that guy is *not* a good lawyer!"

"You put in a few cents' worth on the subject this morning."

"Agggh! I just proved he didn't know how to defend himself against a man who'd been trained to fight. The other matter—it wouldn't be hard to prove Mo is a bad lawyer and certainly not fit to hold public office. He lets personal prejudice guide his conduct. He's been fighting me, you know damn well, not as the doctor I am, but—" With a sigh, Grady closed his lunch box, got up from his bench and after a polite, "Excuse me, Joe," he walked away from his boss.

At three, along with a hundred other men on that shift, he went home. He found that his room was again his to use, and he got out his medical bag to put some Merthiolate and adhesive upon his bruised knuckles. Like any surgeon, he was especially careful of his hands. Tommy came to the door of his room, leaned against the frame and watched what Grady was doing. "Could I help?" he asked.

"If you shut the door and pulled down the shades," drawled Grady, handing him the spool of tape.

Tommy regarded the skinned knuckles. "Fight?" he asked.

"You should see the other fellow."

"What happened?"

Grady told him. "Seems our boy—Rogers—did what I'd told him to do, went to the county clerk's office this morning to register the baby's birth. Did they go to the hospital?" he broke off to ask.

"Yes, at noon. By ambulance."

Grady grinned at Tommy's way with that word. "Yep. I told 'em to do that, too." Then he went on to tell of Mo's coming to the plant, of his threat of calling last night's delivery an illegal—

"And you knocked him down," concluded Tommy. "Good!"

"Oh," said Grady, "I don't know whether it was good or not. But it was something I had to do, right at the minute. However, I felt much better the time or two I've been able to beat Mo with my wits. This way—I was trained to personal combat, Tommy. I know about Judo and how to disable a man quickly, completely. Mo—he just counted on his size."

Tommy leaned back to study the bandaged knuckles. "You must have hit him hard."

"I did. That was temper. Anger. But the men at the plant think I'm good because Judo let me throw him down and be in a place where I could have killed Mo Chronister."

"Did you want to?"

Grady's mouth was rigid. "Yes," he said softly. "Yes. I wanted to kill him."

Tommy stepped back. "My *friend* . . ." he said urgently.

Grady nodded. "I know," he agreed. "I know. I've decided that I must clear out, away from that danger. It's his big chance of winning this war—and—well, now I've got to clear out. I've known I must; that's why I sent for you, but—well—I think you know how I feel about June Cowan, and—"

Tommy's homely face was beautiful with the smile which he turned upon his friend. "I know how she feels about *you!*"

"Yes," said Grady, his face tight again with hurt, frustration and despair. "And what do we have to look forward to? Why, Tommy, here it is, the week before Easter, and I can't go to church with her, nor send flowers for her to wear proudly. I've no right to make plans for her or with her. I've no right to *have* a girl!"

"But after next week . . ." Tommy offered in comfort.

The hearing for the lawsuit had been set for the week after Easter. Judge Cowan had his case prepared, and Grady— "I'll see that through," he promised. "Of course."

He and Tommy went out for their supper, and then Grady went to see Miss Nellie. He did this four or five times a week, wanting to do what he could for his friends, since he was denied the right to perform the service which he would have liked to do.

Miss Nellie had visited with "Brother" that day and could tell Grady that the doctors thought he might come home before too long. "And you'll watch him then, won't you, Grady?"

"I'll do anything I can, Miss Nellie." No need to disturb the little old lady either with his plan to leave the Hollies or the matter of the lawsuit. Should the judgment go against him, his license would be taken away, for a time. And—well . . .

At eight, he drove to the Cowans', with a heavy sense of doing a cherished thing for the last time. He sat for a minute in his car, looking at the gracious home, at its fence and lawn, the tall trees, the shrubbery, the light beside the front door and the glow behind the windows.

Aaron admitted him, said Miss June was at practice for the Easter morning choral service, but the judge was in his study.

"It's the judge I want to see, Aaron."

The judge's study was a pleasant place, paneled in walnut, two walls were glowingly lined with books. There were deep leather chairs, green-shaded lamps, a bowl of apples and walnuts, a tray with decanters and glasses— and Candy to welcome the doctor when he came in.

"Full of good will and generous with dog hair," laughed the judge, extending his hand. "Glad to see you, Grady. Sit down. What can I offer you?"

"My usual—though I heard today of something called a Wisconsin Martini—made very dry, with an anchovy-stuffed olive."

"Oh, my," said the judge, his eyebrows up.

"Doesn't say much for Wisconsin," Grady agreed, taking his highball.

The judge also mentioned the choir rehearsal. "We all feel that you did wrong to give up that association, Grady."

"Well—"

"I understand the impulse. But the padre argues that you should have given the people of the church a chance to exercise their Christian brotherhood toward you."

Grady nodded. "I've made all sorts of mistakes, sir. You see, I hadn't expected to handle just this situation when I came to the Hollies, and—I've blundered about— hurting much more than I've helped. Myself, or anyone."

He leaned forward to set his glass upon the tray. "That's why," he said almost briskly, "that I decided today that it was folly to plan on staying here."

"What prompted the fracas today?" asked the judge keenly.

Grady looked at him admiringly. The judge's mind was like a well-drawn map, clear and definitive.

Relaxing, but only a little, Grady sat back in his chair and gave the details of the trouble he'd had with Mo on that day. He explained the occasion for it.

"Pearl thought she was doing the only sensible thing, and she was! To bring that woman in labor to a house where two doctors lived. But for that matter I thought I was doing the right thing when I brought Tommy here to serve the medical needs of the town—"

"Almost everything which has developed in this affair, Grady," said Judge Cowan thoughtfully, "has been on such a narrow ledge of right and wrong that it is an en-

grossing mental exercise to detect what small considerations have made the difference."

"It's engrossing," said Grady morosely, "unless you happen to be the unlucky chap hanging by a tuft of grass
above the abyss."

"Tommy comes so close to being an acceptable doctor . . ."

"Or if I'd just used my fists on Kopp last Christmas
instead of keeping them for Mo today . . ."

"Joe Perry says it was a beautiful fight."

Grady laughed. "Then he must have been in my corner."

"He was. D'you hurt Mo?"

"Oh, he probably has a sore jaw. Mainly I overthrew
his vanity. I'm sorry. It isn't much fun to beat up a
bully."

"No?" The slight, elegant man was honestly surprised
at this admission.

"No, for like today, they are seldom fair fights. The
airborne taught me Judo and how to defend myself against
real fighters. So Mo didn't have a chance. I'm sorry I gave
way to my anger—"

"I'm not sorry," said the judge emphatically. "Mo
needed just what he got. You needed to express yourself—
and the Hollies needed that fight, too. Those who don't
care about or understand the fine ethical points of your
troubles, can understand that fist fight, and a lot of them
are ready to believe now, with evidence, that you are a
good man."

But Grady sat shaking his head from side to side. "The

point is, sir, I came here to get away from human con-
flict of that sort. To avoid it."

"You can avoid it now by leaving town. You could have
left after Christmas. You can leave now or next week."

"You make it sound very easy."

"It is easy. Or easy enough. If you consider only that
aspect. But something you said to Joe Perry this afternoon makes me think—"

"That I can't consider it," said Grady tightly. "That I
can't leave."

Years ago, as an intern, Grady had served on ambulance
duty and had gone to the scene of a sewer cave-in, where
a man had been buried by tons of sand.

Now, tonight, he felt much as that man must have felt—
if he'd had any feeling at all! Each grain of sand was as
nothing, but the weight of its mass . . .

Tonight, in this minute, suddenly all the hurt, the mis-
understandings and the frustrations, the attacks upon him
—they all piled down upon Grady, crushing the breath
from his body, unbearably weighting him.

With a gesture of struggling upward against these
grains of sand, he got to his feet, his head back, his hands
clenched against his chest. "I can't leave," he cried in
protest, "because I've a score to pay . . ."

Stiffening with protest, Judge Cowan half rose from
his chair.

"Against that vindictive swine," cried Grady hoarsely.
"The Hollies have allowed him to live, and become vindictive. They've honored him with public office; they

laugh at his cruel jokes; they stand back and say nothing
when he takes their doctor from them.

"That's why, Judge Cowan, my first task, and my last,
may be to make the Hollies see what they have let him
do to me. They're all in it, to an extent. My so-called
friends, and the ones who don't seem to care one way or
another. But they are all in it, or they would not let
one man do what Mo Chronister has done.

"Yes, I know. You think the trial next week will clear
me. I think it will, too. So—I'll be cleared. Maybe I'll
open my office again, and these same people will be my
patients. And I'll attend to them. But there will be a great
difference, Judge Cowan. For they won't trust me, and
I won't trust them. Unless, in some way, the town knows
and acknowledges that they have persecuted an innocent
man."

The judge had settled back in his chair; his eyes
watched the big young man who paced the rug before
the fire.

Finally, Grady talked himself out, and the judge suggested that he refill their glasses. The doctor did, his
face still stern, but his manner again quiet and restrained.

"I'm a great hand," said the judge then, turning the
glass against the glow from the fire, "to handle things one
at a time. Matters will take their course at the trial, Grady
—and then will be time enough to decide upon your next
step."

He plainly meant to say more, but just then June
came in, very glad to see Grady. She wore a red coat,

with a filmy scarf about her hair. It had been cold down
at the lakeside, she said. Yes, they'd gone out there to be
sure they knew their places.

She turned to Grady who had risen when she came in,
and still stood beside his chair, his eyes upon this girl
whom he loved. June slipped out of her coat, stooped to
tug Candy's whiskers, brushed her fingers across her
father's shoulder and asked Grady, "Please, won't you sing
with us at Easter sunrise service?"

Grady mashed his cigarette into a tray. And shook his
head. "I'm afraid not, June."

"Oh, why not? I thought you liked to sing! We sound
pretty good—there's about sixty of us, and it is a wonderful experience, singing as the sun comes up . . .   You'd
like it, Grady. I know you would."

He nodded. "I suppose I would, June. But—well, it
seems all a part of my life pattern these days that I can't
do or have much of anything I want to do—or have."
His voice flattened on the final word, and he turned
abruptly toward the door, went into the hall, where he
picked up his hat and topcoat and went out to the porch,
down the steps. . . .

June had followed him, and now her shadow lay long
upon the brick wall before his feet, cast far by the light
beside the door.

Grady saw it, and stepped to the grass, then risking a
glance over his shoulder, he stopped, turned and ran to
her, hungrily reaching his arms for her, hungrily kissing
her . . .

He'd told Tommy that he must leave.

He'd told the judge that he must stay.

But it would be June who would decide. June, the woman he loved . . .

CHAPTER *eleven*

ABOUT HALFWAY between the Hollies
there was a stretch of beach which formed a semicircular
bow. There the sand had heaped into dunes; scrub pines
and grasses held it in place. A pier had been built into
Green Lake at this point, and a dance hall stood at the
water end of it. By summer the place was loud with juke
box music, and the beach was dotted with swimmers, sun
bathers, children, old people and those in between.

In the winter the pavilion was boarded up and only the
gulls went out to it. On Easter morning, it had become
a custom in the Hollies to erect a platform at the center
of the half-circle formed by the hillocks of sand; behind
this a scaffolding was built on which would stand singers
from the various church choirs; their white-robed figures
would form a cross, facing east. Children of the churches
centered the cross.

The people of the community congregated upon the
sandy beach; some came in cars, many were on foot. Some
brought chairs, most stood. These people began to as-
semble before dawn; as day broke across the mist-

shrouded lake, their figures were defined in ghostly manner.

"It must be miserable on a cold day," thought Grady, who had taken a stand on one of the smaller dunes which overlooked the scene. That morning, however, promised to be fair; the sun already had flung pink banners upward across the sky, touching the white choir robes and the faces of the singers with a glorious light.

It was a simple scene, and magnificent. The ministers of the churches stood upon the rough pine platform; the living cross rose behind them. There were no flowers, no organ music—the hundreds of people on the beach were dark forms wrapped in heavy coats and scarfs.

The waters of the lake lifted, rolled whispering to the shore, creamed upon the sand, fell back—as the waters had been doing for centuries before this day, as they would continue to do for centuries to come. Life was timeless, and the Resurrection in springtime was a miracle, ever new.

Grady had brought his binoculars, and he used them in the growing light to pick out the faces of his friends. Sixty singers, June had said. June he found in the group which formed the left arm of the cross, her face serene—all the faces were serene. Ted and Orpha Kent, who owned the jewelry store in Green Holly, and who never missed a single meeting at their church. Billy Howe from the Presbyterian Church—he dealt in real estate and insurance and was enormously fat. They should not have put the tenors—and Billy Howe—so high upon that jerry-built scaffold.

Because of June, Grady wished he had checked the structure; from where he stood it looked rickety, though surely competent carpenters had erected it. And certainly the picture it made was effective; his glasses moved on. There were the Mitchells—Bud managed the lumber company, his handsome wife taught music in the schools. There were the four towheaded sons of the rector—Oren Kopp, from the German church—and June again.

The sun popped up from behind the dune where Grady stood, and its light gilded the group of singers into beauty, touched the familiar faces of his friends with dignity.

Alleluia!

Watching through his glasses, he saw the lips move, before the music and the singing came to his ears—thin, elfin, utterly lovely. His throat swelled at this voicing of the Easter miracle in song; he closed his eyes to squeeze back the emotion which crowded in upon him.

And opened them again—to horror and to disbelief. The sound came, belated, to his ears. His eyes stared unbelieving at the chaos of what had been a gilded cross of singing people. He heard the crash, the shouts and the roar of the collapse. And even as he heard it, and not believing it, he began to run.

And as he ran, stumbling, slipping, falling, getting again to his feet, his eyes never left that tangled mass of timbers and human bodies. The pink and gold light of Easter morn still lay tenderly upon the scene and upon the people who had sung. Running, Grady tried to find his friends again. June—the Cook boys—the Kents—Billy Howe—

For a breathless moment, everything was very still, no

sound came to him at all, no movement could be seen. Disaster had frozen the scene in horror.

There was time to see it all, to mark the single long spar of raw lumber and study the heaped bodies at its base; he could search among the semicircle of people who stood black upon the sand; he could look even at the waters of the lake, the waves lifting, falling, lace-edged in pink, the blue surface of the lake beginning to sparkle now in sunlight.

But now, after no more really than a second of shocked immobility, all was movement, all was confusion.

People ran, people shouted, people screamed. They pulled at timbers, they pulled at human limbs, seeking to drag out those who were caught underneath the weight of the mass, pulling, screaming, shouting, cursing—some praying in voices that were terrible to hear.

And still Grady ran and ran and seemed to get nowhere, his feet leaden, his breath grating in his lungs and throat. It was as if he slept and repeated a nightmare-dream, over and over. The familiar became distorted; the limbs of the men and women in that heap of crushed flesh, the limbs of those who milled about, were the strangest things in the world to him. They were as things which Grady had never seen before, nor imagined. His terror increased; as he reached the edge of the crowd, the faces before him became vindictive and strange—as if he had never seen *them,* had never seen a human face before. And he wondered at what he saw.

Even June—he located her while still 500 yards away; she lay a little to one side of the main mass, her head upon

the sand, her limbs weighted with the timbers of the
scaffolding, her body twisted, the white robe stained with
crimson. He ran and he ran and he *ran* toward her—sobbing aloud in his effort to run faster, to reach her . . .

And then, at long last, he did reach her, and with the
inexorable cruelty of all such nightmares, he must stand
and watch another man lift her head in his arms and seek
to draw her limbs . . .

"Let her alone!" Sound came at last, croaking, from
Grady's throat. *"Let her alone!"*

By sheer strength, he forced Mo's hand to release her,
to let her lie upon the sand.

Teeth bared, the two men faced each other. *"You* let
her alone!" roared Mo. "You'd better not touch anyone!
Doctor!"

Mo took a step backward from that which he saw in
Grady's face. A step away—Grady's eyes met other eyes,
his ears heard the voices which called to him, begging
him—he looked at the still-heaped and tumbled bodies, at
the bloody hands and faces of those who had struggled
free; he even looked again at June where she lay uncon-
scious upon the sand, and then he shut his eyes, he
straightened his back and he walked like a man of iron
or stone or some such hard thing, away from the hurt and
the injured, away from those who pled with him to
help. . . .

I won't, he said to himself. *They wouldn't let me before.
And now—I won't. I can't!*

The people watched him go, unbelieving. His hair was
turned to copper in the sunlight—and his face was that

of a man who had spent time upon his own sort of cross.

He went clear down to the edge of the water and walked along the sand where it was wet and darkened by the incoming waves.

And then he began to hear again, behind him, the voices, the shouts and pleadings, the screams of pain and the terrified weeping of children.

His step became slower and slower and finally stopped. His head was down now between his shoulders—then slowly, as a man lifts a weight far beyond his strength, every muscle straining, he lifted his head, turned and walked again up the slope.

He lifted timbers; he tore the choir robes into strips of cloth and bound them about torn and bleeding limbs, twisting them into tourniquets with splinters of wood. He did not speak, nor heed the things which others said to him. He worked steadily, methodically, silently.

Cold, frozen, he attended to one injured person after another; he gave them first aid. When the ambulance came, he helped lift the injured to the stretchers, and did it again on each trip which their ambulance made. He helped the less-hurt into cars; he laid the eldest Cook boy upon blankets in the bed of a station wagon.

And would not speak.

I won't! His nerves zinged in his head. *I can't! I won't!*

Not speaking, he stood and watched them take June away, with Mo Chronister beside her, pressing the folded handkerchief which Grady gave him against the puncture wound on her temple.

And Grady stood back, frozen faced, silent, cold. . . .

I WON'T. I WON'T!

Soon, Judge Cowan came from town in search of him; he took his arm and led him to his car. Dr. Barton, some- one had said, was acting very queer . . .

"We need you, Grady," said the judge. "We're using your clinic as a first-aid hospital. We need you there."

Without speaking, Grady went with him. When he seemed inclined to balk at going into the clinic building, the judge's hand was firm upon his forearm. And the two men went inside.

The hurt and injured were ranged about the outer rooms; some lay upon pallets and stretchers, some sat in chairs, miserable. In the examination room, a surgical setup was being arranged under Tommy's direction. The autoclave was going, and Tommy was already at work, his slight frame engulfed in one of Grady's white smocks. The sleeves were folded back, and folded again. On one of Tommy's arms—a thin arm, as black with hair as a monkey's—there showed a bare patch with numbers startling against it. It looked like a badge, a brand.

A-3715.

Grady stared hard at that mark. Stanley Tomyanovic would carry the shameful tattoo always. But, if allowed, he would forget it was there. This morning, he forgot it.

Pearl was there, helping Tommy, and Grady's instru- ments were set out and ready.

I won't, I won't, I won't. The bitter sound of resent- ment clanged on in the hurt man's brain.

Tommy, the judge said, watching Grady's face—perhaps he too could hear that gong—*Tommy* was working hard.

But Tommy was not afraid to work hard. Tommy couldn't lose what he didn't have anyway. While Grady —he was angry, he was scared, he was desperate. His first impulse had been to run, first toward the disaster, then away from it. And now he stood in its very presence. In his mind the disaster which had befallen the town became one with his own disaster. It was as if his own hurt shone as white here in this place as did Billy Howe's tibia through the bloody flesh of his leg.

Grady could set Billy's broken bones and heal his torn flesh. What could Grady do for the hurt which was *his?* *I won't touch it,* cried his bitterness. Even as his doctor-hands took splints from Tommy and his doctor-feet led him to the stretcher side.

After a glance at Grady's face, Tommy took charge. He told Grady what to do in exactly the same tone as he told Pearl. He sent all others out of the room. "Too big a crowd—no good . . ." He threw out comments like corn from a popper, and the town watched him, smiled upon him and talked about him as they waited out in the street.

With first aid given at the scene, the doctors could now take each case in turn. They had a contusion and cuts; they had a spouting artery—they put on clamps and sent the patient away to the hospital. By now an ambulance had come from Elmore. They had an abrasion, a man whose whole left side, from brow to ankle, was skinned raw and filled with splinters. The poor devil was put under sedation for further attention later. They had three cases of shock to varying degrees—for these he needed blood. There was no time to type, to transfuse.

As the cases came under their hands, the doctors must decide whom to send to the hospital, whom to send home —what emergency aid to give, and how much.

They had broken bones—ribs, legs, an arm—a badly crushed hand—and there had been at least one concussion. June Cowan.

Grady had sent her home. With Mo. He had wanted to go with her. "Get a doctor from Elmore," he had barked at Mo. *"Do what I say!"*

He'd wanted to stay with her; he wanted to go to her now. He remained in the clinic, hearing the cries of fear and pain, the pleas. . . .

"Take care of my boy, Doc! Take care of him!"

Tommy was in charge, but Grady worked, too, and as he did the things that must be done, his thoughts whirled. His hands were clumsy as he washed syringes and put them to sterilize. He set things handy for Tommy who had a dozen injured still to screen, to treat. His own shock beginning to clear, Grady wondered what they had done with June, for June. If they'd followed his directions . . . His hand clenched white. *If Mo had not. . . .*

Fighting against a return of feeling that would blur his eyes and shake his hand, he broke open packs of gauze dressings, holding his attention to what he did. He had got into a white smock. He held clamps, he wrapped gauze and stretched adhesive—he took a tray of hemostats into the operating room and thought about what he was

doing rather than give his full attention to the child whom
Tommy had upon the table. It was one of the Cook boys.
Charles. And his crushed leg needed expert care, at once.

Tommy, white-faced, looked up at the other doctor—
pleadingly.

"Thank God," Judge Cowan had said as they drove
to the clinic. "Thank God, we have you two doctors!"

Grady had said nothing then; he said nothing now to
Tommy. His head down upon his breast, his ears strained
to listen to the last faint murmuring of that gong's re-
frain. *I won't. I won't. I won't.* For another minute,
he stood sternly silent there beside the table, as a man
stands when he examines his heart or prays to his God.

Tommy was getting very tired. Besides, he was not,
obviously, a practiced surgeon. He hadn't the required
strength, for one thing. Grady's fingers and wrists ached
to take over, to handle that mangled flesh and the crushed
bone-ends. Charles would be sent on to the hospital in
the next ambulance, but his limb must now be placed
in some sort of traction, and the bleeding arrested.

Then, on the stretcher by the door, waiting to be cared
for next, was another child. She had a cut on her cheek
and lip. She was a pretty little girl, and preventive measures were called for that scarring be avoided.

So—slowly Grady's head lifted from his chest, he turned
toward the sink, took one step, another . . .

Tommy's two hands clenched into fists and pressed
hard against his mouth.

Let nothing stop Grady! Let nothing. . . .

And the door flew back upon its hinges, and Mo Chronister charged into the operating room. "What's going on here?" he roared.

Grady turned.

"They tell me out on the street you won't work, Doc! And I'm here as a peace officer to order you to *get* to work!"

Neither looking at Mo nor answering him, Grady walked around the man and leaned across the operating table to speak to Dr. Tomyanovic. "Have the parents of these children signed releases for surgery, Doctor?" He spoke in a voice as cold as ether upon the skin. "For if you don't have their consent . . ."

The strain was too much for Pearl. "Quit it, Doc!" she screamed, "Oh, quit it!"

Grady looked at her and smiled. Pearl relaxed, gazing at him adoringly, even as she sobbed with relief to know that Doc was "back." Beaming, she went into the next room for towels.

Mo Chronister just stood there.

Tommy was cleaning the little girl's cut mouth and cheek; as he did this he talked to Grady about the surgery which he would do, or would not—

"The wrong stitches would be only added keloid . . ."

"Dr. Barton!" Mo tried again.

Grady glanced at him.

"You are a doctor under oath, are you not?"

Grady's eyes brightened.

"You are also a doctor under contract to this town, with

this town. So far as I am aware, Dr. Barton, that oath and that contract have never been abrogated . . ."

It was the word—

Grady's head went back, his mouth opened, and he laughed. And with his laughter, all hatred and bitterness poured away from him in a surging flood. He laughed louder and louder—and then he stopped. For a second, he just stood, tired and drained. His limbs relaxed, his mind empty.

But very soon really, though it seemed an hour to those who watched him, he straightened. He flexed his fingers and rolled his arms in his shoulder sockets.

It was *good* to be himself again, his own man, a free man—

He walked over to the sink to scrub and turned his gaze sternly upon Mo Chronister. "What did you do with June?" he demanded.

And Mo acknowledged Grady's right to ask.

"I took her home," he answered quietly, "and phoned Elmore. A doctor came with another ambulance, but June is at home, in bed. With a nurse. To be quiet, and under observation. He said he thought there was some concussion. She's all right."

Grady nodded and scrubbed his hands, beginning to chuckle again. Tommy looked at him in wonder, his head shaking from side to side. "Americans," he announced, when Grady came up to the table, working his hands into gloves, "they are crazy people."

Grady took the suture needle and bent over the little girl. "Yes," he said in a quiet, though somewhat exalted tone. "We are—crazy. Of course. Trouble comes—" he glanced up. "—when we forget that."

He had run, he had stood stubborn against his trouble and now he would fight. Now he could fight. Which was the better way, for a man.

For two hours the doctors worked in the clinic, finishing up the cases which remained. A heap of stained linen mounted on the floor, the doctors' gowns became wet with perspiration, draggled and stained. Occasionally, people came to the door of the room, gazed at the scene—at the table, at the patient upon it, at the two men helped by Pearl until another nurse came from the Elmore hospital to take her place.

Word was getting out of the disaster at the Hollies. Highway police, reporters and then other doctors, came to help.

And Grady and Tommy worked on; they fixed up the little girl and her sister with a broken arm. Kopp had a broken arm and a huge splinter under his thumbnail. Grady pulled it out "without hurting a damn bit!" marveled Kopp, protesting when the doctor ordered him to the hospital for X-rays, but going just the same.

Dr. Messmer from Madison phoned to ask if Dr. Barton wanted a surgical team. Grady sent a message of thanks and a promise to call upon him if necessary.

"We don't need them," the people out in the street told each other. "We got two fine doctors already here in the Hollies."

They did have, for that day—and that day was what

mattered. That day there were lives to be saved, injuries to be healed, pain to be allayed—and their two doctors could do those things. Forty of the sixty upon the scaffold had been hurt to some degree . . .

At noon, finished in the clinic, Grady and Tommy made the rounds of the injured who had been sent to their homes; they went to see June who was resting and doing all right. Grady inspected her puncture wound and reassured the judge about the girl's blurred vision, the slight paralysis of her hand and foot.

"All a part of concussion," said the doctor comfortingly. "It'll clear up."

He went on to the Elmore hospital and checked on things there, faint stirrings of doubt beginning to rise like foam in his mind. He still was without a license; he'd not want to embarrass the hospital . . . he said.

"Don't talk like a fool," snapped the surgeon in charge. "If you didn't have your M.D. at all, today would grant you one."

"What about Tomyanovic?" asked Grady.

"What about him? He's a trained doctor. This morning, who cared where he learned?"

"Don't count on nobody caring tomorrow morning." Tommy was the one to caution Grady, as the two men prepared for bed on that Easter night, the strangest Easter the Hollies would ever know. "To a man with a belly ache, a doctor is always a saint. Tomorrow—it will be different."

CHAPTER *twelve*

AND TOMORROW CAME, of course.

A day of reflection, of thanksgiving that no one had been killed, that the injured were being cared for and doing well. A day of reaction and sober second-thought for a lot of people.

In mid-afternoon, Dr. Grady Barton came to Judge Cowan's home, and a smiling Aaron took him up to see "his patient."

"She's doing very well, doctor," said the nurse, rising from her chair.

"She looks it," said Grady, smiling at the girl in the four-poster bed, her eyes still shielded with dark glasses; but her cheeks were pink, and her parted lips were healthily red.

After what June called a bit of professional funny business, the nurse tactfully withdrew, and Grady sat down in the chintz armchair, sighing a little.

"Tired?" June asked, stretching her hand to him.

He took it. "Tired," he agreed. "Washed out. But with it all, very content."

Her fingers tightened in his.

"Now that I know you're going to be all right," he went on. "Does your head ache?"

"A little—and my hand's numb. But—well—like you, I'm happy enough."

He bent toward her and kissed her soft lips. "June . . . ?" he began, then looked over his shoulder, for Aaron had come to the door.

"You wanted on the phone, Dr. Barton," said the house-man.

Grady hesitated.

June's hand pushed him away. "Answer it and come back," she said, smiling.

He was gone for five minutes, and she watched him when he returned to the room. It had been months since Grady had walked in just that manner, assured of step, spine and head erect, his mouth firm, but not tight.

Again her hand reached for his, and he moved the arm-chair closer to the bed. The big room was pleasant with ruffled organdy and chintz, tulips in pots upon the window sills, daintiness and soft colors.

Grady sighed.

"What was the call?" June asked him.

He looked surprised, then nodded. "Oh—a child at Neighbors. Sore throat, some fever—"

"Aren't you going over?"

"That was the idea—but, no, I don't think I'd better, June."

"But why not? Dad says your contract, and your license, are all in good order. He said that your license had only been suspended—contingent upon litigation, or some such phrase—and that Kopp has dismissed the lawsuit—or charge—or whatever it would be—so the license trouble is over. Didn't you know that?"

Grady nodded. "Yes, I knew it." Knew too that a committee of citizens had called upon Mo Chronister with a resolution of confidence in their doctor. . . .

June sought to lift herself from the pillows, and his hand pressed her back. "But Grady!" she persisted. "It means you can stay here and work."

"Yes, I suppose it does," he said gravely. "But I think I have a better idea, June. I'd like to be able to give this place to Tommy. He—"

"They say he was wonderful yesterday!"

Grady smiled. "He was. Though any doctor is wonderful if he's on the spot to handle an emergency—and we certainly had just that yesterday. But seriously, I think this may be Tommy's chance. I'm sure I can get him a locum license now. And the people here are in a mood to make a fight to get him permanently licensed. So— what with the examinations he's already passed, his application for citizenship—I couldn't think of anything more to do for the guy except marry him to an American girl . . ."

"We can," said June confidently. "We can marry him to Pearl, and—"

Grady leaned away from her, his face wary. "Women!" he cried. "Incorrigible matchmakers!"

"But you just said . . ."

"I know—and marrying an American girl would ease

things. Pearl's a good prospect, too; she thinks he's cute."

June giggled, and the doctor looked at her warningly.

"An American wife," he went on consideringly, "will make getting his final citizenship easier—and I think we could draw up some sort of special appeal to the State Medical Society. He did a very swell job yesterday for the people of these two towns and surely earned some kind of reward. Maybe your Dad will know how to do it . . ."

"Oh, he's sure to. He was saying this morning how much the towns owed Tommy. But, Grady, that goes for you, too. They owe you even more . . ."

"That may be true—except that I have other plans in mind. And don't you dare sit up!"

She smiled at him. "Then tell me!" she warned.

"I mean to. Because you'd be in those plans—I hope."

"Grady . . ."

"I am telling you, June. I think I'm going back into city practice."

"Chicago?"

"No. Madison. If I do it. To surgical service at a new teaching hospital there. It's a doctors' hospital, built by doctors, for doctors. I could go in as assistant to the present surgical chief."

"When did you make all these plans?"

"I'm in the process of making them now, though I had this offer some time ago."

"You didn't tell me."

"When I was first asked, I thought I'd rather work here. Then—I had things to clear up. But now I mean to accept.

I hope you won't think I'm a coward, June, darling, or overly bitter. Though I've eaten a deal of bitter fruit in these past months and the taste of that isn't lost to a man, overnight. Besides, I doubt if I could work here again. Because there's a thing which claim-conscious patients—*and* their lawyers—don't recognize. And that is that suing a doctor for malpractice is definitely not the same as trying to collect damages for a bashed-in fender. From the minute of accusation, the doctor suffers irreparable damage to his reputation. Even if a trial proves the charge unfounded, that it was malicious—as Kopp *was* malicious, or vindictive—as—er—his attorney *was* vindictive—the public always remembers the charge longer than they remember its injustice."

"But the people here *know* they need you! That's been proved to them."

"Yes, but—"

"Won't you try it?"

"I have tried it, June. After the original suit, remember? And—it didn't work."

She sighed.

"Medicine is a somewhat exact science, June," he said gravely, "but the people we apply it to are not exact. And every time I would seem to make an error—oh, like treating a man for pneumonia and having him die of a coronary—the people here would remember this suit, and . . ." His broad shoulders lifted in a shrug.

"The people here," she repeated softly, her pretty face troubled.

"*Here,*" he agreed. "In a small town, June. Where everyone lives intimately with everyone else, where the state of your bridgework is common knowledge, where everyone knows how much you borrowed to build your new house—*and* how often your name has appeared on a police court blotter. Small towns are like that, darling." His brow was wrinkled, his manner anxious, and she laughed at him gently.

"There are some good things here, Grady," she teased.

"Yes, ma'am!" he assured her. "And I plan to take the best of them away with me. The thing, really, that I came to the Hollies to get. Remember? The girl with the boat . . ."

"I like being called a 'thing,'" she challenged.

"I hoped of course that you'd like to go to the city with me."

"Why, Grady! I'd even stay *here* with you."

And, laughing, they were in each other's arms. He held her gently, lovingly. "Get well fast, darling," he urged. "I want to marry you. *Soon.*"

"Oh, I am getting well, Grady. But—just now—wasn't there a call for Dr. Barton?"

He laughed and stood up—tall and strong. He took his bag, hefting its weight in his left hand, then he came back to bend over June and kiss her.

Smiling, she watched him walk out of the room, his head up, his shoulders straight, the bag swinging from his hand. Pride filled her heart. Grady would lose all bitterness and be his own man again—her man.

He'd been that—from her first sight of him—one day way last fall when she'd raked leaves with Candy. She'd never told him about that. And she must—some day. *Soon.*

ELIZABETH SEIFERT'S first novel, YOUNG DOCTOR GALAHAD, won the $10,000 Dodd, Mead-Redbook Prize. Since then she has written more than a score of novels about American doctors and their problems—professional, social and domestic. The medical world, with its breath-taking accomplishments and its very human weaknesses, has been a source of endless fascination and unfailing inspiration to her, both as a woman and as a writer. She wanted to study medicine, but was thwarted by poor health and family disapproval. She did, however, take courses in anatomy, physiology and medical dietetics, and later worked as a clinical secretary in a hospital. From this background of training and experience comes the richness of realistic detail which is characteristic of all her books. From her natural gifts as a storyteller come the vivid and heartwarming plots and characters that have made her novels so successful.

Elizabeth Seifert was born in Washington, Missouri, attended the public schools in St. Louis and was graduated from Washington University. In private life she is the mother of four children and the grandmother of six. Her husband, a hero of World War I, is a member of that gallant wheel chair brigade about which she wrote with especial feeling in HOSPITAL ZONE. With her children grown up and scattered halfway around the world, from New Mexico to Pirmasens, she has time now to get down on paper the abundant story material produced by a tirelessly creative, narrative mind.